TIDES OF CHANGE

SEACLIFF COVE
BOOK 2

LISA LINDEN

Editing: Peter Senftleben, PES Editorial

Proofreading: Abbie Nicole

Cover design: Natasha Snow Designs

Photography: Eric McKinney, 6:12 Photography

Model: Michael S.

CHAPTER ONE

GARRETT

I opened the door to The Coffee Cove, and the bells on the door jingled a familiar melody. The rich, potent scent of freshly ground beans hit me immediately, and the sibilant hiss of steam from the espresso machine delivered a jarring noise to the otherwise quiet morning. I inhaled deeply and let the coffee-scented air invigorate my flagging steps. The morning had been uneventful—just a few parking citations to show for my time—and the weight of Monday sluggishness settled in my bones. I stifled a yawn and gave myself a mental shake. The life of a deputy sheriff wasn't always the stuff of action-packed movies, but I'd learned to appreciate the calm days. Too much excitement usually meant someone's life had taken a turn for the worse.

And yet…something told me my calm day was about to be wrecked.

I waved to Cooper, the shop's owner, who operated the espresso machine. Coop acknowledged me with a chin lift. I approached the cashier at the counter, already cluttered with miniature pumpkins and faux leaves, even though it was only the last week in September. But Halloween would be here before I knew it, and Noah and I hadn't yet picked out his costume. I mentally kicked myself. I had to get on with that.

"Morning, Deputy! The usual?" Jessica chirped from behind the register and bounced on her toes like she'd mainlined caffeine since dawn. Her purple-tipped blonde ponytail swayed with her movement, and her smile was as bright as the fall decor.

"You know it." I paid for my black coffee and dropped a tip in the jar while the bells jingled behind me.

"Deputy!" someone called from the shadows deeper in the shop.

I bit back a groan and turned toward the speaker. Frank Ehrhart perched on a stool at the bar along the wall. Frank was eighty if he was a day, with a permanent scowl etched into his craggy face and arms folded across his barrel chest like he was ready to wage war on the world.

I took a deep breath, fixed my face into something that approximated a smile, and strolled over to him. My boots scuffed lightly on the hardwood floor. "Morning, Frank." I braced myself for a tirade.

His eyes narrowed behind his thick glasses. "Martha's dogs are shitting on my lawn again. What are you going to do about it?"

I hooked my thumbs in my belt and gave him my best disarming grin. "Well, Frank, as I've mentioned before, that's something you'll need to take up with Martha."

"Coffee's up, Garrett," Cooper called.

Frank huffed, and his leathery skin wrinkled further as he muttered under his breath.

"What was that?"

"I said, every time I go over there to complain, she asks me in for coffee and then sends me home with cookies, or a pie, or some damned thing. How am I supposed to yell at her when she does that?"

I nearly choked on my laugh but turned it into a cough. "So, let me get this straight, Frank—you're telling me that every time her dogs poop on your lawn, you go over there, and she's baked something for you?"

His face twisted into a deeper scowl, though I caught the faintest flicker of uncertainty in his eyes. "Well, yeah."

I scratched my head and tried to keep my expression neutral. "Frank, I think she's setting you up."

"What?" His head jerked back. "Why would she do that?"

"Think about it," I said and gentled my voice to soften the blow. "She lost her husband last year. I think she might be lonely. Maybe she wants the company."

His eyes widened, and he scrubbed a weathered hand down his face. "Well, hell."

I clapped him on the shoulder and felt the weight of his realization settle. "Why don't you try visiting her on your own? Maybe that'll stop the dog problem."

Frank muttered something incoherent and reached for his coffee cup, clearly still processing what I'd said.

"Ethan! Order's up!"

I strode to the pickup counter and grabbed a to-go cup.

"Garrett—" Cooper began.

I took a large sip, only to nearly spit it out. My mouth flooded with sugar, the sweetness and spice so overpowering it made my teeth hurt. I grimaced and forced it down. "What the fu—dge is this?" I held the cup up and glared at it like it had betrayed me.

A deep chuckle drew my attention to the tall man who had stepped up to the counter. "It's my pumpkin spice latte," he said quietly, amused. Lips surrounded by a short, trim beard curved into a grin. Soft-looking dark-auburn curls escaped the crisp new ball cap pulled low on his forehead. Ray-Bans hid his eyes. "Not to your taste?"

"Go—sh, no." I gave an exaggerated shudder. "Sorry to take your drink. I'll buy you a new one."

Cooper sighed from behind the counter. "You did it again, Garrett. Pay attention to the names on the cups." He shot me an exasperated look before he turned to the man. "I'll make you another latte."

I dumped the sugary abomination in the trash. "You're my new neighbor across the street." I extended my hand to the man. "Garrett Whitlock."

He pulled off his sunglasses. Deep brown eyes met mine and sent a curious heat through my chest.

"Ethan." He gripped my hand in a firm shake.

I tried to ignore the tingle in my spine as his snug hand met mine. But the cop in me noticed Ethan only gave me his first name. Why was that?

"How was the move?" Noah'd had a restless night, so I'd seen Ethan arrive in the wee hours of Sunday morning. He'd unloaded two suitcases into the rental house, and I'd hardly seen him since.

"—didn't bring a coffee maker."

I mentally shook my head and tuned back into the conversation.

Ethan spread his hands to encompass the coffee shop. "So, here I am." He shrugged. "Is there any place in town to buy one?"

I shook my head. "Not unless you want to take a trip over the mountains to a big box store."

He winced. "Looks like Amazon it is."

"Welcome to small-town living along the Pacific coast." I sipped my black coffee and savored the sting of heat that spread through me. No sugar, just the sharp, bitter kick I needed. "Where did you come from?"

"East Coast," he said, but the way he said it—the slight hesitation—made something in my gut tighten. There was more to that story.

"And what brings you here?" I tried to sound casual and studied his reaction.

His lips quirked into a teasing smile. "Small-town living along the Pacific coast."

I chuckled. "Touché." I raised my cup in salute.

Cooper slid a fresh coffee across the counter. "Here you go, Ethan."

"Thanks." He grabbed the cup and took a sip while he held my gaze. He hummed, a full, rich sound. "Mmm."

I burst out laughing. "You'll do fine here." Before I could dig further into the mystery of my new neighbor, my radio crackled to life. Duty called. A house alarm was blaring and needed to be checked out. I gave Ethan a brief nod. "Nice to meet you."

But as I left the shop, I couldn't shake the feeling that Ethan wasn't just any new guy in town. Something about him was…off. Guarded. Like he was hiding something.

And my cop instincts rarely failed me.

CHAPTER TWO

ETHAN

As I juggled my pumpkin spice latte and keys, adrenaline prickled the back of my neck. It was irrational—Seacliff Cove was a quiet town, the very definition of safe—but the faint, ever-present sense of being watched had followed me here. It settled around me like a thin fog. I quickly opened my front door. With a breath to steady myself, I pushed it shut and slid the deadbolt home. The cold metal thudded into place with a satisfying *click*. I held it there for a moment longer than necessary, just until my heartbeat slowed. A home security company was due this afternoon to install a system, and I'd feel safer when that was done.

I threw my ball cap—my poor attempt at a disguise—onto the back of the couch. The slip-covered ivory sofa was not my style, but the furniture was functional and comfortable. I'd only had a few requirements when I hired the property manager to furnish the house for me: a quality mattress to sleep on, a sturdy desk to work at, and an ergonomic desk chair that wouldn't ruin my back. Everything else that mattered—my laptop, research materials, a few clothes—I'd brought with me. I'd had to leave my Keurig behind.

I took a sip of my coffee, which had cooled but still delivered a soothing blend of cinnamon and nutmeg. I grinned at the deputy sheriff's reaction to my pumpkin spice latte. Maybe I shouldn't have engaged, since my goal was to stay as invisible as possible. But Garrett Whitlock had broken through the caution I'd wrapped around myself. The amusing, gregarious man had gotten past my defenses.

The tight grip of his handshake had been like electricity zipping up my arm, like a lightning bolt to my chest. And his piercing blue eyes had mesmerized me. Had I seen a spark of interest in his gaze?

It was probably wishful thinking. I'd seen him across the street with his son, his adorable carbon copy. While making an assumption about someone's sexual orientation was inappropriate and most likely inaccurate, I couldn't help but think he was straight. I'd seen a woman let herself into the house—was she the boy's mother?

But I knew one thing for sure. Garrett hated pumpkin spice lattes. With a passion. I snorted a laugh into the silent house.

He probably drank coffee as pitch black as the night I saw him peeking through his blinds at me. I'd abruptly left New York on Saturday night and had arrived in Seacliff Cove in the early hours of Sunday morning.

No one in New York knew I was here. No one. I'd texted my neighbor on Sunday and asked him to keep an eye on my apartment. I'd broken up with my boyfriend months ago, so I didn't owe him an explanation. My editor lived in the city, but we usually worked via email. And my family thought I was on a writing retreat. I was here until the threat passed.

If there *was* a threat, and I wasn't simply being paranoid.

But I couldn't deny I'd had strange things happen, things

related to the series of thrillers I'd written. A black feather on my doorstep mimicked the calling card of the murderer in my first Jake Slate novel. Just a random feather, I'd tried to tell myself. Someone could have tracked it in on their shoe. But then, there was the copy of my second book on my usual coffee shop table, lying open at a scene in which the killer spied on the victim through binoculars. My spine had tingled at the reference. Next was the cryptic flyer left on my windshield from the clearly made-up Mr. Lee's Trees. It echoed the victim of my third novel, a landscaper named Lee. I'd called the phone number on the paper, but it was disconnected. Was the flyer an innocent advertisement and the phone number an honest typo? I shuddered. It might not have been.

Separately, I could have dismissed each occurrence. But all together... A chill coursed down my body and left goosebumps in its wake. The references had given me an escalating sense of dread and hinted at a familiarity not just with my books but with my home and habits.

And then there had been the final straw—a sticky note on my apartment door that read, *Guess who's next.*

I clutched my cup tightly, and it threatened to crush in my hand. I'd spent hours down a rabbit hole of rental listings, casting a wide net across the country—big cities, sleepy towns, anywhere far from the threat. Dozens of applications were sent into the void. The first reply? A Realtor in a tiny coastal town I'd never heard of—Seacliff Cove, California. One email later, I had a lease. Just like that, I was on a flight to San Francisco.

I moved through the house, my footsteps thudding on the hardwood floor. The quiet amplified every sound—the soft hum of the fridge, the cry of a distant seagull. I left the neutral-toned living room, the bare walls a contrast to the colorful, overfilled shelves of my apartment in Brooklyn.

I pushed open the door to the back bedroom I'd turned into my makeshift office, furnished sparsely with a standard desk, an adjustable lamp, and an ergonomic desk chair. My laptop and file folders sat on the desk, a comforting reminder of home, even if it felt strange to have them here.

I placed my latte on the desk and dropped into the chair. I stared at the laptop, closed and silent, rubbed my eyes, and pushed down the dread. This was supposed to be my sanctuary, the place where I could pour my thoughts into words, into Jake's world. Writing was my escape, my calling, and more than that, my career. I'd been one of the lucky ones. My books reached readers around the world. But today, layers of unease buried the joy I usually felt.

Was someone out there studying each word, analyzing my plots, and taking them to heart in ways I'd never imagined? Had I met them in passing at a book-signing, or maybe exchanged emails, only to have them fixate on my work? If I kept writing, would it feed their obsession and pull me deeper into their twisted reality? Would it ever end? If so, how?

My books featured stalking, kidnapping…and murder.

I shivered despite my sweatshirt and wrapped my arms around myself.

CHAPTER THREE

GARRETT

Noah burst into the Tides & Tales bookstore, and his excitement radiated through the quiet shop like an electric spark. His sneakers pattered against the polished floor. He streaked past the display of recent bestsellers and made a beeline for the counter. Barely slowing, he announced, "Mr. Mason! Mr. Mason! I'm going to get a Halloween book!"

I trailed behind and soaked in the store's scents—crisp paper, fresh ink, and lemon-polished wood.

Noah was the reader in our family. I liked a good story, but I preferred it on-screen, action-packed with explosions and heroes who saved the day in under two hours. A new thriller series was coming to a streaming channel—starring a crime-solver named Jake Slate—and I couldn't wait to watch. Quiet movement on the second level caught my eye. My breath hitched, and I stuttered to a stop. A tall man searched the shelves on the balcony upstairs. Auburn hair curled around the edge of his ball cap. *Ethan.* I'd only seen him coming and going since our encounter at the coffee shop the previous weekend. I couldn't help it—my gaze roamed from his curls, down his broad back, to his sculpted ass cupped by fitted jeans.

My thoughts screeched to a halt. What the hel—eck?

I hadn't really noticed a man's ass in years—not since high school, when I'd had an ill-advised crush on Leo, the center to my quarterback position. He'd had an easy swagger and a grin that made my stomach flip. But in the locker room, under the weight of machismo and expectations, attraction was dangerous. I'd kept my eyes forward, my mouth shut, and my hormones buried beneath pads and bravado.

But I'd also found myself drawn to the head cheerleader —the way her breasts bounced, the way her laugh lit me up. She was safe. Acceptable. I asked her to Homecoming, played the part, and from then on, I only dated women. I suppressed the other side of myself.

So, what was it about Ethan that cracked something open?

I mentally shook myself, forced my gaze away, and ambled to the counter. I tried to act unconcerned even though my heart raced with a weird, restless energy.

"Garrett." Mason greeted me with a casual nod and a smile. He glanced at Noah, chuckled, and handed him a basket. "Go on back to the children's nook, kiddo. I have some new books for you to look at."

Noah flashed Mason a grin and took off, the basket swinging crazily at his side.

"We're only buying two books!" I called after him.

Mason laughed, and his eyes twinkled with amusement. "Good luck with that. I bet you leave with eight books."

I shook my head. "Three."

"Five."

I rolled my eyes. But encouraging Noah's love of books was worth the hit to my wallet.

As I followed Noah, I took a moment to drink in the sight of my kid. He sat on a colorful carpet, surrounded by picture books, and his small fingers carefully flipped through the pages. There was a warmth in my chest, a mix of pride and love that had stuck with me since the day he was born. My girlfriend had shocked me when she told me she was pregnant. We'd always used a condom. But Noah was proof that condoms failed, and he was the best surprise that ever happened to me. He was a little miracle disguised in messy hair and scraped knees.

He placed a book into the hand basket, and I smiled. We would be buying five books.

Ava and I had broken up over her drinking habits. She'd been dry during her pregnancy—thank Go—odness. But her excessive drinking afterward had given me full custody of Noah.

Ava had died in a solo drunk-driving accident when Noah was two.

I'd been the first on the scene and had been as crushed as her car. She was an alcoholic, and she'd needed the help I'd encouraged. She didn't deserve to die from her disorder.

Noah didn't remember his mother, and my mom and sister had stepped into the role. But every once in a while, he asked why he didn't have a mom like his friends at kindergarten. Every time, the question was an arrow to my heart.

He threw a book into a discard pile. "Be gentle with the books, bud."

Blue eyes so much like my own met mine, remorse in their depths. "Sorry, Daddy." He was the best kid I could have asked for. Sure, he was a picky eater and begged for a few more minutes at every bedtime, but those were typical of five-year-olds. He had my heart wrapped around his little finger, and he knew it.

Just as I settled onto the floor beside Noah and relaxed, a loud gasp from the counter snapped me back to attention. Mason's startled, "Oh my God!" cut through the quiet hum of the store and sent alarm surging down my spine.

"Stay here, Noah," I ordered, my heart in my throat. I leaped to my feet. I had my badge with me, but I wasn't carrying. That wouldn't stop me from going to Mason's aid, though. I pulled out my phone, and my thumb hovered over the keyboard, ready to call for backup.

With quiet footsteps, I approached the corner of a bookshelf where I'd have a view of Mason and the counter. I peeked around the edge and frowned, confused.

Ethan stood at the counter with a finger pressed to his lips, signaling for silence. His frantic gaze darted around the store.

I stepped out of hiding, strode to the desk with long strides, and aimed for calm authority. "Is there a problem?" I asked in my most commanding cop voice.

"Garrett!" Mason whisper-shouted. "This is Ethan Quinn!" He practically vibrated with excitement.

Oh, was that his last name? I drew my brows together. "So?"

He rolled his eyes and blew out a breath. "He's the author of the Jake Slate novels! And he's here! In my store! Can you believe it?"

My eyes flew wide. I wasn't familiar with the books, but meeting the creator of the show sent a thrill through my stomach. "Really?"

"Can we keep it down?" Ethan pleaded and glanced around the shop like he half expected a mob of fans to rush him. "I'm just Ethan Cole here. I don't want attention."

Mason's gasp was audible. "You come to Seacliff Cove often?"

"I'm…visiting," Ethan replied hesitantly, quietly, as

though he chose his words with extra caution. He shot me a glance, something between curiosity and wariness flickering in his eyes. I figured I knew what he was thinking—was I going to tell Mason he was my new neighbor?

I shook my head and kept his secret with an amiable smile. Still, something felt off, a silent uncertainty beneath the casual exchange. Ethan was hiding more than just a pen name, but it wasn't my place to pry. Not yet anyway. I wondered, though, how long he'd be staying. Would he move out abruptly in the middle of the night like he'd moved in?

Why did the thought sink like a stone in my gut? I didn't even know the guy.

"I'm Mason Carter." He placed a hand over his heart. "And I own this bookstore." With reverent awe, he said, "Let's have a book-signing! I have an events room that—"

"No!" Ethan exploded, and he sounded almost panicked. He quickly recovered and murmured, "No, thank you. I'm not…making public appearances right now." He placed a thick hardback on the counter. "I'll just take this and leave." His fingers tapped anxiously as Mason rang up the book and slipped it into a paper bag.

As Ethan made for the door, he turned back, and his eyes found mine for a split second longer than necessary. He nodded. "Garrett."

"Ethan," I nodded in return, and the odd gravity of his gaze pulled at me.

As soon as the door closed behind him, Mason whirled on me, betrayal written in the scowl on his face. "You *met* him, and you didn't *tell* me?"

I shrugged. "We met at Cooper's, and I didn't know who he was. It's not like he had a flashing neon sign above his head that read, *Famous Author*."

Mason grumbled, "Well, you might have recognized him if you read something other than children's books."

An idea—probably a stupid one—formed in the back of my mind. "Where…?" I lazily searched the store with feigned nonchalance. "Are his books?"

Mason pointed. "Right there on the front display. They could have bitten you when you walked in."

I strolled over to the rack and kept my steps casual. Sure enough, eight of Ethan Quinn's Jake Slate books lined the top shelf. I grabbed the first book in the series. I peeked at Mason and returned his smirk with a glare.

I made a show of ambling through the bookstore as if I didn't have a care in the world and tossed Mason a look of indifference when I passed the counter. I ended up in the children's nook. Noah sat cross-legged, utterly engrossed in a Halloween picture book, his brow furrowed in concentration. Around him lay a small fortress of books.

"Time to clean up, buddy." I crouched beside him. A swell of pride swept through me as my eager reader quickly set his current book aside to sort through his piles. The smell of new books, that sharp scent of binding glue, wrapped around us.

"But, Daddy," he whined. His hand darted protectively over the stack he'd already gathered. "I need *all* of these." He fixed me with wide, pleading blue eyes.

I huffed a sigh and pretended reluctance. "You know the rule. We'll save some for next time." I gently coaxed the pile down from ten to five, allowing him to debate each one, his lip between his teeth as he made his hard choices.

He darted toward the counter. "Mr. Mason! I got five books!" He held up his hand in a proud display of five fingers.

Mason gave me a smug grin. But he gave Noah a kind, approving smile as he took the basket and rang up the books. "All good choices, too."

I slid Ethan's book onto the counter alongside Noah's stack.

A quirk pulled at the corner of Mason's mouth. "Do you know how to read anything but picture books, or is this your first dive into big-kid literature?"

I grunted and glared at him. "Ha-ha," I shot back. "For your information, I know how to read perfectly well."

But I had additional plans for that Jake Slate book.

CHAPTER FOUR

ETHAN

I stared at the screen of my laptop, arms crossed, and the flashing cursor on the blank page mocked me. *Blink, blink, blink.* I'd glared at that cursor for hours and willed the words to come. Yet, dread crept up my spine like icy fingers. The fear of feeding my alleged stalker's delusions paralyzed me. My throat tightened with anxiety that I was writing bait, but I had a deadline to meet.

I placed my fingers on the keys and began, *Slate vaulted the—*

The doorbell interrupted the silence, and a notification from my security app stole my attention. My breathing stopped, and the familiar pulse of adrenaline kicked in. There shouldn't be anyone on my porch—no deliveries, no visitors. For a scary moment, I simply eyed the alert on my phone, my mouth dry as I braced myself. I tapped the camera feed, half prepared to see some shadowy figure or threatening gift. Instead, I exhaled, and relief coursed through me as my screen revealed Garrett and his son.

I couldn't stop the grin that spread across my face. I

dropped my phone onto my desk and padded through the house in thick socks that hushed my steps. The residual tightness in my shoulders loosened.

As I reached the door, I heard the boy's muffled, enthusiastic chatter, punctuated by Garrett's deep murmur. Another chime rang through the house, followed by impatient giggles. Despite my fears and the need for privacy, my contrary mood lightened with anticipation as I disarmed the alarm system.

I swung the door open and found the little man bouncing from foot to foot. His hands clutched a picture book against his chest, his wide-eyed grin aimed up at me.

"Looking for me?" I teased and struggled to rein in my laughter at his intense excitement.

"Mr. Ethan!" he squealed and clutched his book even tighter. "I'm Noah! I'm five years old and I live across the street!" He spun on his heel, his sneakers scuffing against the pavement of the porch, and jabbed a small finger toward his house. He whipped back around. "Daddy told me you write books. I broughts my book for you to sign!" His enthusiasm radiated off him as he stretched the book up toward me.

Garrett stood behind him, and one hand ran self-consciously along the back of his neck. A blush dusted his cheeks. "I told Noah you only signed your own books, but he insisted."

I chuckled. "I'd be honored to sign his book." I pointed to the paperback Garrett had tucked under his arm. "And it looks like you brought one of mine, too." Heat unfurled in my chest at his interest in one of my novels.

"Come in." I shifted and welcomed them into the house. As they stepped inside, Garrett's gaze drifted around the room. "The new owner did a great job of renovating the place." He tapped the floor with the toe of his sneaker. "The refinished hardwood floors are beautiful."

"I got lucky to find such a nice house." Especially since I rented it and moved in at the last minute.

"You did." He turned in a circle. "I'm working on my home, but it's slow. I inherited it from my grandmother when she passed away." He shook his head. "She couldn't keep up with it in her final years."

A pang of sympathy hit me in the chest. "I'm so sorry for your loss."

He shrugged and tousled Noah's hair. "At least she got to meet Noah." He gave his son a fond smile, who ducked out from underneath his hand.

"Da-ad. I'm not a baby," he whined.

Garrett rolled his eyes, and I grinned.

"Let me get a pen, and I'll sign your books." I hooked a thumb toward my office.

Garrett handed me a Sharpie with a quick, confident flick of his wrist. "Came prepared." A hint of a grin tipped his lips.

I raised a brow and accepted the pen. "Were you a Boy Scout?"

"Yes, but I'm a deputy sheriff now. We're even better prepared than the Boy Scouts." A glint twinkled in his eye.

I snorted a laugh and plucked the pen from his fingers. "Have a seat."

Garrett settled into the club chair, and Noah jumped onto the sofa next to me. "Sign mine first!" His little face peered up at me, wide and hopeful.

"Please," his dad admonished.

"Please," Noah said sheepishly and ducked his head.

I opened the book to the title page and asked, "Do you know how to spell your name?"

He nodded. "N-O-A-H."

"Very impressive. *To my friend, Noah*," I printed. "*Happy Reading!—Mr. Ethan*. There you go."

As I handed him the book, his eyes grew impossibly wide, and he clenched the signed copy. "I'm going to show my teacher!" he declared, pride in his voice.

"Buddy, we're going to keep the book at home," Garrett said gently.

Noah's expressive face scrunched up like a prune. "Why?"

"Because Mr. Ethan is very famous, and he doesn't want people to know he lives here."

Noah turned to me, confusion in his gaze. "Why?"

How could I explain my reticence to a child when I couldn't even tell Garrett the truth without sounding like I was paranoid? My words tangled in my throat, and I stumbled to explain. "Umm—"

Garrett jumped in. "He wants quiet time." Relief poured through me at his simple answer, suitable for a young boy.

"Oh." Noah's eyebrows raised. "We have quiet time at school," he said matter-of-factly, as if everyone knew about quiet time.

A smile tugged at my lips. "Yes, like that." I nodded and tried to match his seriousness. It was impossible not to be charmed by his earnestness.

His head tilted a bit, and his gaze considered me. "Do you have playtime, too?" he asked innocently, as if the idea of a world without playtime was both baffling and a little tragic.

A chuckle escaped before I could stop it, and I pressed a hand to my chest as if that might help contain it. "No playtime," I said finally and grinned at him.

"Well, you should." His little face became thoughtful. Then he lit up. "I know! You can come to our movie night tonight."

"Buddy, Mr. Ethan probably doesn't want to watch a Disney movie," Garrett said. Yet hope lived in the depths of his eyes.

"Who doesn't like *Frozen*?" My lips twitched. "But I don't want to impose upon your family. And...shouldn't you ask your...wife...first?" I was blatantly fishing for information, but I was curious about the woman I saw at their house in the evenings. Garrett had seemed to give signals that he returned my interest, which was confusing if he had a woman in his life.

Garrett's brows drew together, and the awkwardness deepened. "Oh, Harper? No, that's my sister. She watches Noah when I'm working evenings and weekends."

Relief filled me, and I couldn't stop the quiet smile that slipped onto my face. Perhaps Garrett felt the buzz between us after all.

"Auntie Harper makes blanket forts! With different rooms in them!" Noah's voice rose with excitement. His eyes sparkled, and his entire face lit up like he'd just shared the world's best secret. It was impossible not to get caught up in his enthusiasm; the way he looked at me, so expectant, so utterly convinced that blanket forts were the pinnacle of happiness, made my chest tighten with affection for my new little friend.

"Auntie Harper sounds like a lot of fun," I said with a gentle smile. The words came easily, but behind them was a pang of longing I hadn't expected. When was the last time I'd felt the joy Noah radiated?

"Yeah!" Then the light in his eyes dimmed, and he kicked his dangling feet against the sofa. "But then she makes me go to bed." His lower lip stuck out in a pout.

I bit back a chuckle and pressed my lips together to keep from laughing outright. "Does she read you a story at bedtime?"

He gave me an incredulous look, like I'd asked the dumbest question. "Of course," he said, as though I'd broken some unspoken rule of bedtime routines.

"Then it's worth going to bed," I said weightily, as if I imparted the wisdom of the ages.

His lips pursed with the exaggerated thoughtfulness of a child. He finally let out a dramatic sigh. "I guess," he mumbled and slumped back against the couch in defeat.

"And tonight..." I nudged him gently with my elbow. "You can read the new book I signed."

His entire demeanor shifted in an instant. He sat bolt upright, and his eyes lit up like the lights on a Christmas tree. "Hey! Yeah!" he exclaimed, full of the pure, unfiltered excitement that only kids seemed to pull off. He bounced on the cushion, his earlier sulk forgotten.

I turned to Garrett, who watched us with a fond smile, and held out my hand. "Want me to sign your book so you can read it at bedtime?" I winked.

Garrett threw his head back and laughed, a deep, full sound I felt in my chest. He handed me the book and his fingers brushed against mine for just a second—enough to send a zing up my arm.

My heart raced, but I outwardly composed myself. "*To Garrett. Happy bedtime reading—Ethan.*" I tried not to think of Garrett in bed, wearing nothing but a pair of sleep pants, his abs and broad shoulders on display. And failed.

Garrett accepted the signed book with thanks, grinned at the inscription, and stood. "So...pizza and a movie at six?" His piercing blue gaze bore into mine, as if he could see my desire to spend time with him.

"I'll bring the popcorn." My heart raced with the promise of an evening with the little family—and with Garrett.

CHAPTER FIVE

GARRETT

The whir of the vacuum drowned out Noah's chatter as he sorted through his Hot Wheels cars, precisely lining them up on the coffee table. I maneuvered the cleaner over the carpet and zeroed in on the cracker crumbs from this afternoon's snack. Noah had insisted on Goldfish—extra cheddar, of course—and now the light-gray carpet I'd installed was paying the price. Thank fu—dge for STAINMASTER.

When I inherited the house, it had been a time capsule of the seventies—threadbare carpet in some rooms, curling yellowed linoleum in the kitchen and bathrooms. Fixing the flooring had been my first project. I'd spent weekends ripping up the old floors and putting down carpet and tile. It wasn't fancy, but it was clean and functional.

I powered down the vacuum, gave the sofa's throw pillows a quick fluff, and arranged them neatly on the kid-friendly couch. It wasn't the sleek leather kind Ethan probably had in the city, but it was stain-proof and built for a five-year-old's acrobatics. I stood back and took in the room. It wasn't perfect, but it would have to do.

"Time to put away the toys, bud," I said while I stowed the vacuum in the small entryway closet.

Noah's face lit up. "Is Mr. Ethan coming soon?" He buzzed with excitement.

"Yep." I kneeled beside the coffee table. Together, we tossed the fleet of cars and trucks into their storage bin, and my thoughts drifted to Ethan. He was due any minute. He was coming for pizza and a movie—nothing big. But the more I thought about it, the more nervous I got. My house felt cramped and outdated compared to the remodeled rental Ethan was staying in. What would he think of my place?

What would he think of me?

The thought made my hands slow. I wasn't used to second-guessing myself, but Ethan…Ethan confused me. I liked him, that much was clear. He was smart, funny, and easy to talk to. And…was I attracted to him? It had been years since a man had made my pulse stumble. So long that my attraction to Ethan felt…new. Fresh. Welcome.

The doorbell rang and snapped me out of my thoughts. Noah shot up like a spring, his excitement palpable. "I'll get it!" He bolted to the door.

"Noah, wait!" I surged to my feet and my heart thudded in my chest. He was already at the door, fingers fumbling with the latch before I could reach him. My stomach tightened at the possibilities.

Noah swung the door open with a bang against the wall and revealed Ethan. The sight of him—his light smile and warm brown eyes that crinkled at the corners—loosened some of the tautness in my shoulders.

"Hi!" Noah sang and bounced on the balls of his feet.

"Hey there, buddy," Ethan said, as if they were best friends. He crouched down to Noah's level. He held out a red and yellow box like it was a prized treasure. "I brought popcorn."

Noah hopped from foot to foot. "Extra butter?"

"Is there any other kind?" Ethan said mock-seriously.

I stepped forward and placed a firm hand on Noah's shoulder. "What have I told you about opening the door without checking with me first?"

Noah's excitement dimmed, and his narrow shoulders slumped.

"Sorry, Daddy," he mumbled and tugged at my heart. "I thought it was Mr. Ethan."

I weakened. "It's okay. Just remember for next time, all right? You don't know who might be on the other side."

Noah nodded, chastened, but was quick to recover. "Okay!"

Ethan rose to his full height, and his gaze flickered between Noah and me. "Sorry if I caused any trouble."

"Not your fault." I stepped aside and gestured. "Come on in."

As Ethan moved past me, the faint scent of his body wash—maybe cedarwood?—lingered in the air and frazzled me. My nerves, barely calmed from the door incident, flared back to life at his presence.

Noah's excitement returned full force and brightened the space. He buzzed around Ethan as he slipped off his shoes. Noah chattered about the popcorn, and Ethan chuckled and handed it over. I shut the door and leaned into it for a moment to collect myself. But when Ethan's eyes met mine, a peculiar twist gripped my chest.

What the hell was happening to me?

A knock jolted me from my spiraling thoughts.

"It's here!" Noah practically vibrated with energy. His begging gaze caught mine as he silently asked for permission to open the door.

I couldn't help but laugh. "Hold on." I peeked through the peephole and spotted the delivery driver. "Go ahead." I stepped aside as Ethan moved to give Noah room.

Noah yanked the door open. "Yay! Pizza!" The savory aroma of garlic and spices spilled into the entryway.

The young deliveryman grinned and handed the hot, fragrant boxes over Noah's head. I took them with a nod of thanks and passed him a tip while Noah darted toward the kitchen table. His shout of "Come on, Mr. Ethan!" echoed through the house.

"Wash your hands!" I called after him. He let out an exaggerated groan but veered toward the bathroom. The sound of rushing water followed.

Ethan stayed by my side. His gaze followed Noah's retreat with a light chuckle. "He's got enough energy to power the entire block."

"Don't I know it," I said, my fond exasperation clear. Ethan's quiet laugh did something to me—something I wasn't ready to unpack.

In the kitchen, I set the pizzas on the table, and their rich aroma made my stomach growl. "I didn't know what you liked." I pointed to the boxes. "Got pepperoni for Noah, plus a veggie, just in case."

"Not picky." Ethan shook his head. "But thanks for thinking of me."

"No problem," I muttered. My cheeks heated—was I actually *blushing*? This man had me so off-kilter that I was in danger of falling on my face.

"What can I do?" Ethan asked.

"You can have a seat." I gestured to a chair. "And let me know what you want to drink. I've got water, sparkling water, soda, iced tea, and lemonade."

Noah ran into the room. "I want lemonade, Daddy!" His

enthusiasm burst through the calm like a firecracker. He gripped the edge of the table as he jumped in his seat.

I raised an eyebrow and tried to suppress a smile. In his excitement, he'd forgotten the manners I'd worked so hard to instill. "Please don't interrupt," I reminded him gently. "Mr. Ethan is our guest. Let him choose first."

Noah's face fell momentarily. "Sorry, Daddy." But he recovered with the resilience only a kindergartener could muster. He turned to Ethan. In his wide eyes, I could see his hopes rising. "But you want lemonade, don't you, Mr. Ethan? Huh? It's the bestest!"

Ethan's lips twitched with the effort to keep a straight face. "Sure." He nodded with mock solemnity. "If it's the bestest, how can I say no? We can be twinsies." His eyes sparkled with good humor.

I bit the inside of my cheek to keep from laughing. Ethan had an easy way of indulging Noah without a hint of condescension, a quality that made my chest tighten in an unfamiliar, complicated way. His kindness touched me deeply, and I wasn't ready to examine that too closely. That's just how friends felt about each other.

Right?

"Two lemonades, then." Ethan glanced at me with a small smile. "Can I get them?" He half rose from his chair.

"Thanks, but I've got it." I waved him off. "Help yourself to pizza." Truthfully, I was grateful for the excuse to step into the kitchen and steady my nerves. I poured the sweet and tart drink into two glasses. A punch of citrus hit my nose and mingled with the comforting aroma of hot pizza. I grabbed a bottle of cold water for myself, took a deep breath, and returned to the table.

Ethan had already taken over and distributed slices. Noah happily munched on a piece of pepperoni, a streak of sauce smudged on his cheek. A slice of each pizza sat on Ethan's plate.

"I didn't know what you wanted." He nodded toward the boxes.

The savory aroma made my stomach growl audibly. I grabbed two slices of pepperoni, and the cheese stretched as I lifted them to my plate. The first bite was heaven—gooey, salty, and rich. I groaned loudly, the sound escaping before I could stop it.

Ethan raised a brow, and his brown eyes twinkled with amusement. "Good?"

I swallowed quickly, and heat crept up my neck. "Excuse me," I mumbled, embarrassed by my lack of restraint. "I was hungry."

"You're excused," Noah said primly, his face the picture of disapproval. "But don't do it again."

Ethan turned his laugh into a discreet cough, and the sight of his barely contained smile sent a fresh wave of warmth through me. He had a way of making everything feel easy.

"So, Noah." Ethan leaned forward. "Tell me about school."

It was all the encouragement my son needed. "My teacher is Mr. Matsumoto, and he's *so* funny. He tells jokes all the time!" Noah rose to his knees. "Knock-knock!"

"Who's there?" Ethan asked. His mouth quirked as he braced for what was coming.

"Boo!"

"Boo who?"

"Don't cry—it's just me!" Noah exploded into a belly laugh, his joy infectious. I laughed, despite having heard the joke roughly, oh, a gazillion times.

Ethan chuckled along and nodded appreciatively. "That's a good one. Knock-knock."

Noah's face lit up, surprised and delighted that Ethan was playing along. "Who's there?"

"Cow says."

"Cow says who?" Noah's face wrinkled in confusion

"No, silly. A cow says moo!"

Noah squealed with laughter and nearly toppled off his chair. Ethan laughed with him, the sound rich and full. I watched the two of them, my heart swelling at how seamlessly Ethan fit into the scene. His patience with Noah, his genuine interest—it disarmed me, to say the least.

As Noah rattled off stories about school, his words tumbled over one another. Ethan listened attentively and asked questions that made Noah light up even more. I couldn't help but admire the way he handled my son, like it was the most natural thing in the world.

After Noah finished his second slice and drained his lemonade, he looked at me expectantly. "Can I be done?"

"Yeah, buddy. Take your plate and cup to the kitchen and we'll watch a movie."

"Yay!" He threw his hands up in the air and nearly knocked over his cup. With all the speed and energy of a five-year-old, he dumped his dishes by the sink. In no time, he bounded onto the couch.

I shook my head, and a smile quirked my lips. He was a handful, but he was my handful, and I wouldn't trade him for the world. As I turned back to the table, Ethan was watching me, his expression gentle, almost unreadable.

"What?" I asked quietly.

He shook his head, and his smile returned. "Nothing. You're a wonderful dad, that's all."

The compliment meant more to me than I expected, and I had to look away. I busied myself with clearing the table and ignored the tightness in my chest. I brushed off the praise with, "Ready to watch *Frozen* with a hyperactive five-year-old? Brace yourself."

CHAPTER SIX

GARRETT

The buttery scent of popcorn filled the air as I carried the bowl from the kitchen and placed it on the coffee table. Noah vibrated with impatience, perched on the couch with his legs folded under him. He bounced as he rattled off every detail about *Frozen*—his favorite parts and characters, and how many times he'd seen it.

"Too many times," I groaned and plopped onto the couch beside him.

"Not enough times," Ethan countered. A grin tugged at his lips as he settled on the other side of Noah. Ethan nudged Noah with his elbow. "This is one of my favorites. I could quote the whole movie by heart—I've watched it about a thousand times with my niece. Let's see if you can keep up with me."

That earned him a beaming smile from Noah, who seemed thrilled to have found a fellow *Frozen* aficionado. I grabbed the remote, queued up the movie, and hit play.

The opening notes of "Frozen Heart" filled the room, the

deep voices of the ice harvesters singing as they worked. Noah narrated and explained every character and scene, like he was giving Ethan a personal tour of Arendelle. Ethan hung on every word, nodded, and asked questions that only fueled Noah's enthusiasm.

When Anna sang "Do You Want to Build a Snowman?" Noah and Ethan joined in, loud and off-key. Ethan, for all of his virtues, had a cringeworthy singing voice. The two clicked their tongues like a clock, and Ethan flicked his eyes back and forth like Anna peeking through the keyhole. That sent Noah into a fit of giggles, and I chuckled.

I noticed Ethan's energy. He wasn't just tolerating the movie for Noah's sake—he was fully into it and dramatically gasped when Hans made his first appearance.

Noah solemnly declared, "He's the bad guy."

Ethan clutched his chest. "What? No! He seems so nice!" and earned another round of laughter from Noah.

My spirits lifted at their interactions, and I sat back and enjoyed the fun.

By the time the snow creature showed up, the intensity on the screen had Noah sliding closer to Ethan. When the creature roared, Noah covered his eyes and snuggled into Ethan's side. Ethan froze for a moment and his hand hovered uncertainly above Noah's back. He glanced at me and his eyes silently asked, *Is this okay?*

I nodded, and Ethan gently rested his hand on Noah's back. He rubbed small circles as he murmured, "It's okay, bub. I've got you."

The simple gesture punched me in the gut. I watched Ethan care for Noah so naturally and thoughtfully, and an ache stirred within me—an ache that was unfamiliar and yet settling.

For the rest of the movie, Noah stayed glued to the edge

of his seat, practically shouting at the characters as if they could hear him. "No, Anna, don't trust him!" He threw his hands up.

I gave Ethan a knowing look and mouthed, "See what I mean?"

Ethan smirked in return, but a fondness lit his eyes.

When the movie ended and everyone in Arendelle had their happy-ever-after, Noah flopped back on the couch like he'd just finished a marathon. "That was awesome."

I couldn't agree more, though my thoughts weren't about the movie. Ethan fit so effortlessly into our little family dynamic, which left me with a tug to know him better.

"All right, kiddo." I ruffled Noah's hair. "Bedtime."

Predictably, Noah groaned. "But I'm not tired!"

"You just flopped like a snowman melting in the sun."

Noah frowned. "Okay, maybe I'm a little tired. But can Mr. Ethan read me a story?" He turned to Ethan. "Pleeease?"

Ethan looked at me, his expression unsure, as if worried he was intruding upon our bedtime routine.

"Your call," I said with a shrug.

Ethan nodded, smiling gently. "We can read the book I signed."

"Yay!" Noah launched off the sofa and his feet pounded the floor as he disappeared down the hall, a whirlwind of renewed energy. His laugh trailed behind him and lit up the house.

"Brush your teeth and go potty!" I called after him.

A glum, "Okay, Daddy," floated back, muffled by the distance.

Ethan's mellow laugh followed me as I headed toward Noah's room. The sound wrapped around me, low and warm.

Inside Noah's room, I helped him into his dinosaur-print

pajamas, the colors faded from countless washes but still his favorite. Ethan respected our privacy and waited quietly in the hallway. I appreciated his consideration. Noah wiggled eagerly when I handed him the book.

"You can come in now." I glanced over my shoulder.

Ethan stepped inside, and his hesitant smile caught me off guard. Shy yet sincere, it sent a ripple through my chest. I furrowed my brows, confused by my reaction to Ethan. It had been so long since a man's smile affected me.

Ethan tilted his head, and concern dimmed his expression. "Everything okay?"

I forced my features into something more neutral. "Everything's fine. Thanks for doing this." I stepped back to give him room. I leaned against the doorframe and tried to recover from the odd sensation.

"My pleasure." He perched on the edge of Noah's bed, his tall frame out of place in the cramped room overflowing with stuffed animals and storybooks. He cleared his throat theatrically, cracked opened the book, and tilted it so Noah could see the illustrations.

Then Ethan began to read. His voice dropped an octave, his tone resonant and deep, and he slipped seamlessly into the role of storyteller. He gave each animal a distinct form of speech, from a grumpy bear to a squeaky squirrel, and even added exaggerated gestures. The effect was magical.

Laughter bubbled out of me before I could stop it.

Ethan utterly captivated Noah. His giggles rang out, pure and light, as he clung to every word Ethan read. When Ethan reached the last page and closed the book with a dramatic flourish, Noah sighed in contentment.

But then mischief entered his eyes. "Another!" he begged.

I shook my head and bit back a grin. "That's enough for tonight, buddy. It's way past your bedtime."

Noah's shoulders slumped, and his lower lip pushed out in an overblown pout. "Aww."

"Say thank you to Mr. Ethan for reading the story." I crossed my arms.

Noah perked up, bright with a zeal that was equal parts gratitude and a stalling tactic. "Thank you, Mr. Ethan!"

Ethan stood and carefully placed the book on the shelf. "Goodnight, Noah. Sweet dreams," he whispered. He retreated to the hallway to allow us to finish our bedtime routine.

I tucked Noah in, smoothed the blankets, and pressed a kiss to his forehead. His dark hair smelled faintly of baby shampoo, and for a moment I lingered, overwhelmed by the quiet love that always seemed to swell in moments like these. "Sleep tight, buddy. I'll see you in the morning."

"Night, Daddy," he murmured, already drifting off.

I shut off the lamp, made sure his nightlight cast a glow over the room, and pulled the door until only a crack remained open. Ethan waited in the hall. A strange mix of gratitude and a deeper pang twisted in my chest. The house felt a little fuller, a little brighter. And it wasn't because of Noah.

Ethan nodded briefly, a warm smile on his lips. He turned, made his way to the front door, and stepped into his shoes. "Thank you for a fun evening."

I was reluctant to let him go, though I didn't have the excuse of Noah's invitation to prolong the evening. A connection between us sparked in a way I hadn't expected but couldn't ignore. Ethan made me laugh—not just polite chuckles, but genuine laughter. His sharp mind kept me on my toes. And the way he'd been with Noah—kind, patient, and unhurried—had struck a chord. It wasn't just that I admired him. I liked him. I wanted to know more about the man.

The thought of the evening ending left a hollow ache, as if I'd be letting go of something that mattered before I even fully understood it. I wasn't ready to say goodbye—not yet. My pulse picked up, and my words stumbled out. "Stay for a beer?"

CHAPTER SEVEN

ETHAN

Garrett's question hung in the air, simple but loaded—
"Stay for a beer?"

I froze with my hand on the doorknob. The correct
answer was *no*. I should leave. I had my reasons—too many
of them.

But my chest tightened with the weight of the isolation
I'd carried for months. Garrett's home was warm, inviting,
and full of life—clear in the faint, lingering aroma of shared
popcorn and the memory of Noah's laughter. My house
was…empty. Quiet to the point of suffocation.

The logical side of me shouted its objections: he's a
deputy sheriff. If he finds out about the stalker, it'll
complicate everything. I'm here temporarily and might have
to leave at a moment's notice. What's the point of forming
friendships if I'm just going to sever them?

And the most important argument—what if I
endangered Noah if I got closer to the little family?

My hand tightened on the doorknob.

But then there was Garrett. The openness in his

expression, the hint of nervousness in the way he shoved his hands into his pockets. He wanted me to stay. For a beer. For company. For…something more?

The thought sent a flicker of warmth through me, battling against the impersonal voice of reason. We had chemistry, no denying that. The way he smiled, the way his deep laugh filled my chest—he drew me in, made me forget the walls I'd built.

And maybe his presence could keep the stalker at bay. Not that I wanted to use him. I didn't want that. But maybe he could provide a shield of safety, and if I ever told him everything, Garrett might offer the support—professional, emotional—I couldn't find anywhere else.

Still, the risk loomed large. What if the stalker escalated? What if I brought danger to his doorstep? I couldn't do that. I wouldn't forgive myself.

But then, maybe I was just being paranoid, and there were no negatives.

Garrett spread his hands wide, and his voice pulled me from my spiraling thoughts. "Hey, it's okay…"

The hesitation in his tone hit me like a blow to the chest. He was giving me an out, but it felt like a fragile thread was stretching between us, one I could either strengthen or snap.

I gave him a touch of a smile and dropped my hand. "A beer sounds good."

Undeniable relief lit Garrett's face, and my resolve to distance myself weakened further. One beer. I'd stay an hour and then go home to my empty house.

He clasped his hands and rubbed them together. "Great! Have a seat."

By the time I'd toed off my shoes and settled on one end of the couch, Garrett had reappeared from the kitchen, necking two bottles of beer in one hand like a practiced pro. The bottle he handed me was cool to the touch, the amber glass sweating in the cozy glow of the living room lamp.

"Cheers," I murmured and tipped my bottle to his. The first sip was icy and crisp, with an earthy richness. I studied the label and raised my eyebrows at the unfamiliar design. "This is excellent. Barnacle Brews?"

"It's made right here in Seacliff Cove. I'll take you to the brewery and introduce you to Callum."

I froze for half a heartbeat. He was already talking about a next time and meeting his friends. Despite my better judgment and the rational defenses I'd built, the words hit me like a warm rush of pumpkin spice latte. My chest tightened as I struggled to hold him at arm's length. I couldn't dwell on wishful thinking and wanting something I might not be able to have. I needed a safer topic. "Maybe someday," I said under my breath. Then louder, "Why did you become a deputy sheriff?"

"I was born to be a deputy sheriff," he said with a sheepish chuckle. "My father was one—retired now—and he named me after Pat Garrett."

I couldn't help it; the corner of my mouth twitched upward. "The sheriff who shot Billy the Kid?"

"Exactly." He took a long pull from his beer, his throat working with a rhythm so hypnotic that I had to drag my gaze away.

Why was that so suggestive? So maddeningly sexy? The heat that surged through me was entirely inappropriate. My fingers tightened around the neck of the bottle, the condensation damp against my palm. I forced my mind to stop wandering down paths it had no business exploring. He'd offered me a beer, not a—I cleared my throat. "If you followed in your father's footsteps, does that mean you didn't really want to be a deputy?"

"Oh, no." His denial was instant, his voice full of

conviction. "Being in law enforcement was the only thing I ever wanted to do. I looked up to my dad. Wanted to wear a uniform just like him. In my childish mind, it was all about putting away the bad guys."

As he took another sip, I forced my attention to the sturdy texture of the sofa fabric and not the stretch of his throat or the languid way he leaned against the couch.

"The reality is, it's not a thrill-a-minute. It's a lot of paperwork and minor complaints, punctuated by moments of adrenaline-packed emergencies. But I believe in protecting and serving my community." He shrugged, an unassuming gesture. "That's probably more than you wanted to know."

I almost said, *I want to know everything*. But I clamped my lips shut, terrified of revealing too much. Instead, I offered a crooked smile. "I'm always interested in people and their stories. It's the writer in me. Who knows? You may end up in a book one day." I put a period on the statement with a wink.

He grinned in reply. "Just don't kill me off."

The humor in his words slid right past me as a chill ghosted down my spine. My smile faltered, the weight of his safety heavy on my chest. *Not on my watch.*

He raised his bottle, pointing it toward me like a casual invitation. "What about you? Did you always want to be a writer?"

"God, no." I swigged my beer, the tang hitting my gut. "I wanted to be a pediatrician."

Garrett tilted his head, studying me with his perceptive blue eyes. "I can see that. You're good with Noah. What changed your mind?"

My fingers tightened around the bottle. "I took creative writing as an elective. My professor thought I had talent and became my mentor." My lips quirked at the memory of Professor Halpern's unruly hair and blunt critiques. "I entered a few contests, published some short stories, and ended up loving writing." I shrugged. "By the time I graduated with a degree in biology, I knew I was in the wrong field. I wanted to write."

But that wasn't the whole truth. The rest was a familiar weight in my chest. The nights I spent hunched over my laptop after endless hours at my day job in a sterile lab, my dreams poured into chapters when everyone else had long gone to sleep. It had been grueling, a balancing act that sometimes felt impossible. But when the Jake Slate series finally took off, I knew it had been worth it.

Garrett nodded, his expression thoughtful. "Where did you go to school?"

I paused, the words catching on the edge of caution. Telling Garrett where I went to college meant giving away a piece of where I came from. But something about him— steady, grounded—made me want to take the risk. "Columbia University," I said, and let it hang there between us.

Garrett's eyebrows lifted slightly, the only real sign of surprise. He leaned back on the cushion, eyes narrowing— not with suspicion, but with new curiosity.

"Impressive," he said. His voice was calm, measured, but I could see the wheels turning behind his gaze. "East Coast, then."

I gave a small shrug, not ready to fill in the blanks.

"That niece you mentioned earlier—does she live on the East Coast?"

I nodded, fondness blooming quietly in my chest. "Yeah." I stared at the brown bottle in my hand, turning it slowly as doubt twisted in my gut. Then, with a quiet breath and a glance toward Garrett, I made the choice—I was going to trust him. "Brooklyn."

His gaze flicked toward me, and I could tell he was

tucking the detail away, careful not to press too hard. I appreciated that more than he knew.

"My sister's a single mom," I added. "Her ex—well, he didn't stick around. Never really stepped up. So, I fill in the gaps where I can. I'm the uncle who picks her up from school, helps with science projects, reads bedtime stories. Kayley is...everything to me." I ached for her—her bright smile, the way her excited chatter filled a room. Every day I stayed away felt like I was missing something irreplaceable. And yet...I wasn't ready to go back. Not while danger still lingered in the corners of my life. I wanted to be there—I *needed* to be. Brooklyn called to me, but right now, home didn't feel safe.

Garrett didn't say anything right away, but the softness in his expression said he got it.

"The rest of my family's there, too," I said after a pause. "Parents. Cousins. Old neighbors who still wave when I pass their stoop. It's all back east."

"So," he said, voice low and deceptively casual, "why'd you come to Seacliff Cove?"

The question hit harder than it should have. My fingers tightened around the neck of my bottle, the chill of the glass suddenly grounding me.

I could feel the weight of his eyes, waiting for an answer I wasn't ready to give.

My heart kicked up.

Not yet.

I wasn't ready to hand over that part of the story

I aimed for a light voice. "Writing retreat," I said. "Needed a change of scenery to finish my latest book."

Garrett nodded slowly, the corners of his mouth tipping into something warm. "Can't argue with the view."

I forced a smile in return.

And I hated how easy the lie had come.

He sipped his beer, then tilted his head slightly and curiosity lit his eyes. "Where do you get the ideas for your books?" The way he cocked his head, as if genuinely interested, sent a satisfying pulse through me.

For a pragmatic, down-to-earth deputy sheriff, I understood why he'd ask. "News stories. Life. My imagination."

Garrett whistled, low and long. "Eight books? That's some imagination."

My face heated, and I looked down, fiddling with the label on my bottle. Pride swelled in my chest despite myself. "I hope to keep going for at least eight more, as long as readers stick with me." I shifted the focus. "But tell me about your job. I admire what you do."

His stories were a mix of absurdity and heart, painting Seacliff Cove with vivid strokes. The dog-crap feud between Frank and Martha had me laughing. The flood of clueless tourists during the summer boggled my mind. A rash of unsolved pranks plagued the town. But it was the way Garrett spoke about his friends—Cooper at the coffee shop; Mason, the owner of the bookstore; Caleb, director of The Coastal Light Gallery; Declan, owner of the diner; and Landon, the manager of the boutique hotel—that struck me. Fondness laced every word. I couldn't help but envy those connections. Under different circumstances, I would have liked to meet them.

Before I knew it, eleven o'clock was approaching.

Garrett stretched, the movement lazy and unguarded. "Excuse me." His mouth opened in a jaw-cracking yawn. "I'm usually in bed by now. Noah's up early."

My stomach dropped. Had I overstayed my welcome? I pushed to my feet, wiping my palms on my jeans. "Sorry for keeping you up."

He stood and shook his head. A small smile curved his

lips. "Don't worry about it. I enjoyed this evening. Thanks for staying." His voice was low and rough, each word wrapping around me. His blue eyes darkened, the shift so subtle I might've missed it if I wasn't so attuned to him.

My pulse kicked up. Was I imagining the pull between us? Garrett took a hesitant step forward, and I held my breath. But then he veered toward the door. I followed, the disappointment sharper than I wanted to admit.

In the entryway, I slipped on my shoes. "Thanks for a fun evening. I had a good time," I said softly. *More than you know.*

"We'll, uh, do it again," Garrett said, rubbing the back of his neck. His gaze darted to the floor before lifting to mine, uncertainty shadowing his usual confidence. "Maybe… without Noah next time?"

Was this his way of asking me out? Maybe that magnetic pull I'd been feeling wasn't just in my head. A thrill ran through my stomach. "I'd like that," I whispered. "See you again." I twisted the knob and stepped out into the chilly night, my porch light a beacon in the dark.

I crossed the street, and my shoes scuffed softly against the pavement as the night wrapped around me. The faint, rhythmic *whoosh* of distant waves provided a sense of calm as I walked up the path to my door. When the motion-activated floodlight flared to life, its brightness splashed across the porch and illuminated an object resting on the welcome mat. I sucked in a breath, and a frisson of fear snaked down my spine.

I slowed my steps, and my muscles tightened with a mix of dread and reluctant curiosity. I squinted against the harsh light, and I willed it to be nothing more than a stray leaf blown in by the sea breeze. But deep down, I knew better. I crept closer, my heartbeat hammering harder with every step until I halted at the edge of the doormat. My lungs hitched as my gaze locked on the thing that waited for me.

It wasn't a leaf.

My stomach clenched like a fist. I turned in a full circle and scanned the darkened street for any sign of movement. Shadows stretched along the quiet road. My ears strained for the sound of footsteps, the rustle of leaves, anything—but the silence was absolute, except for the distant crash of waves.

I turned back to the thing on my porch. A costume Bowie knife—plastic blade smeared with thick, fake blood—the kind you'd find in a Halloween store.

It lay at an odd angle across the welcome mat, gleaming wetly under the floodlight as if it had just been used. My skin prickled, heat rising up the back of my neck before being chased away by a deep, chilling unease.

A knife.

The weapon the killer used in my fourth Jake Slate novel.

Was this a prank? Part of the rash of stunts Garrett had been talking about? If so, why was it left at *my* door?

A sour taste crept into my mouth. Was it something more ominous? Did I truly have a stalker, and this was a warning? A message that they'd found me, even across the country in sleepy Seacliff Cove?

I glanced over my shoulder; the floodlight cast my shadow long and distorted against the porch. Across the street, Garrett's house glowed with reassuring warmth. His porch light was still on, like a lighthouse shining in the oppressive darkness. My legs moved before my brain caught up, my hand tentatively reaching for the handle of the plastic knife as if the blade might slice me. I plucked it up, the texture cold and unpleasant in my grasp, and crossed the street with my heart pounding in my ears.

I knocked lightly on Garrett's door, my breathing shallow, my thoughts racing. What if this was nothing?

What if it was everything?

When Garrett opened the door, his smirk was instant. "We're keeping the rest of the pop—" His words cut off, and he reared back, his expression twisting in horror. "What the *fudge* is that thing?"

"It's a plastic knife painted with fake blood." My voice came out steadier than I expected, though my chest still felt like it might implode. "I found it on my doormat. Is this the kind of prank you've been seeing?"

"Heck, no." Garrett shook his head, his brows furrowing. "That's just disturbing. We've had mailboxes filled with marshmallows, toilet-papered trees, rearranged yard decorations…that sort of thing. This doesn't fit."

My stomach churned, and a knot tightened. My muscles stiffened with the effort of holding myself together. This couldn't be happening. Not here. Not now.

Would I have to run again?

No. Not yet. I forced air into my lungs, willing my cramped muscles to relax. "Would you keep an eye out for more incidents like this?"

"Yeah, no problem," he said, all business. "Wait a sec." He disappeared into the house and returned a moment later with a plastic bag, in full cop mode. "Put that in here. I'll take it to the station and show it around. Ask if anyone else has seen anything like this. Ask everyone to be on the lookout."

Relief flickered as I dropped the creepy toy into the bag. The weight of it was no longer in my hand, but its implications lingered. "Thanks," I mumbled. "Let me know." I recited my phone number. He sent me a text, so I had his number.

We said goodnight—again—and I retraced my steps across the street, the house feeling impossibly far away. My eyes darted toward every shadow, my breath quick and shallow.

When I reached my door, I unlocked it with trembling fingers and stepped inside. I closed the door with a muted *thud*, then reset my security system. I pressed my back to the solid wood.

What had just happened?

The question ricocheted in my mind, unanswered and relentless. My pulse thundered in my ears, and I swallowed hard, trying to force down the rising panic. Was it just a prank? A cruel joke? Or something more menacing?

Then a thought hit me—I retrieved my phone from my pocket and saw a security alert I must've missed while watching the movie. *Shit.* I pulled up the camera feed.

There.

My breath hitched. At nine-sixteen p.m., a hooded figure stepped into view. The black-and-white footage revealed little —the hood obscured the face and a baggy sweatshirt and sweatpants concealed the body. It could have been a man or a tall woman. They bent, placed the knife on the doormat, and vanished into the darkness.

I texted Garrett, quickly summarizing what I'd found. His reply came almost instantly:

Send me the footage.

My fingers trembled as I attached and sent the video, urgency sitting like a weight on my chest. There was a long pause, then:

I'll see if anyone recognizes them.

The silence in my house felt heavier than ever, and I told

myself the shiver crawling up my spine was just the chilly night air.

I lied.

CHAPTER EIGHT

GARRETT

When Noah and I reached the head of the path that wound its way from our neighborhood down to the beach, I toed off my tennis shoes. The coarse sand sifted cool and gritty beneath my toes, a refreshing contrast to the unseasonably warm afternoon sun. The ocean breeze carried the faint tang of salt and seaweed, ruffling Noah's hair as he bounced on his feet beside me.

"Give me your shoes, buddy." I held out my hand, and he shoved the sneakers into my grasp, his excitement barely contained. I hooked them with two fingers.

He hopped from foot to foot, and his energy vibrated like a live wire. "Can I run ahead? Huh? Huh?"

I nodded. "Not too far."

Noah didn't need to hear it twice. He was off like a rocket and his laughter spilled out behind him in high-pitched squeals. I followed at a moderate pace and savored the feel of the sand shifting under my weight and the rhythmic crash of waves in the distance.

It was peaceful—until it wasn't.

Up ahead, Noah skidded to a halt. My gaze sharpened as he approached a man standing on the path. Without hesitation, my son reached up and slid his small hand into the man's much larger one. The sight sent an icy bolt straight to my chest. My heart stuttered, then lurched into a gallop.

I broke into a dead run, adrenaline prickling at the base of my neck. The man turned slightly, his head swiveling as if searching for someone. The brim of his ball cap cast a shadow over his face, but the glint of auburn hair curling out from beneath it caught the sun. Recognition washed over me, and I exhaled sharply, the tension in my shoulders easing as I slowed to a walk.

"Look, Dad!" Noah's voice was pure joy as I closed the gap between us. He held up their joined hands. "I found Mr. Ethan!"

My relief melted into exasperation. "I see that. But remember the rules about stranger danger."

Noah's face scrunched in confusion. "But he's not a stranger."

Ethan's brows knitted together above the dark frames of his sunglasses. "Did I just cause a problem again?"

"Hi, Ethan." I gave him a quick chin lift, still catching my breath. "No problem on your end. This guy"—I shot Noah a pointed look—"nearly gave me a heart attack until I realized it was you."

Noah's smile fell. He slumped a little, dragging his toes through the sand. "Sorry, Daddy."

I mussed his hair, the short, soft strands slipping through my fingers. "Next time, just run back and tell me first, okay?"

"O-kay." He drew the word out. His eyes darted back up to Ethan, and lit up like someone had flipped a switch, his guilt short-lived. "We're going for a walk! Wanna come with us?"

"What a coincidence." Ethan's lips quirked. "I'm going for a walk, too."

Noah's grin spread wide, his excitement a force of nature. "We can go together!" He cast a hopeful glance my way. "But can I run ahead?"

Ethan chuckled, his laugh low and warm, and crouched to Noah's level. "Doesn't that kind of defeat the purpose of walking *together*?"

I snorted, unable to hold back my amusement. "Yes, you can run ahead. *But*"—I leveled him with a stern look—"no talking to strangers. And stay out of the water until I get there."

"O-*kay*, Daddy." He dropped Ethan's hand like it burned and took off again. "Race you!" floated back on the breeze.

I shook my head, half in exasperation, half in affection. Ethan straightened and fell into step beside me, his pace effortlessly matching mine. The ocean came into view, and the sun sparkled off the rushing waves.

I was keenly aware of the man at my side—the way his height just edged past my six feet, the breadth of his shoulders, the strength in his stride. The way his T-shirt clung to his chest and hinted at lean muscle that didn't come from sitting at a desk all day.

Why was I noticing these things? Why now? Why Ethan?

My stomach gave an uncomfortable twist, and I glanced at his hand swinging at his side. A traitorous thought whispered through my mind. Would it feel strange to reach out and take his hand, the way Noah had done? How would his large, strong hand feel in mine?

Heat crawled up my neck, and I shoved my hand into my pocket, curling my fingers into a fist. Would Ethan welcome the gesture? Was he even gay? He'd said he'd like to see me again—just the two of us. Had he picked up on what

I was really asking? That maybe I wasn't just looking for friendship?

We hardly knew each other, despite our easy conversation the previous evening. But I liked what I knew, and he drew me to him unlike anyone—woman or man—had before.

We joined Noah at the edge of the wet sand, where the waves crept up, pulling the ocean's chill onto the shore. The rhythmic roar of the surf wrapped around us like a living heartbeat. I took Noah's hand in mine, the warmth of his fingers a stark contrast to the icy Northern California water we stepped into. A jolt shot up my legs as the cold water washed over our feet, the grit of sand shifting with the tide's pull.

Beside us, Ethan approached the water. The instant it touched his toes, he hissed and leaped back onto the dry sand. "That's fu—friggin' cold." His shiver was almost theatrical, and his reaction wrung a laugh out of me.

"Come on, Noah." I tugged his hand gently, and we stepped out of the surf. "Let's go for a walk. This way." I nodded toward the north, where a towering cliff, jutting into the water on a spit of rocky land, loomed in the distance. The promontory formed the northernmost curve of the cove.

"Yeah! I can show Mr. Ethan the sea cave!" Noah's hand slipped from mine as he bolted ahead, his energy boundless as the waves themselves.

"It's high tide, buddy," I called after him and raised my voice to be heard over the crash of the surf. "The sea cave will be underwater. Don't go anywhere near it."

Ethan's gaze followed Noah; his brow furrowed as if he was judging the danger.

"Sometimes I feel like I'm constantly telling him what not to do," I admitted and exhaled a breath of exhaustion.

Ethan's smile was small but sincere. "I assume that's part of being a good parent. You care, so you guide him." He shrugged, as though the answer were obvious. "You love him."

His simple observation hit me like a wave, a swell of emotion rising in my chest. "I do." Though the words didn't convey the depth of it.

Noah sprinted ahead, pausing now and then to pluck a seashell from the sand or hurl a piece of driftwood into the surf. The ocean returned the sticks, each wave depositing them back onto the shore. He flung the wood again, like he was playing fetch with a dog.

Ethan snorted a laugh. "He sure has a lot of energy."

"Tell me about it. That's why we're taking a walk—to burn some of it off. This morning, we drove over the mountain to buy a Halloween costume, and he's been bouncing off the walls in it ever since." My tone was wry, but the fond smile tugging at my lips probably gave me away. "At this rate, he'll tear a hole in it before Halloween even gets here."

"Is he going trick-or-treating?" Ethan glanced at me.

"Yeah, I'll take him around the neighborhood." Our steps fell in sync again as we moved closer to the cliff.

"Well, stop by my house. I want to see him."

Warmth spread through my chest, not just at the invitation, but at the way Ethan had quickly woven himself into our lives. "Will do." After a few moments of companionable silence, I asked, "What brings you out today? Enjoying the sun?"

He shrugged. "I walk when I'm working out a sticky plot point." He chuckled, the sound light against the heavier crash of waves. "So, I walk a lot."

"Can't help you with sticky plot points." I shot a quick look his way. "But I can walk with you if you ever want company." My shoulders tensed, and I wanted to take the words back. I might have overstepped and assumed he wanted more time with me.

His head turned toward me, his gaze hidden and unreadable behind his sunglasses. "I'd like that."

Relief loosened the tension I was holding.

We caught up to Noah, where he gestured toward the base of the rock face. "Look, Mr. Ethan. There's the sea cave!"

I followed his pointed finger to where the waves ebbed and revealed the triangular top of the cave, only for the next swell to crash and swallow it again. "It's carved about one hundred feet deep into the cliff," I explained, "narrowing, twisting, and branching off. It's a labyrinth. At low tide, people sometimes explore, but..." I hesitated and lowered my voice. "Not all of them make it out."

Ethan shuddered and rubbed his arms. "I'd never go in there, anyway. Claustrophobia."

"Smart choice. Walking, enjoying the sun, playing volleyball—those are all much safer beach activities."

Noah wandered nearby, his dark head bent as he searched the sand for treasure. He occasionally picked something up, only to discard it. The sight of him, his boundless curiosity now tempered by a growing tiredness, filled me with tenderness.

"Ready to go home, buddy?" I called.

He trudged to my side. "Yeah, Dad." He lifted his hopeful gaze. "Can I watch *Bluey*?"

"Sure thing." The three of us began the trek back, and this time, Ethan and I had to slow our steps for Noah as he lagged.

Ethan and I fell into an effortless conversation about the town and its quirks—the hitchhiking ghost, the town's renowned, reclusive artist Austin Beaumont, the summer's town-wide scavenger hunt. Occasionally, I exchanged greetings with someone I knew—the perks of being a local deputy—but Ethan remained reserved, his face shadowed by the low brim of his cap and sunglasses.

When we reached our house, I opened the door for Noah, who stumbled inside.

Ethan lingered on the path, his hands in his pockets. "Thanks for the walk."

"Did you work out your sticky plot point?"

He smiled and his lips quirked to one side. "No. I got distracted. But I had a good time."

He pivoted to go, and I knew I should let him, but the thought of not seeing him for days, maybe weeks, left a hole in my chest. Before I could stop myself, I blurted, "Noah's staying at my parents' next Saturday night. Want to visit that brewery I was telling you about?"

Ethan turned back around and cocked his head, his expression hidden behind his sunglasses.

Had I overreached?

"I'd like that," he said warmly.

The thrill that coursed through me was as unexpected as it was intense. Friends could grab a beer. It was only a date if he wanted it to be. Otherwise, it would just be two people getting to know each other.

At least, that's what I told myself.

CHAPTER NINE

ETHAN

By early afternoon on Monday, I typed the last sentence of the chapter. My fingers hovered over the keyboard, and a tremor of satisfaction rippled through me. The weight of the unresolved plot point that had haunted me for days had lifted after my walk with Garrett and Noah, and the words had flowed effortlessly. I leaned back in my chair and savored the rare moment when creativity felt easy.

A smile tugged at my lips. It wasn't just the writing, though. If I were honest with myself, I'd been smiling a lot since the walk the previous day. Their laughter, their acceptance, their warmth—it lingered in my mind like the scent of salt air on the breeze. It surprised me how quickly they'd begun to feel like more than casual acquaintances. Like a connection I hadn't dared to hope for when I came to Seacliff Cove.

But the memory was bittersweet. As much as I enjoyed Garrett's company, a quiet unease curled in the back of my mind. My—alleged—stalker. I'd taken every precaution to keep my presence here discreet. I was using my real name—

one only a handful of people, those who knew me before the books were published, would recognize. I'd left my apartment in Brooklyn without a word, not even telling my personal assistant where I was going. My friends, family, and editor all believed the same lie: that I was tucked away on a writing retreat in the Catskills, finishing my latest novel. But now, with the shadow of a stalker possibly tracking me even here, in Seacliff Cove, the illusion of safety began to crack. If someone had found me despite all my shields, what did that mean for the people around me? For the man and his innocent son, whom I was starting to care about? Could I really justify letting myself have moments of happiness—knowing something dangerous might be waiting just beyond the edges?

Perhaps I shouldn't have accepted Garrett's invitation to the brewpub, but he drew me to him. When we were together, I was keenly aware of his attractiveness, his protectiveness, and his sense of humor. Our conversations were engaging and comfortable.

I backed up my writing to the cloud. My work deserved a reward—a pumpkin spice latte sounded perfect. I stood, stretched the tension from my shoulders, and grinned at the memory of meeting Garrett over the coffee mix-up.

I stepped out into the cool morning air, set the alarm, and locked the door. The scent of sea salt filled my head. For a moment, everything felt still—ordinary, even. The kind of coastal calm I was trying to convince myself I belonged to.

But then I saw it.

A single photograph, fluttering lightly in the breeze where it was tucked beneath the windshield wiper of my car. I froze.

I crossed the driveway slowly, each step tightening my chest. My fingers felt numb as I reached for the photo, already knowing it wasn't something harmless—because nothing left for me like this ever was.

My stomach dropped.

It was a candid shot of me and Garrett walking along the beach yesterday—just the two of us. His hand brushing against mine. My face tilted toward him mid-laugh. The moment was soft, private. And someone had captured it like they were watching from a distance.

The world tilted around me.

My pulse thundered in my ears as I searched my surroundings. The security camera above my door faced the porch—not the driveway. Whoever left this knew that. They knew where the blind spot was.

I gripped the photo tighter, the glossy edges crumpling in my fist. This wasn't just a threat. It was a taunt. A challenge. And worst of all—it meant whoever was behind it wasn't just watching me.

They were watching *us*.

A primal instinct, sharp and unrelenting, gripped me. I scanned the street, every shadow and corner suddenly suspicious. The back of my neck tingled, and the fear of being watched prickled my skin. The neighborhood was quiet and still, though, not even the nonstop hum of lawnmowers that I noticed as soon as I left the city. Eerie.

I retreated into the safety of my house and bolted the door behind me. My pulse thundered in my ears.

What now? Moving seemed futile—they'd already shown they could track me. My mind raced, scenarios spiraling out of control.

I stared at the photo, its glossy surface catching the light. My stomach churned. The air felt too thin in my lungs.

Garrett needed to know. He was captured in the picture, and he'd know what to do. But telling him meant opening a door I wasn't sure I could close again.

But not telling him? That felt reckless. Cowardly, even. Because whoever left this knew where I lived. Knew what I looked like with Garrett. Knew how to get close without being seen.

I dropped the photo onto my entryway table as if it had scorched my fingers. I pulled out my phone with a shaking hand and typed out a message.

> I got something I think you should see. Can you come over?

The response came quickly.

> On my way.

Five minutes later, Garrett stepped through my front door, and his eyes scanned the room before they landed on me. Concern furrowed his brow the moment he locked his gaze with mine.

"What is it?" he asked, all business.

I gestured toward the table. "It was tucked under my windshield wiper this morning."

He leaned over and peered at the photo—not touching it—eyes narrowing as he studied it.

"Jesus," he muttered. "Do you have any idea who could've done this?"

I shook my head, swallowing hard. "No. I mean…not really." I hesitated. There were things I could say—*should* say. The other messages, the lingering sense that someone had been watching me even before I left New York. But I wasn't sure those were connected. I didn't want to drag him into a deeper storm if this was just some unhinged local prank or a fan gone too far.

So, I lied by omission. "Not that I can think of."

Garrett gave me a long look, like he knew I wasn't telling

him everything—but he didn't press. Instead, he pulled an evidence bag and nitrile gloves from his jacket pocket. He carefully slid the photo inside. "I'm taking this in," he said. "I'll run it by Detective Ballard, see if we can lift any prints."

I nodded, but the guilt twisted in my chest. If this really was connected to the past I thought I'd outrun, Garrett was walking straight into danger with his eyes half-closed. And not just him—Noah, too.

That thought settled my decision like a stone in water.

"I'm canceling Saturday," I said quietly. "The brewery. Our…date."

Garrett turned his head sharply toward me. "Why?"

"Because I don't want to put you or Noah in danger," I said, forcing the words out even as part of me screamed to take them back. "Until we know who's doing this, or what they want, it's not safe. I couldn't live with myself if—" I swallowed. "I just couldn't."

He studied me for a moment, jaw tense. "You're not doing this alone, Ethan. Not anymore."

I wanted to believe that. God, I wanted to. But the past didn't let go easily. And if it had found me here, it wasn't done yet.

———

By Friday, I couldn't hide in my house any longer. I'd written thousands of words, scrubbed the kitchen until its surfaces gleamed under the overhead light, and organized my books on new shelves with a precision that bordered on obsessive.

The refrigerator was bare. My stomach was staging a loud rebellion, and I was craving the warm comfort of a pumpkin spice latte. In short, I had cabin fever.

I pulled up the door cam feed on my phone and studied every inch of the porch. Nothing. The sidewalk beyond lay empty, save for the occasional breeze stirring leaves. Still, my heart hammered like a bass drum as I settled my ball cap snugly on my head, grabbed my keys, and opened the door. As I rearmed the security system, I glanced up and down the street, hyperaware of any movement. Nothing suspicious. Just normal.

I hurried to my car and glanced over my shoulder as I slid into the driver's seat and locked the doors. My eyes flicked to the rearview mirror as I pulled away and scrutinized every vehicle behind me. My chest remained tight, my breathing shallow. But when it became clear no one was tailing me, relief seeped in like warmth after a plunge in the cold ocean.

By the time I parked near The Coffee Cove, the tension had dulled to a low hum. I stepped inside, immediately enveloped by the rich aroma of freshly brewed coffee. The lunch rush had passed, and the shop was quiet except for the older gentleman from the other day, seated at the bar along the wall and nursing a cup of coffee.

Cooper greeted me with a friendly smile as he wiped the counter. "Afternoon, Ethan." He tossed the cloth aside and washed his hands in the steel sink. "Medium pumpkin spice latte?"

"Make it a large this time." My voice sounded steadier than I felt. I peered into the refrigerated case. "And I'll take the turkey, provolone, and pesto on a ciabatta." The sight of the sandwich with its thick layers made my mouth water.

I paid the cashier and moved to the pickup counter as Cooper worked. I couldn't help the tug of disappointment that Garrett wasn't here. It was probably for the best—how could I explain why I'd turned down his invitation without unraveling into a mess of evasions?

When Cooper placed the plate and latte on the counter, the scents hit me—warm bread, tangy pesto, the earthy sweetness of cinnamon and nutmeg. "Thanks," I murmured. The simple act of holding the warm cup in my hands brought a flicker of calm.

I carried my lunch to a small table near the window and tucked myself into the corner so that passersby would barely notice me. The sandwich was every bit as satisfying as it looked, and I devoured it with a focus that bordered on ravenous. The latte, sweet and spiced, was like a balm against the nerves still simmering beneath the surface.

After finishing the sandwich, I pulled out my phone to check my author email account, the latte cradled in one hand. Most of the messages were typical fan emails—praise for my books, questions about my writing process. My assistant would handle them later.

But my finger froze over one particular email, from EyeSeeYou. My blood ran so cold no latte could warm it.

You can't escape me.

The words stared back at me, ominous in their simplicity. My mouth went dry, and my pulse slammed into overdrive. The air in the café seemed to thin, the once comforting scents now cloying and suffocating.

I shot a glance at the street outside, my gaze darting over every figure. A car rolled by, its driver oblivious. A woman pushed a stroller, her pace unhurried. A shopkeeper swept her storefront with lazy strokes.

No one looked at me. Yet my skin prickled as though a thousand unseen eyes were trained on me.

I shot to my feet. The chair scraped across the wood floor and nearly toppled. The sound was loud enough to draw Cooper's attention.

His brows knit together in concern. "Everything okay?"

"Yeah," I croaked, my voice tight and unconvincing. "Gotta go." I quickly cleared my table.

My steps sped up as I left the coffee shop, and I scanned

the street with every turn of my head. By the time I reached my car, I was practically jogging.

My errands couldn't wait, though, no matter how much I wanted to retreat. At the post office, I felt exposed under the fluorescent lights, and my heart raced as I picked up the mail forwarded to my PO box.

A Priority Mail Express envelope sat at the bottom of the stack, having arrived sometime last week. My breath hitched the moment I spotted it.

My name—Ethan Cole—and address in Brooklyn were printed neatly on the label, with the post office's forwarding address label underneath. The return address on the envelope was from a real estate company in Brooklyn.

My grip tightened around the cardboard envelope as a cold current slid down my spine. I stepped outside, heart thudding, the sounds of gulls and passing cars suddenly distant.

Hands unsteady, I tore the envelope open.

Inside was a glossy flyer from a real estate agency I didn't recognize. The kind you'd find stacked near the front desk of an apartment building—professional, sleek, harmless-looking. But across the top, scrawled in large, loopy handwriting, was a handwritten message:

We have a customer interested in buying your apartment. Please give me a call.

This had to be another message, disguised as something mundane. Like the gardener's flyer, left just so. But I didn't have any real estate agents in my Jake Slate books. There was no fictional breadcrumb this time. Still...I didn't trust it.

I yanked out my phone and Googled the company's name.

A website loaded. Clean, modern, real. Full of smiling headshots and staged living rooms. I found the agent's profile, her phone number, her office address. Everything matched.

I let out a breath I hadn't realized I was holding.

Legitimate. A coincidence. Real estate business as usual.

But as I tucked the flyer back into the envelope, unease still lingered.

I hastened to my next errand. The grocery store was no better than the post office—every aisle felt too open, every fellow shopper a potential threat.

When I finally locked my front door behind me, my knees nearly buckled with relief. The house wrapped around me like a cocoon, but even its walls felt thinner. I leaned against the door, my breaths ragged and uneven.

The email had shattered my fragile sense of security.

———

The blinking cursor on my screen seemed to flash a warning. I'd been staring at the same unfinished sentence for nearly an hour, my thoughts too tangled to form anything coherent. The story was there, but it was hiding beneath layers of anxiety and the oppressive weight of the previous day's email from EyeSeeYou.

I sighed, rubbed my temples, and glanced at my phone for the hundredth time. No new messages. No new notifications. I tapped the screen anyway and scrolled through the same list of unread fan emails. My chest tightened with the name of every sender. There was nothing new from EyeSeeYou. Was I relieved? No.

The silence was almost worse.

My coffee sat untouched on the desk beside me. I picked it up, took a sip, and grimaced at the cold, unappealing brew. My gaze drifted to the window and the tightly closed blinds that shrouded the room in shadows. It felt wrong to be so cooped up in my own house.

I clicked over to my social media accounts and scanned the notifications. Most were harmless: comments, likes, a few new followers. But each one felt like a potential threat. I closed the apps with a shaky exhale, leaned back in my chair, and stared at the ceiling.

What was I supposed to do? Should I tell someone? Tell Garrett? My stomach churned at the thought. What would I even say? *Oh, hey, Garrett, I think I have a deranged fan who's stalking me and leaving cryptic messages. That's normal, right?*

The sharp chime of the doorbell made me jump so violently that I nearly knocked my coffee onto the keyboard. My heart pounded as I reached for my phone and pulled up the door cam feed with trembling fingers. Relief flooded through me when I saw Garrett and Noah standing on the porch.

Noah grinned up at the camera while Garrett stood behind him, hands tucked into the pockets of his jeans and looking sheepish. I set my phone down and rushed to the door, my pulse racing, but for a different reason.

When I opened the door, Noah beamed. "Hi, Mr. Ethan!"

Garrett cleared his throat, his expression apologetic. "Sorry to drop by unannounced. Noah wanted to come say hi…" He glanced away briefly, adding under his breath, "And, well, I guess I did too." He looked over his shoulder. "But don't worry, I scanned the street before we came over. Just Mrs. Hendershot walking old Bernie."

A small, genuine smile broke through my tension. "I'm glad you're here."

Noah looked up at me, his face animated. "I'm going to Grandma and Grandpa's house for a sleepover tonight! We're gonna bake cookies and watch a movie. Grandpa lets me stay up super late."

"That sounds like so much fun." My smile softened as I crouched to his level. "What kind of cookies are you going to make?"

"Chocolate chip! Grandma says we might even do oatmeal raisin, but raisins are gross." As he spoke, Noah glanced down. "Oh!" He squatted to grab something from under the doormat. "Here, this is for you."

The smile froze on my face as he handed me a piece of paper. I stood and unfolded it with trembling hands. A cold dread crept through my chest. It was a torn page—ripped straight from the fifth Jake Slate novel. The one where I'd typed *The End*. Beneath those two words, scrawled in jagged red letters, was a message that made my blood run cold: *You'll never see The End coming.*

The ground seemed to shift, and my breath came in shallow gasps. My fingers shook as I stared at the page, and the paper quivered in my hand.

"Ethan?" Garrett's voice cut through the fog, sharp and concerned.

I met his gaze, unable to hide my fear.

"What is it?" It was a command couched as a question.

Wordlessly, I handed him the page. His jaw tightened as his eyes scanned the writing. "What the heck?"

I shook my head; my throat was too tight to speak.

Garrett's face darkened, and his voice dropped, steady and furious. "We'll talk about this later. Do you have a Ziploc bag?"

I retrieved a bag from the kitchen and handed it to Garrett. He slipped the paper inside, like evidence at a crime scene. I supposed it was.

"I'll be here at six. We'll figure this out."

I managed a weak, "Okay," my body still shuddering.

Garrett turned to Noah and softened. "Time to go, buddy. Grandma and Grandpa are waiting."

Noah waved cheerfully as they left, completely oblivious to the tension. "Bye, Mr. Ethan! See you!"

I forced a smile and waved back as they crossed the street to their car. Garrett glanced over his shoulder and his eyes locked with mine, questions in his gaze.

As I threw the deadbolt, the severity of the situation hit me like a wave against the cliffs. I stumbled to the couch and sank into it. My pulse pounded in my temples, and my vision narrowed. *Breathe, Ethan*, I reminded myself. *You're not in this alone.*

I wasn't sure what terrified me more—the stalker's growing boldness or the thought of Garrett getting caught in the crossfire.

CHAPTER TEN

GARRETT

I knocked on Ethan's door at six sharp, the warm bag of takeout releasing mouthwatering aromas of char-broiled beef, tangy barbecue sauce, and crispy fried potatoes into the evening air. In the crook of my arm, four chilled bottles of craft beer clinked together. I adjusted my grip, suddenly very aware of the tightness in my shoulders. It wasn't just the weight of the food—it was the weight of the conversation we were about to have.

The door opened, and Ethan stood there with a hesitant smile that didn't quite reach his eyes. His face looked pale, the usual spark in his expression dulled by…fear, maybe.

I lifted the bag, putting on my best attempt at an easygoing grin. "Special delivery from Barnacle Brews."

His smile widened, genuine this time. "Bringing our evening out…in?"

"Exactly." He moved back, and I stepped inside and kicked off my sneakers near the door. I looked around for direction. "This way?" I asked, gesturing toward a door off the living room.

"Yeah." He closed the door behind me and locked it with a firm twist.

I crossed the living room and entered the kitchen. A teak table sat tucked into the corner, its polished surface reflecting the soft glow of the overhead light. I grabbed a paper towel from a roll on the counter and placed the greasy bag on it.

Ethan inhaled deeply. "Something smells good."

"I brought a cheeseburger, a barbecue pulled pork sandwich, and fries. Take your pick, and I'll eat the other choice."

Ethan grabbed a couple of plates from the cabinet and slid them onto the table. "I'll take the pulled pork."

We worked in unspoken sync, unpacking the food and popping the caps off the IPAs. The sound of clinking bottles and rustling paper filled the space. The moment felt normal, comfortable.

As we sat down and dug in, I kept my tone casual but firm. "Enjoy your dinner because you're coming clean afterward."

The words sounded harsher than I had intended. I winced as Ethan choked on a bite of his sandwich and his face went red. He reached for his beer to wash it down.

"Sorry." I softened my voice. "Didn't mean for that to sound like a threat."

He shook his head and gave me a wry smile. "It's fine. You're not wrong."

I changed the subject to lighten the mood. "I finished reading the first Jake Slate book. That plot twist at the end? Didn't see it coming."

His face lit up, and the glow of it hit me square in the chest. I hadn't realized how much I missed seeing him animated and confident. "Glad you liked it! I'd give you book two, but I didn't bring books with me when I came here. Traveled light."

The mention of his arrival in the wee hours of the morning sobered me. "I guess that'll happen when you move across the country with only two suitcases."

Ethan's smile faltered, and a flush crept up his neck.

I instantly regretted the reminder. "Sorry," I muttered. "That was insensitive." I mentally kicked myself. Again.

He waved it off, though his voice was quieter. "It's okay." He hesitated, then added, "I worked out my plot point, though. The walk we took helped clear my head."

"I'm glad." I casually leaned back, trying to ease the mood again.

"What did you do this week?" He dunked a fry in ketchup.

"The usual—helped old ladies cross the street, tied knots, set up camping tents…"

He laughed, the sound rich and warm, exactly what I'd been hoping for. "Boy Scout," he teased.

"So," I said, leaning back in my chair with a grin, "if I'm the Boy Scout in this setup…what are you? And how'd you end up writing about murder and mayhem?"

Ethan smirked as he wiped his hands on a napkin. "You mean besides the obvious darkness lurking beneath this mild-mannered exterior?"

I chuckled. "Exactly."

He took a long sip from his bottle, then set it down. His thumb ran along the label like he was thinking through his answer.

"I write thrillers," he said finally, "because I've always liked puzzles. Even as a kid, I wanted to know how things fit together."

He sat back, his body loose but his voice careful. "Thrillers let me explore that. You start with a mess—something bloody or brutal or broken—and you peel it apart, layer by layer. You get to make sense of chaos, even if just for a few hundred pages."

I watched him for a beat. He wasn't putting on a show. This wasn't a press interview answer. It was quieter than that. More real.

"Was there something that made you want to start?" I asked.

He hesitated. "I guess... I wanted to know why people make the choices they do. Especially the bad ones. Writing let me ask the question without having to live the answers."

I nodded slowly. "Makes sense. You're the one shining the flashlight into the dark corners."

Ethan's smile was small but real. "I like that."

We finished eating and cleaned up together in a rhythm that felt surprisingly natural. Then, with beers in hand, we settled onto the couch in the living room. The soft cushions dipped under our combined weight as we sat side-by-side, and our thighs brushed. I shifted away, but not by much. I suspected he would need support and comfort during the coming conversation.

I set my bottle on the coffee table with a clink and pulled out my phone. I clicked on a notes app and poised my thumbs over the keyboard. "Tell me everything," I ordered.

Ethan's brow furrowed as his gaze flicked to the phone in my hands. "Is that necessary?"

"Yes," I said, unyielding. "If I can't convince you to file a report, then at least I'll have the details for myself." What I didn't tell him was that I'd unofficially put the word out to watch for anything suspicious. But darn it, I didn't want this to stay unofficial. This needed a proper investigation. "Start from the beginning. Dates, times, events. Everything."

Ethan exhaled, his breath shaky. "I think it all began Tuesday, four weeks ago," he said, low. "I found a black feather at the door to my apartment around two in the afternoon."

A chill ran down my spine, and I straightened, my thumbs hovering over the screen. "Like the feather the assassin used as a calling card in your first Jake Slate novel?"

His lips pressed into a thin line, and his hands curled into tight fists on his thighs, knuckles white. "Yes. But I thought I was being paranoid. Someone could've carried it in on their shoe."

"But…" I prompted.

He brought me up to speed on the other creepy gifts.

The hairs on the back of my neck prickled, and my scalp tingled. Taken separately, each incident could be dismissed as a coincidence, but together, they painted a darker picture.

I asked gently, "What made you leave the city?"

Ethan didn't answer right away. His jaw worked for a moment, like he was debating whether or not to say the words aloud. Then he exhaled—quiet, resigned—and met my gaze.

"I found a sticky note on my door that read, *Guess who's next*."

The words hit me like a punch to the sternum. I reared back, every protective instinct firing at once. "Fudge, Ethan," I said, my voice low. "That's not just creepy. That's a threat."

He gave a shrug and slid his gaze away from mine. "It was the final straw."

"So, you packed up and left."

Ethan nodded. "Yes. In less than twenty-four hours." His voice was a whisper, heavy with exhaustion and fear.

"Who knows you're here?"

"No one. Not even my family."

I exhaled sharply and anger bubbled beneath my surface. "Was the plastic knife next?"

He hesitated. "Well, maybe. Did anyone else report pranks like that?"

I hated to be the one to crush any hope he might've had. "No. We caught the kids who'd been pulling those stunts. They swore they didn't do it."

His shoulders sagged, and he grabbed his beer, gulping it like a man desperate for courage. "A knife is the murder weapon in my fifth book."

I leaned forward and narrowed my eyes. "Anything else?"

His hands trembled as he placed the empty bottle back on the table. "Yesterday, at The Coffee Cove, I got an email from an account called EyeSeeYou." His voice wavered, and he shuddered visibly.

"Forward it to me." A low growl slipped into my tone. "We don't have a tech department at the station, but I'll send it to headquarters." I frowned. I already anticipated the delay; forensics was perpetually backlogged.

He took his phone out of his pocket, tapped the screen a few times, and my phone dinged with a notification. "That's everything I've got to give you. You already have the video of the door cam from the evening they left the knife, but you can't see much. Just a vague person in baggy sweats." His tired voice sounded like he'd reached his limit for the evening.

"I just don't understand why anyone would stalk me," Ethan said, his voice tight with confusion. "I can't think of a single encounter—no angry fan, no confrontation—that would push someone over the edge like this."

He ran a hand through his hair and let it fall limply to his side. "I mean…I'm just an author. My life's so routine it borders on boring. As Ethan Cole, I'm openly gay. But under the Ethan Quinn pen name? I keep my personal life private. He doesn't talk about sexuality. He doesn't really talk about anything but the books."

His eyes flicked up to meet mine, searching. "Do you think this could be about that? Homophobia?" He exhaled and spread his hands in helpless frustration. "Honestly, who even knows that Ethan Quinn is Ethan Cole? It's a short list."

I shook my head. "Nothing about this feels like a hate crime. No slurs. No targeted messaging. It's all been about your work—your stories, your characters. Whoever this is, they're fixated on your writing."

That didn't seem to offer him any comfort.

Ethan's shoulders sagged like the weight of it all had finally pressed too hard. "Then why does it still feel so personal?"

Watching him try to make sense of something senseless, I wished I could give him an answer. "Here's what we're going to do." I straightened my spine. "First thing Monday morning, I'm going to type up your statement. I'll pick you up mid-morning, bring you to the station to sign it, and open an investigation. Then I'll bring you home." I raised an eyebrow, daring him to contradict me.

Ethan sighed heavily, but he nodded.

The resignation in his expression cut me deeply. "You're not going anywhere alone. As your friend, I'll accompany you to the grocery store and anywhere else you need to go. We'll even pick up pumpkin spice lattes." I grinned, trying to lighten the edict.

His mouth opened, likely to argue, but I cut him off with a raised finger. "Not up for debate."

He shook his head and said firmly, "I can't endanger you and Noah by being seen with you."

"I can take care of myself, and I'll have my sister look after Noah. He'll enjoy spending extra time with Auntie Harper." And as a bonus, I'd get to spend extra time with Ethan. Too bad it was under such circumstances.

I rose from the couch and tucked my phone into my

pocket. I grabbed our empties and wandered into the kitchen to dump them in the recycling bin. "Call me immediately if anything else happens." Ethan followed me to the front door, where I slipped into my shoes.

I turned back to him, and the sight of his ashy, drawn face twisted my gut. I gripped his arms gently. "Hey, it's going to be okay," I said quietly. "We're going to catch this person."

He didn't respond, just nodded mutely. His vulnerability hit me like a punch to my already twisty gut, and without thinking, I put an arm around his shoulders in a bro hug. He whimpered.

I wrapped both arms around him and pulled him closer. Hard chest to hard chest. My pulse picked up.

He stiffened, but after a moment, he circled my waist and laid his head on my shoulder.

And it felt…right. Grounding. I enjoyed having Ethan in my arms, tight against me.

CHAPTER ELEVEN

ETHAN

Garrett's sheriff's department SUV rumbled as it pulled into my driveway and brought a tangle of emotions to the surface. I was nervous—terrified, even—but I was also ready. For too long, I'd let fear dictate my every move. I was taking the first step in reclaiming my life. I locked my front door behind me.

Garrett climbed out of the SUV; his crisp uniform stretched across his broad shoulders. His presence was commanding, yet calm. He glanced at my Subaru, parked on one side of the driveway. His brow furrowed, and he crossed his arms.

"Why don't you park in the garage?" His tone was casual, but the sharpness in his eyes suggested he was already forming an opinion.

I sighed and ran a hand through my hair. "It's full of debris from the renovation. The landlord never took it to the dump."

His lips pressed into a thin line as he propped his hands on his hips. The morning light caught the badge on his chest, making it glint as he shifted his stance. "Have you asked Carl to remove it?"

"Of course I have. Several times." A touch of exasperation crept into my voice. "He keeps saying he'll do it, but then never does."

Garrett's jaw tightened, and his gaze drifted back to the garage as if he could see through its closed door. "I'll have to see if that's some kind of violation," he muttered under his breath, though loud enough for me to catch.

I shrugged, trying to deflect the tension with nonchalance I didn't quite feel. "I was just glad to get the rental on such short notice."

His head snapped back toward me, his expression softening just a fraction. "Still. You shouldn't have to deal with that kind of crap." There was a quiet intensity in his words, a protectiveness that I found comforting.

The moment hung in the air, and his concern settled over me like a warm, unexpected blanket. I didn't know how to respond, so I tucked my keys into my pocket and forced a smile. "I guess it comes with the territory."

Garrett didn't reply right away. Instead, he let out a slow exhale. His posture relaxed as he gestured toward his SUV. "I'll leave it be—for now. Ready?"

"As ready as I'll ever be." I slid into the passenger seat, the onboard computer system between us.

The drive to the station was quiet, but comfortable. Garrett had a way of making me feel like everything was going to be okay, even if I wasn't entirely sure I believed it yet. I stared out the window and watched Seacliff Cove's streets roll by, the quaint charm and orderliness of the town at odds with the storm brewing in my life.

When we arrived at the bland, nearly windowless station, Garrett parked in the visitors' lot. I followed him up the concrete ramp to the glass doors, my palms damp. Inside, the reception area was simple but efficient—a long counter with a male uniformed officer sitting behind it, typing something into a computer.

"Jones," Garrett greeted him with a short nod.

The officer looked up and his eyes flicked briefly to me before he nodded back. "Whitlock."

Without missing a beat, Garrett moved past the desk and punched a code into the keypad beside a door. The lock clicked open. He held the door for me, and I stepped through into a hallway that smelled faintly of burned coffee and copier toner.

The bullpen wasn't far. The space was utilitarian, with pairs of desks arranged in clusters, cluttered with computer monitors, keyboards, cables, and phones. A half-empty coffee cup and a forgotten granola bar wrapper sat on one desk we passed. The hum of fluorescent lights buzzed softly overhead. Only one other deputy sheriff was present. He muttered to himself as he two-fingered his keyboard.

Garrett led me to a desk in the corner, where he pulled up a chair and motioned for me to sit. "This is us."

I sat down, and the hard plastic chair creaked beneath me. Garrett pulled a folder from a filing tray and extracted a sheaf of papers. He laid them on the desk in front of me. I tried to ignore the way my heartbeat quickened, like the printout was a snake ready to strike.

"Your statement." He tapped the pages. "I need you to read it over. If everything looks right and you don't have any changes, sign on the last page."

"Doesn't a detective normally handle stalking cases?" I asked, curious.

Garrett didn't answer immediately. Instead, he crossed his arms as he leaned back in his seat. "Yes," he said finally, edged with a hint of frustration. "But we only have one detective.

He's overwhelmed right now. I got permission from my sergeant to take the case."

I caught the flicker of tension in Garrett's jaw. The sense of calm he usually carried seemed thinner, like he was balancing on a tightrope.

He leaned forward and dropped his voice to a near-whisper. "I didn't tell him we're…friends." His gaze locked with mine, serious and unwavering. "It's imperative that we keep that between you and me, or Sarge will take me off the case. I could face disciplinary action."

The words settled like a weight in my chest, and a tangle of emotions tightened my gut. Relief that Garrett was willing to take this on personally, guilt for being the reason Garrett might face scrutiny or even get into trouble. And then there was something else—something warmer—that I wasn't quite ready to unpack.

"Friends," I repeated softly, the word feeling strange on my tongue, yet strangely right. I hadn't missed the pause Garrett had given it, the unspoken acknowledgment that our connection might be more complicated than that simple label.

I dropped my gaze to the table, wary of the papers in front of me and the tension in my body. "You didn't have to do that," I said quietly. "Request to take the case, I mean. You're risking your career."

Garrett's brow furrowed. "Ethan, I'm doing this because I want to. I'm not allowing you to face this alone. Not when I can do something about it."

I looked up, and the sincerity in his expression struck me like a physical force. My breath caught, and the uncertainty faded.

"Thank you," I said, the words barely audible but carrying the depth of my gratitude.

His lips quirked into a faint smile. "You don't have to thank me. Just promise you'll keep me in the loop, okay?"

I nodded, swallowed hard, and picked up the papers. The words blurred for a moment before I blinked and forced myself to focus. It was all there—the black feather, the coffee shop book, the gardening flyer, the sticky note, the knife, the email from EyeSeeYou, the end of the book. Seeing it laid out so plainly made it feel more real than ever, but it also gave me a strange sense of validation.

I reached the last page, and the signature line waited. "It's all correct," I said, my voice solemn.

Garrett handed me a pen, and my fingers tightened around it as I hesitated. Then, with a deep breath, I signed my name.

I set the pen down, leaned back in the chair, and exhaled slowly. Relief mingled with pride as a weight lifted off my chest. "I should've done this sooner." I met Garrett's steady gaze. "I'm done hiding. The stalker is going to make a mistake, and we're going to catch them."

Garrett's jaw tightened. "I'm not using you as bait, Ethan."

I shook my head, and my resolve hardened. "I'm not talking about bait. I'm talking about taking back control of my life. I'm not letting them keep me locked in my house, afraid of my shadow."

His eyes softened in understanding. "I promise I'll do everything I can to protect you. Now you have the force behind you. Patrol units will be watching your house at night. And I'll be watching even closer."

His confidence settled something inside me. For the first time, I felt like I wasn't fighting this battle alone.

As we returned to the SUV, the crisp morning air filled my lungs, a sharp contrast to the stifling fear that had consumed me for weeks. Garrett opened the passenger door like a gentleman, and I slid into the seat. He shut the door with a solid *thunk*, rounded the hood, and climbed into the driver's side. The engine rumbled as he pulled out of the lot, but instead of heading toward my house, he turned onto Main Street.

"Where are we going?" I asked, sharper than he deserved. The tension of the morning still thrummed under my skin.

"I'm kidnapping you," Garrett said, deadpan.

I grimaced.

He glanced sideways at me and winced. "Too soon?"

"Way too soon." Despite myself, I chuckled.

He pulled into a spot in front of The Coffee Cove, the sign over the door swaying gently in the ocean breeze. "We're taking a break." He toggled his shoulder radio and called in a code seven.

Inside, the familiar warmth of the coffee shop soothed my frayed nerves, though I still found myself glancing over my shoulder at the people passing by. Everyone seemed to blend seamlessly into the easy rhythm of a small tourist town, and I let out a breath of relief.

The scents of freshly brewed coffee and baked goods wrapped around me like a comforting hug. Garrett approached the counter with the same casual confidence he carried everywhere, greeting the barista.

"Hey, Jessica. Medium black coffee and…" He turned to me, his eyebrow raised in mock expectation. "Pumpkin spice latte?"

The corner of my mouth twitched. "You know me too well."

I instantly caught myself, my cheeks warming. Garrett and I were friends—I'd opened up to him about the stalker—but I didn't want to assume too much. Friendships, especially ones formed under pressure, needed time to grow naturally.

He winked, his grin softening the tension inside me. "I've got your back."

The words landed differently than they should have. They weren't just professional—they were personal. I wasn't just his job. He genuinely cared. Something as small as ordering my favorite drink reminded me of that.

When Cooper handed us the drinks a few minutes later, the familiar scent of cinnamon and nutmeg drifted through the air. Garrett passed me the cup, his fingers brushing mine briefly and sending a buzz through my core.

"Thank you," I murmured, wrapping my hands around the warm paper. I stared out the shop's wide window at the bustle of Main Street. People strolled past, chatting and laughing, oblivious to the storm brewing in my life. Somewhere out there, my stalker could be watching. Yet, for the first time in weeks, I didn't feel like prey. "This feels... normal," I admitted softly. "Something I've been craving."

"Good," Garrett said firmly. "We're going to take back your life."

The words settled over me like a shield.

We climbed into the SUV, and Garrett drove us home. When he parked in my driveway, I reached for the door handle, but he was already at my side. He opened my door and gestured for me to lead the way.

"I'll walk you to the door."

"I can—"

"It's not up for discussion."

I nodded and led the way. As I approached the door, my steps faltered, and my stomach twisted sharply. My scalp prickled as my gaze locked onto the object sitting on my doormat.

"What's—" Garrett started and stepped past me. His sharp intake of breath. "Fudge!"

There, resting half-hidden in the fibers of my doormat,

was a silver locket—small, delicate, and unmistakably out of place. The chain was broken, the links jagged like they had been yanked free. My blood turned to ice.

"I know this," I whispered, throat tight. "This is from my sixth book."

Garrett turned to me. Questions and fury warred in his expression.

Numb, I continued, "Inside was a photo of her husband. He was the next target."

Garrett straightened his spine, all business now. "Don't touch it. I'll grab my gloves and a bag."

He jogged to the SUV while I stood frozen on the porch, staring down at the twisted chain and trying not to let my imagination spiral. But it was too late for that. Because if this was what I thought it was, someone wasn't just reading my books—they were using them as a blueprint.

Garrett returned quickly, gloved up, and took photos from several angles with his phone. Then he knelt again and gently picked up the locket, holding it steady as he clicked the clasp open.

My breath caught.

Inside the locket was a photo—small, curled slightly at the edges, but unmistakable.

Me.

My face stared back from within the polished metal. One of my author headshots, the kind you could find online with a quick image search.

A cold wave of dread washed over me, and my heart thudded in my chest.

Garrett looked up, jaw set. "This isn't just a sick prank."

"No," I said quietly. "It's scary."

And suddenly, every step I'd taken to disappear didn't feel like enough.

I pulled up my door cam footage on my phone, hoping

for answers. Instead, static filled the screen for the minutes the stalker left the locket. I showed it to Garrett, and my frustration mounted.

"They used a jammer," he muttered with restrained rage. "Illegal, but that's the least of their crimes." He blew out a sharp breath. "I'll check other cameras in the neighborhood, but if they used the jammer along the entire street…" He shook his head. "Go inside, lock the door, and call me if anything else happens. If you need to go anywhere, I'm coming with you." His lips twitched into a small, determined grin. "Also, plan on getting together this weekend. We're not allowing this person to run us to ground."

I blinked at him, the words taking a second to settle.

We're not allowing this person to run us to ground.

The "we" lodged in my chest like a flare of warmth and fear colliding. For a moment, I didn't know what to say. Part of me wanted to argue, to protect him and Noah by keeping my distance. But another part—the part that was tired of hiding, of flinching at shadows—clung to his conviction.

I nodded slowly. "Okay," I said, voice rough. "This weekend. Just…don't let me pull away if I start to panic."

Garrett's expression softened. "I won't."

And for the first time in days, I almost believed I didn't have to do this alone.

CHAPTER TWELVE

GARRETT

I rang Ethan's doorbell, leaning into the field of the camera with what I hoped was a reassuring smile. The early afternoon sun cast deep shadows over the porch, but it did nothing to ease the tension knotting my stomach. My feet ached in my boots from hours spent canvassing the neighborhood, and I felt the sting of failure in the pit of my gut.

The lock clicked, and Ethan opened the door, his hesitant smile a reflection of my own reservations. "I hope you have good news."

I exhaled deeply, letting the breath settle my thoughts. "May I come in?"

Ethan's smile faltered. He stepped aside, his movements stilted, as though bracing himself for disappointment.

Inside, I stopped in the entryway, his familiar cedarwood scent wrapping around me.

His brow knit with worry. "Did you find anything?"

I propped my hands on my hips, and frustration simmered just below the surface. "Someone jammed the door cams all up and down the street around the time they left the locket on your porch."

Ethan's lips pressed into a tight, colorless line, his shoulder brushing against the door as if steadying himself.

"But I found a witness. Barbara Hendershot, three doors down." My hope had soared for a moment, to be dashed. "She saw a person walking along the sidewalk wearing a baggy hoodie, ball cap, and oversized sweatpants. About five-ten. Carrying a black device in their hand. Said she thought it was a man because she didn't see any hair sticking out from under the cap and hood."

Ethan's gaze grew distant for a moment, his eyes clouded with thought. Then, with a small nod, he murmured, "A man. Sounds about right." His focus sharpened, and his eyes locked onto mine. "Anything else?"

I shook my head. "Sorry, that was it. They probably came in from the beach path. No suspicious vehicles in the area."

"Okay," he said softly, the weight of the news clear in his voice.

He stepped over to the side table, picked up a glossy tri-fold brochure, and held it out to me like it explained everything.

I frowned. "A home security system? You already have one."

"I'm upgrading to a wired camera," he said, voice low but steady. "No more jamming."

I met his eyes and gave a short nod. It was a smart move —but the fact that he had to make it twisted my gut. "Good idea." I hooked my thumb toward the door. "I'll head out. Let me know if you need anything."

He didn't say a word, just offered a tight smile as I stepped onto the porch. I waited until I heard the deadbolt slide home before turning back toward my SUV, every instinct in me on edge. Because someone had made him feel unsafe. And I wasn't going to let that stand.

An hour later, I sent him a text.

> What would you like to do on Saturday?
> Any errands you need to run?

> Could you take me to the farmers' market?
> I need some organic foods.

I started typing *It's a date* and immediately erased it, shaking my head. What the hell was I doing? We were just friends—I didn't date men.

But…did I want to?

The thought landed like a slap—sharp, unexpected, impossible to ignore.

Since my high school crush on Leo had been buried under the weight of locker room expectations and silence, I'd only been with women. Dated them, even had a child with one. I'd never questioned it. Not really.

Not until Ethan.

He shook the foundation of everything I thought I knew about myself. It wasn't just his looks, though I'd be lying if I said he wasn't attractive. It was the way he made me feel— like we meshed. It was the pull toward him that defied logic.

Maybe I shouldn't take so much for granted. Maybe Ethan had slipped past my defenses before I'd even realized it.

> Come over at 10.

> See you then.

I tossed my phone onto the passenger seat and sighed. I

needed to clear my head, but one thing was certain: Ethan wasn't just another case.

I couldn't wait for Saturday.

CHAPTER THIRTEEN

ETHAN

I retrieved my shopping cart from the back of Garrett's Escape, the metal frame cool and solid in my hands. The parking lot buzzed with the hum of car engines, the chatter of families, and the occasional bark of a dog. The gray sky stretched overhead. A chill brushed against my face, and I tugged on my sweatshirt, the soft fabric offering a welcome layer of warmth.

The cloud cover might have rolled in off the ocean like an unwelcome guest, but it couldn't touch the anticipation swirling inside me. Spending a few hours with Garrett—just the two of us—was enough to brighten the day. It was ridiculous how much I looked forward to these moments, how the thought of his presence could lift my spirits.

I unfolded the cart, its joints squeaking, as Garrett closed the hatch of the SUV with a soft thud. He locked the vehicle with a quick press of the fob, and a short honk cut through the surrounding noise.

"You came prepared," he teased as he gestured to the cart.

I shrugged. "I'll fill it up. I like to shop organic and support local farmers when I can."

"At our house, we're fans of Kraft Mac 'n Cheese."

I clutched my chest dramatically, pretending to shudder in mock horror. "Blasphemy."

Garrett laughed, the sound warm and unguarded, wrapping around me like a shield against the chill. I couldn't help the smile that tugged at my lips in response.

The strains of a cover band floated through the air, their rendition of a classic rock song rising above the murmur of voices. The familiar melody mingled with the earthy scents of fresh produce, yeasty baked goods, and the salty tang of the sea.

We moved into the crowd, Garrett's broad shoulders parting a path as we wandered from booth to booth.

The vibrant colors of the market seemed to bloom in contrast to the overcast skies—crimson tomatoes, leafy greens, baskets of bright oranges, and the soft pastels of homemade soaps.

I stole a glance at Garrett as he paused to inspect a crate of apples, his brow furrowed in consideration. He seemed so at ease in a way I envied. My pulse quickened when he turned, catching me mid-stare.

"What?" His lips quirked into a half-smile.

"Nothing," I said quickly. I averted my gaze and focused on a nearby display of pumpkins.

The crowd thickened as we made our way toward a booth selling artisan bread. My cart bumped against a rogue rock on the pavement, jarring my grip, and Garrett's hand shot out instinctively, steadying the handle.

"Careful." His hand lingered for a second longer than necessary, and I felt a warmth rise to my cheeks that had nothing to do with the sweatshirt.

"Thanks," I murmured, barely audible over the market's noise.

We moved on and slipped into the rhythm of the day, but I couldn't help the flicker of awareness that lingered, a subtle but undeniable pull toward the man walking beside me.

I didn't know where this was going or what it meant. All I knew was that the ominous clouds, the crowd, the stalker lurking in the shadows of my life—they all seemed to fade for a little while, leaving only Garrett and the quiet strength of his presence.

Garrett's hand landed on the small of my back again and again, a brief but steadying touch that sent a ripple of heat through me. His casual gestures—placing his fingers lightly on my elbow or brushing against my shoulder as we walked —seemed so natural, yet they branded me every time. Did he realize how often he touched me? Did he notice the way my breath hitched?

I found myself leaning closer to him as we moved through the crowd, drawn to his presence. The air was rich with the scent of fresh herbs, but all I could focus on was Garrett—his warmth, his strength, his quiet protectiveness. "Where is Noah today?"

"He's with Ava's parents. They live down the coast. Hopefully, getting him out of town will keep him out of sight, out of mind."

My stomach churned at the thought that just being connected to me might have put him in danger. The thought of Noah—innocent and full of life—being caught in the crossfire made my chest tighten.

I scanned the crowd, my gaze flitting over faces and movements, looking for anything out of place. No one seemed to pay us any attention, but unease wrapped around me like a shroud.

Garrett noticed, of course. His hand found my back, this time rubbing gently in small, soothing circles. "I haven't seen anyone following us," he said, low and steady. "Relax."

The tension in my shoulders melted under his touch, and I let his strength bolster me. For a moment, I felt safe.

"Good morning, Garrett," a man passing by greeted him with a nod.

Garrett straightened immediately and put a noticeable distance between us. The warmth of his touch vanished, replaced by a hollow ache in my chest. Disappointment settled like a weight in my stomach, heavy and unwelcome.

Was he ashamed of being seen with a man? With me? The thought stung. But then again, he'd been touching me all morning—in public, no less. He was confusing, a swirl of mixed signals and contradictions that left me reeling.

Did he even know what he wanted?

I swallowed the questions, unwilling to let them spoil the peaceful rhythm of the day. I had to be patient and let him decide on his own time.

We continued walking and stopped at booths as we browsed. I filled my cart with jars of pasta sauces, bundles of seasonal vegetables, crusty artisan bread, and a pumpkin for my porch. Garrett added muffins, fragrant apples, and canned fruits to my pile, his choices clearly made with Noah in mind.

By lunchtime, the smoky aroma of grilled chicken led us to a food stand. The scent was irresistible, making my stomach growl audibly, and I treated Garrett to street tacos and cold lemonade served in Mason jars.

"Thanks for taking me shopping," I said as we sat at a small table tucked off to the side.

He gave me a warm smile, and his eyes crinkled at the corners. "It's been fun. I haven't been to the market in years, but I can see why you like it." Garrett took a bite of his chicken taco. "You know, I'm starting to think you might actually be in a committed relationship—with organic food."

I lifted an eyebrow. "I like knowing my tomatoes weren't raised on chemicals."

He grinned around his sip of lemonade. "Do you interrogate your produce before buying it?"

"Only if it looks suspicious," I said, deadpan. "If a zucchini makes direct eye contact, it's not coming home with me."

Garrett laughed, shaking his head. "You're unbelievable."

"You're one to talk," I shot back. "Your pantry probably has six emergency boxes of neon-orange mac and cheese."

"That's because it's the food of champions. And children. And exhausted single dads."

I mock-gasped. "Do you at least add anything to it? Pepper? Real cheese? Dignity?"

He leaned back and smirked. "Sometimes I throw in hot dogs. That count?"

I pressed a hand to my chest. "You wound me."

"Please. One box and even you'd forget how to pronounce quinoa."

I grinned and shook my head, warmth unfurling in my chest. The banter was effortless, but beneath it, I felt something more—an unspoken connection I couldn't quite define.

The entire day had been like that: easy, comfortable, but charged with an undercurrent of possibility. I enjoyed being with Garrett as a friend, but I couldn't ignore the part of me that wanted more. Whether that happened, though, was up to him.

On the drive home, I pulled out my phone, my thumb hovering over the email app. My stomach tightened as I refreshed my inbox, half-expecting the familiar jolt of dread that came with seeing a new message from EyeSeeYou.

Nothing.

I exhaled slowly, a knot I hadn't realized I was carrying loosening in my back. No new messages. No threats. For the first time in weeks, I allowed myself to hope.

I had a new security system. Garrett had opened an official investigation. And he'd accompanied me to the farmers' market, his presence a constant reminder that I wasn't alone.

Was it too much to hope that the stalker had finally given up?

CHAPTER FOURTEEN

GARRETT

I sat at my desk in the bullpen and stared at my monitor, unseeing. My fingers hovered over the keyboard, poised for action that wouldn't come. The report I'd started an hour ago still read, *Incident Summary:* and nothing else.

The quiet hum of the station buzzed in the background —phones ringing, chairs creaking, the faint tapping on keyboards—but it all faded into a dull blur. It had been three days since I'd escorted Ethan to the farmers' market, and yet, every detail of that day played on a loop in my mind. The sound of his laughter, low and warm. The way his smile softened his features and made his eyes crinkle at the corners. The way his voice, smooth but with an edge of uncertainty, drew me in like a magnet.

Accompanying him hadn't been a hardship—not by a long shot. I'd enjoyed every minute. I couldn't stop replaying the casual touches I'd let myself indulge in—a hand on his elbow, a brush of shoulders as we maneuvered through the crowd, the steady press of my palm on the small of his back as I guided him toward the vendors. None of it was necessary. All of it felt right.

And yet…why?

What was it about him that pulled me so deeply, like an undertow I couldn't escape? It wasn't just the way he looked, though I couldn't deny his curly auburn hair and warm brown eyes had captivated me from the start. It was something more, something intangible. The quiet strength he exuded, the way his humility never dulled his wit or kindness. He wasn't like any woman I'd ever been with—and that was the puzzle.

Ethan had me questioning my sexuality, something I'd never truly confronted before. The thought rattled me, and yet, it didn't scare me the way I thought it might. It was the uncertainty that ate at me. My mind felt like a battlefield, emotions clashing in waves, leaving me tossing and turning at night as if I were a boat adrift on a stormy sea.

During the day, my thoughts scattered like sea foam in a gale. Even now, I wasn't sure if I should steer toward Ethan or anchor myself far away. Every time I tried to sort it out, I kept coming back to the same question: *What does* he *want?*

A sharp buzz broke through my haze, and my phone lit up on the desk. My chest tightened with anticipation even before I glanced at the screen.

ETHAN

> I owe you dinner and a movie at my house.
> Any chance you're free this weekend?

I stared at the text, and my pulse thudded in my ears. He'd reached out. He wanted to see me. The warmth of his words curled around me and quieted the storm.

My thumbs hovered over the phone's keyboard as I typed, then deleted, then typed again. I wanted to say yes immediately, but I didn't want to seem too eager. Finally, I settled on:

> Pizza and Disney were our pleasure.

I paused, and my heart pounded. Was this the moment to take a leap? The decision felt monumental, like standing on the edge of a cliff, staring into the unknown. My pulse quickened as I typed my next message.

> I'm free on Friday evening. Noah's spending the night with my sister.

The response came almost instantly.

> Building blanket forts?

I chuckled, the tension in my chest easing. Of course, he remembered Noah's words about Harper and their fort-building escapades. That minor detail told me he'd been paying attention to my son, and as a single dad, that warmed me to my core.

> Exactly. What should I bring?

> Yourself.

My lips curved into a smile that I couldn't suppress, the kind that made my cheeks ache.

> 7 okay?

That would give me enough time to pick up Noah from after-school care, drop him off at Harper's, and shower off the workday.

See you then.

I glanced around the station and my fingers tightened around my phone as Ethan's invitation lingered on the screen. A slow, goofy grin spread across my face before I could stop it. Dinner at Ethan's.

If anyone noticed the stupid look on my face, they might ask questions. Questions I wasn't ready to answer.

A quick scan of the room confirmed that no one was watching me too closely, but the weight of what I was doing settled in my chest. I shouldn't be this excited. Heck, I shouldn't even be considering it. This was a bad idea. A really bad idea. Ethan was part of an active investigation, one I led. If Sarge got wind that I was spending time—alone—with the very man I was supposed to be protecting, it would raise red flags.

But darn it, I wanted to see Ethan. Wanted to sit across from him at the dinner table and pretend—just for a little while—that this wasn't complicated. That there weren't risks. That I wasn't walking a razor's edge between what I should do and what I *wanted* to do.

I told myself I'd keep it casual.

But I already knew I was lying.

———

I locked Ethan's door behind me and toed off my Chucks. The soft thud echoed in the cozy entryway. The comfy house seeped into me like a welcome hug. The savory, spicy scent of herbs and garlic teased my senses and made my stomach growl loudly enough to fill the silence. "Mm, something smells good."

Ethan chuckled at my grumbling stomach, the sound rich and low. "I hope you like veggie lasagna. I made it with the ingredients I bought at the farmers' market."

His brown eyes caught the golden glow of the living room lamps and danced with something that looked an awful lot like happiness—or maybe anticipation. The sight stirred something deep in my chest.

"Love it." I grinned. "And I'll bet yours is better than the frozen stuff I buy from the grocery store."

Ethan reared back, and mock offense scrunched up his face. "I should hope so."

I couldn't stop the laugh that escaped me. It felt good. Natural. "I'm sure it is." I held up the six-pack of Barnacle Brews pilsner I'd brought. "I know you said I shouldn't bring anything, but I couldn't arrive empty-handed."

Ethan smiled, and a flicker of warmth passed between us. "It's perfect. Bring it into the kitchen. I don't think the house came furnished with beer glasses, so we'll have to chug it from the bottle."

He led the way, his movements unhurried and relaxed. I followed him through the living room into the kitchen, full of delicious aromas and heat from the oven.

I set the beer on the table, shrugged out of my light jacket, and draped it over the back of a chair. I rolled up the sleeves of my button-down, which I'd paired with jeans. I'd debated what to wear—this evening felt almost like a date.

I was relieved to see he'd had the same idea. His crisp shirt fell perfectly from his broad shoulders, wrapped around toned biceps, and tucked neatly into the waistband of his jeans, which rested low on narrow hips.

When had I started caring what I wore around another man? Or noticing how his clothing highlighted his fit body?

Not since Leo. Not until Ethan.

He held up a cherry tomato, his expression questioning. "Tomatoes okay in the salad?"

I dragged my focus back to his face and nodded. "Unlike some little boys I know, I'm not a picky eater."

Ethan snorted a laugh and scattered tomatoes on top of a leafy green salad. "Well, I can also make chicken nuggets and macaroni and cheese like a top chef."

The playful words warmed the air between us, but my thoughts turned serious for a moment. When would he cook for Noah? Ethan lived in Brooklyn—his life was there. His family was there; his niece was there. The realization he'd leave Seacliff Cove once we caught the stalker weighed in my stomach like a stone. As a single dad, I'd never stand between a man and his family. Instead, I'd focus on the time we had together.

With that thought in mind, I popped open two bottles of beer, and the soft hiss broke the momentary silence. I handed one to him and brushed my fingers against his as I did.

"Thanks," he said quietly. "Dinner's almost ready."

"What can I do?" I moved back and tried to ignore how close we'd been.

Ethan glanced at me, a mischievous glint in his eyes. "Just stand there and look handsome." He winked.

I froze for a heartbeat; the words hit me like a rogue wave, unexpected. Was he *flirting*? Did I want him to be?

I raised an eyebrow and forced my voice to stay light. "Are you objectifying me, Mr. Cole?"

Ethan's eyes widened, and panic flashed across his face. "I'm so sorry. I didn't mean—"

"It's okay," I said, low and husky as I cut him off. "I like that you think I'm handsome."

His cheeks flushed a rosy hue that had nothing to do with the oven's heat. He nodded, and the tiniest smile tugged at his lips as he turned back to the salad. But when he placed the bowl on the table, his arm brushed mine even though he had plenty of room to maneuver. He lingered just long enough to send a shiver down my spine.

The timer on his phone shattered the heartbeat of time. We both startled and stepped apart as if caught in the act of something we hadn't quite admitted yet. Ethan cleared his throat and hooked a thumb toward the oven. "The lasagna…"

I nodded, unable to prevent a small quirk of a smile. "Right. Lasagna."

He bent to pull the bubbling dish from the oven, but I didn't miss the slight tremor in his hands as he slid a sheet of garlic bread inside.

In the quiet that followed, the air between us buzzed with unspoken words, unacknowledged feelings. Something was building, slow and steady, and I wasn't sure whether to stoke the fire or let it burn out.

I sipped my beer, keeping my tone casual. Neutral ground seemed like the safest bet. "Did you write the screenplay for the Jake Slate TV series?"

He pulled plates from the cabinet, the dinnerware rattling. "No, a screenplay writer adapted the first book for the first season of the show, though he consulted me on the script."

I nodded, trying not to get distracted by the way the golden glow of the lights lit up the red highlights in his hair. "That makes sense. Did you have any say in who they cast to play Jake?"

Ethan turned to the oven and pulled out a tray of perfectly browned garlic bread. The scent hit me like a tsunami—garlic, butter, a hint of herbs. My mouth watered at the delicious aroma.

"No." He set the tray on a butcher block on the counter. "But I met Brock Mitchell. They invited me to the first day of filming."

"No shi—oot?" I caught myself and instinctively glanced around the kitchen.

Ethan chuckled, low and warm. "You can swear around me. Noah's not here."

"Best to stay in the habit," I muttered and tried to ignore the way his laughter did funny things to my stomach.

He picked up his phone, swiped the screen, and gave it to me. His hand brushed mine briefly with a spark of temptation.

I squinted at the photo. There he was, standing next to Brock Mitchell, who looked like he could toss Ethan over his shoulder without breaking a sweat. Ethan wasn't small—tall and fit in a way that suggested he exercised—but Mitchell made him look almost fragile. Almost. But I only had eyes for Ethan. Ethan's wide smile in the picture was what really caught my eye, a smile I rarely saw under the current circumstances. It made my breath hitch.

"Wow," I managed, handing the phone back. "He makes a great Jake Slate."

Ethan grabbed a knife and started slicing the garlic bread. "I know, right? They did a good job with the casting."

I picked up the basket he'd filled with bread; the warmth radiated through the fabric napkin in my hands. "When does the show come out?"

"They're wrapping up filming in Ontario. It'll be streaming next fall." He plated generous squares of lasagna, the cheese stretching and oozing. I couldn't wait to dig in.

We carried everything to the table and sat. As soon as I took my first bite, I couldn't stop the groan of appreciation that escaped me. The lasagna was rich, cheesy, and full of flavor, the kind of comfort food that was like a soft bed after a long day. "Much better than mac and cheese and chicken nuggets." I savored another forkful.

"You haven't tasted my homemade mac and cheese and chicken nuggets." A grin tugged at the corner of his mouth.

I raised an eyebrow. "Going to show me up, huh?"

"Wouldn't dream of it." He laughed, and the sound lit up the room.

Over dinner, we talked about the first Jake Slate book. Ethan's passion was obvious as he described the plot twists and character development, his face animated with every word. I hung on every sentence, more invested than I cared to admit.

"I don't plan much when I write." He leaned back in his chair. "The story unfolds as I go. The twist for the first book hit me during a walk in Central Park—an hour away from my computer. I had to stop and type up notes on my phone before I lost it."

"Walks seem to inspire you."

His gaze turned distant. "I never thought about it, but yeah, I guess they do. There's something about the mindless rhythm of my footsteps. It stimulates my thought processes."

We lingered over the meal and traded stories. I told him about Noah's adventures, and Ethan's snickers filled the pauses between my tales.

"One Christmas." I grinned at the memory. "He insisted on wearing his little suit to my parents' house. Used his tie as a napkin for the entire dinner."

Ethan chuckled. "What else are ties for?"

Cleaning up afterward felt strangely natural. We moved around each other in the kitchen like we'd been doing it for years, anticipating each other's movements without a word. There was something…easy about it, something that made me ache in a way I wasn't ready to name.

We carried bowls of Cherry Garcia to the couch. I sank into the cushions, the rich sweetness of the ice cream a perfect end to the meal. Ethan sat close, and his shoulder brushed mine just enough to remind me he was there. Too close, and yet not close enough.

And that was the problem. Ethan wasn't just someone I was getting to know. He was becoming someone I couldn't stop thinking about. And I wasn't sure what to do with that.

Ethan placed his bowl on the coffee table and picked up the TV remote. "Want to watch a thriller?"

"Absolutely. Turn it on, and let's see if it holds up to your book."

Ethan snorted a laugh. "My books aren't the gold standard."

I waved my spoon in the air and flashed a crooked grin. "Pick one, and I'll be the judge of that."

As Ethan navigated through the streaming options, I noticed the faint crease between his brows. He always looked so serious when he focused, and it tugged at something deep inside me—something I was still grappling with.

He paused on a title. "Have you seen this one? It's about a detective searching for a woman who vanished."

"Right up my alley. Let's do it." I finished the last spoonful of melting ice cream, savoring the sweet flavor as I set my bowl next to Ethan's on the table.

The movie opened with a man in shadows stalking a woman. Ethan stiffened beside me, his fingers whitening around the remote. The tension in the room was palpable, and I felt an urge to reassure him.

"Maybe we should watch something else," I offered quietly. My hand hovered over his thigh for a moment before I finally let it rest there, the contact soothing me as much as I hoped it would soothe him. My pulse hammered in my ears. Would he be all right with my touch? Or was I crossing a line?

He glanced at me and, to my immense relief, gave my hand a firm squeeze. "I'm okay," he said, soft but steady.

I pulled my hand back, reassured, but when the man on-screen grabbed the woman, Ethan's muscles tautened. I slid my arm along the back of the sofa and let it span his shoulders. His body was rigid at first, but then he leaned into me, the subtle weight of his trust making my chest tighten.

My heart thundered, not from the suspense of the movie but from the sheer gravity of the moment. This wasn't just about comforting Ethan; it was about what it meant for me —for us. My mind swirled with questions, doubts, and a cautious thrill at the realization that I'd taken a step toward acknowledging the part of myself I'd suppressed.

"…inciting incident."

Ethan's voice broke through my haze. I blinked and glanced at him. "Sorry, what?" I cleared my throat to remove the tremor in my voice.

"That was just the inciting incident. Now we're into the exposition and the introduction of crucial story elements." He turned his head, and his eyes caught mine. Husky and low, he said, "But the rising action and climax are coming, so leave your arm there."

A grin tugged at the corner of my mouth. "Well, when you put it like that…" I dared to let my hand fall to his shoulders, the solid warmth of him under my touch a mix of comfort and exhilaration.

Ethan's lips curved into a small, knowing smile, and his gaze held mine for a beat too long. The sudden blare of a siren on the screen made us both flinch and broke the spell.

As the movie progressed, Ethan leaned against my side, his nearness welcome. He pointed out the beats of the story, his insights fascinating and eye-opening. I knew I'd never watch a movie the same way again.

By the time the movie reached its heart-pounding climax, I was fully engrossed. My palms were damp, and my heart raced—not just from the suspense, but from the subtle, quiet intimacy of Ethan pressed against me. The relief was almost overwhelming when the detective found the woman alive.

Ethan leaned forward to grab the remote and turn off the TV. I reluctantly dropped my arm from his shoulders, the loss of contact disheartening.

"Well, that gave Jake Slate a run for his money." I broke the silence.

Ethan grinned. "I'll take that as a compliment."

I smirked and leaned back into the couch. "Your books are still the gold standard."

"Have you read any other thrillers?" he teased and arched an eyebrow.

I scratched my temple, sheepish. "Well…no."

Ethan burst into laughter. His belly laugh was infectious, and I chuckled at my own expense.

He scrubbed a hand down his face, laughter still bubbling up from deep within. "Oh, God. I needed that." His shoulders shook with residual sniggers, his face lit with an ease I hadn't seen in days.

I watched Ethan laugh, truly laugh, and it made my chest feel buoyant, as if I were finally doing something to lift the weight he carried. I couldn't find his stalker yet, couldn't give him the peace he deserved—but I could give him this. A few hours of safety, distraction, and companionship.

I sobered quickly at the thought of his stalker, but for Ethan's sake, I kept a smile on my face. I vowed silently that I would solve his case, no matter how many leads went cold. He deserved to live without looking over his shoulder.

A rude yawn escaped before I could catch it. I stifled it quickly, embarrassed. "Sorry," I muttered and rubbed the back of my neck. I didn't want the evening to end. Being here, with Ethan, felt right in a way I hadn't expected.

Ethan's hand landed gently on my knee, and his warmth cut through the fabric of my jeans. "You must have had a long day. Don't let me keep you," he said, ever thoughtful. He had a way of putting others first, even when he had every right to focus on himself. It was one of the many things I admired about him.

I stood reluctantly and stretched my arms overhead to shake off the pull of exhaustion. "I do need to get to bed," I admitted. "Noah's coming home early tomorrow morning, and we've got his classmate's birthday party in the afternoon." I rolled my eyes as if it were a burden. "Ten five-year-olds and their parents? Pure chaos."

Ethan's grin was knowing, and his lips quirked upward just enough to make my heart stutter. "You can't fool me," he said, low and warm. "You love being a dad. All of it."

He wasn't wrong. "I'd do anything for that boy." I smiled, unable to hide my love for my son. I moved toward the entryway, and Ethan shadowed me.

I turned to thank him for the evening and caught his gaze. My breath hitched at the intensity I found there—longing, desire, and something deeper that sent a shiver down my spine. My heart thudded, and I wavered as the air between us thickened. He was waiting for me to decide, his stillness an invitation.

Did I want to take a further step toward the decision I wrestled with?

The answer came faster than I anticipated. Yes. I wanted it more than I could put into words.

My gaze dropped to his mouth, framed by his trim beard. Red highlights threaded through the bristles. My fingers itched to touch him, to feel the softness of that beard, to press against the fullness of his lips and taste whatever sweetness lingered there.

I swallowed hard, and my voice dropped into a register I barely recognized. "May I kiss you?"

Ethan didn't answer right away, but his eyes darkened

and his lips parted just slightly. He stepped closer, close enough that his heat seeped into me. His hand rose, hesitated for a moment, and then cupped my jaw. His thumb brushed lightly along the curve of my cheek.

"Yes," he whispered as his breath mingled with mine.

I closed the remaining distance and captured his lips in a tentative kiss, gentle and testing. His lips were soft and yielding, and the unfamiliar texture of his beard sent a thrill skittering across my skin. Beard to stubble, man to man. So different from the silky skin of a woman's mouth, and yet thrilling.

Ethan pressed closer. The kiss deepened, and his fingers slid into my hair as mine gripped his waist.

My heart pounded furiously, and each beat thundered with the realization that this—this moment—was changing something fundamental inside me. Kissing Ethan felt like crossing a threshold, like finding a part of myself I'd been missing.

When we finally pulled apart, our breaths mixing, I couldn't help the smile that tugged at my lips. Ethan's gaze searched mine, his cheeks flushed, his lips slightly swollen. *Sexy*. Passionate. Stunning. More than stunning—he looked like someone I wanted to protect, cherish.

I cleared my throat, my voice thick with emotion. "That…was worth the wait."

Ethan's laugh was quiet, a little shy. "Good," he said softly. "Because I've been waiting for you to do that."

The words settled in my chest where they belonged. We were on the cusp of something momentous.

But I'd utterly failed at keeping the evening casual.

CHAPTER FIFTEEN

ETHAN

I unscrewed the Mason jar of beef vegetable soup from the farmers' market and the lid gave a satisfying pop as it released. The savory aroma of tomatoes, garlic, and herbs swirled up and teased my senses. My stomach growled, but my mind remained detached, far beyond the walls of my kitchen.

I poured the chunky soup into the pan, and the vegetables tumbled out with a muffled plop. I turned on the burner and reached for a loaf of artisan bread. Golden and dusted with flour, its yeasty scent mingled with the simmering soup. My serrated blade sliced through the crust into the soft center.

But I was on autopilot, my movements mechanical, my thoughts consumed by a single, electrifying moment—Friday night's kiss with Garrett.

I'd replayed it in my mind so many times over the past three days that it felt like I could recall every tiny detail. The slight intake of his breath before his lips touched mine. The firm yet tender pressure of his kiss, filled with a confident warmth that had made my heart stutter. The faint, residual sweet taste of cherry ice cream. The way his hands had gripped my waist and settled me, even as an electric charge zipped through my veins.

Was it spontaneous? A sudden burst of courage on his part? Or had he been thinking about it for days, carefully waiting for the right moment? And now that it had happened, how did *he* feel about it? Did he relive it the way I did, or had he pushed it to the back of his mind, chalking it up to a fleeting impulse?

The knife faltered mid-slice, and the question lingered like a weight on my chest. Was he bisexual? Bi-curious? Exploring? Did he regret the kiss?

For me, it was anything but a regret. That kiss was a connection I hadn't dared to hope for. But did it mean the same to him?

I hadn't heard from him all weekend. The logical part of me tried to rationalize it—he'd told me he was spending time with Noah, that it was their father-son weekend. Still, doubt itched at the edges of my thoughts, persistent and unwelcome.

I gave the soup a halfhearted stir and watched the bubbles break the surface. A flicker of something hopeful whirled low in my stomach. Maybe that kiss could lead to something more. Something real. My pulse quickened at the thought, and I imagined what *more* with Garrett might look like—late-night conversations, stolen moments in the quiet safety of our homes, more kisses.

More than kisses.

But the hope came tangled with the same knot of fear that had been tightening in me since I'd come to Seacliff Cove. I'd only be here until Garrett arrested the stalker. Then what? Did I have the courage to see where this could lead, knowing it might only be temporary? And what about the danger? By letting Garrett in, wasn't I putting both of us at greater risk?

Not to mention the risk to his career.

I sighed and gripped the edge of the counter as the beefy aroma of the simmering soup filled the kitchen. My chest ached with the weight of it all—the uncertainty, the fear, the raw, undeniable yearning.

All I knew for sure was that I wanted more. More closeness, more connection.

And more of Garrett's kisses.

The doorbell echoed through the house and shattered the fragile quiet of my afternoon. My shoulders tensed instinctively; the ever-present unease from the stalker lingered like a shadow, even though there had been no incidents lately. My pulse quickened as I plucked my phone from my pocket and tapped the screen to view the front door feed.

Garrett stood on the porch, hands braced on his hips, his ramrod posture exuding authority. It was lunchtime, and my stomach twisted. Was this an official visit or something more personal?

I turned off the burner. The soft beeps of the alarm system as I disarmed it seemed overly loud in the silence. I opened the door to find Garrett's expression carefully neutral, the only sound his tactical gear creaking faintly as he shifted his weight.

"Garrett?" I betrayed a flicker of apprehension. "What are you doing here?"

"May I come in, sir?" he said, clipped and professional.

The formality in his voice sent an uneasy ripple through me. I frowned, and my thoughts raced. What the hell was going on? My gut churned as I stepped aside to let him in. He moved past me with quiet efficiency, the faint scents of gun oil and sporty body wash trailing him.

I closed the door and set my back to it. He placed an arm on the door above me and leaned in. "Do you have anything new to report...sir?"

His lips quirked at the corners, and the anxiety in my chest snapped like a rubber band.

"You bastard." The breath rushed out of me in relief. I grinned as I swatted his hard tactical vest. *Ouch.* "You worried me."

Before I could pull my hand away, he caught and clasped it against him. His thumb brushed across my knuckles in a slow, deliberate motion and sent a shiver skittering down my spine.

"That's battery against a police officer. I should put you in cuffs," he said, low and husky.

A smirk tugged at my mouth. "Oh, you'd like that, wouldn't you?"

His eyebrows waggled, a glint of mischief lighting his eyes. "Only if you would." He paused, his voice softening. "But I really came to do this."

The air between us shifted, charged with unspoken desire. He leaned in hesitantly, his gaze locked on my eyes, and silently asked for permission. My chest tightened, but I gave a small nod, and he closed the distance.

His lips pressed to mine, tentative at first, then with growing confidence. His arms circled around me, drawing me close, and I let myself fall into him. The hard press of his vest against my chest was an afterthought compared to the warmth of his embrace.

The kiss was everything I remembered—and more. A spark ignited and raced down my spine as Garrett's tongue flicked against the seam of my lips. I opened for him, and he deepened the kiss, stealing the air from my lungs and the coherent thoughts from my mind.

I lost track of time—seconds, minutes, eternity—but too

soon, he leaned back. Our breaths mingled as his forehead rested briefly against mine.

"I can't stop thinking about Friday night," he confessed, his voice roughened with emotion. He brushed a light kiss to the tip of my nose, and my heart swelled.

"I can't, either," I said, barely above a whisper.

"I had to come steal another kiss." He nuzzled my face. "Love the feel of your beard against my cheek. Had to make up an excuse to come see you."

A soft laugh bubbled out of me. "Well, you can report that I haven't had any more incidents."

He stepped back, and the sudden absence of his warmth left me bereft. "That's good news," he said, his voice gentle. With one last quick kiss, he turned to go.

"I'll wait on the porch until I hear you lock the door," he said over his shoulder, ever the protector.

I nodded and watched him leave, his movements light for a big man. The soft *snick* of the bolt sliding into place felt strangely final. Moments later, his SUV rumbled to life, and the sound faded as he drove away.

I returned to my soup, and the smile stayed on my lips. My chest felt lighter, as though something fragile and hopeful had taken root. We were moving forward.

But where were we headed?

CHAPTER SIXTEEN

GARRETT

At lunchtime on Halloween, I settled at a corner table at The Coffee Cove, the rich scents of my coffee and savory hot ham and cheese sandwich curling around me. Outside, the crisp fall air carried the tang of salt, and the town bustled with last-minute shoppers. But inside the café, it was warm, familiar…and yet, I couldn't shake the restless energy simmering beneath my skin.

Ethan.

He had been a constant presence in my thoughts for the past four days, ever since I'd stolen that kiss in the middle of my shift. A reckless moment, one I hadn't let myself overanalyze. But I couldn't stop thinking about the way he'd looked at me afterward—like I was something he hadn't expected but wasn't quite ready to walk away from.

I exhaled slowly and pulled out my phone. My thumb hovered over his name, and my pulse kicked up a notch.

> Want to trick-or-treat with Noah and me tonight? He's been asking about you.

It wasn't just about Noah; it was an excuse to see Ethan again. I sent the message, and the seconds stretched out as I waited for his reply.

> Love to.

I grinned, and warmth spread through my chest.

> Pick you up at 6.

> Have Noah ring the bell. I've got candy for him.

I frowned, and my jaw tightened. Had he been out in public without me?

> How did you get candy? I was supposed to escort you to the grocery store.

The thought of Ethan stepping outside—even to cross the street—made my shoulders tense. The stalker had been quiet lately, but silence didn't equal surrender.

> There's this thing called DoorDash delivery...

I barked a laugh, some of the tension easing. Of course, he'd find a way to get what he needed without walking into danger.

> Smart ass.

> See you later. Can't wait!

I stared at the last message, his words replaying in my mind. *Can't wait.* My chest felt light, the usual weight I carried about the stalker momentarily lifting. I pocketed my phone and picked up my sandwich, unable to suppress a smile.

At the pickup counter, Cooper arched a brow and wiped down the surface with broad strokes. "What's that smile about?"

I shrugged, playing it cool. "Going trick-or-treating with Noah tonight. Should be fun."

But Cooper wasn't buying it. He paused mid-swipe, his sharp eyes narrowing. "No, it's more than that."

Before I had to answer, he was called away to fill an order. I exhaled, a mixture of relief and unease swirling in my gut. I wasn't ready to explain the way I felt about Ethan, not even to my closest friends. It wasn't shame. It was... something deeper. Intimate. Personal. And Ethan was a private person. I didn't want to betray his trust.

The day slipped by, and before I knew it, I was helping Noah into his costume. He wiggled with excitement, a ball of boundless energy.

"I can't wait to see Mr. Ethan!" He bounced on his toes.

I smiled and tugged his mask into place. "He can't wait to see you either, buddy."

Pumpkin bucket in hand, Noah darted toward the door. "Let's go!"

"Shoes!" I called. I laughed as he skidded to a stop and hurriedly jammed his feet into his sneakers.

Hand in hand, we stepped out into the chilly October evening, the air tinged with the scent of wood smoke. The neighborhood was alive with the laughter of kids and running feet.

We walked up the path to Ethan's porch. The bright security lights blinked on and lit the way. The porch light cast a warm illumination in welcome, and a carved pumpkin with a goofy grin glowed by the door. Noah enthusiastically rang the doorbell three times.

After a moment, the lock clicked, and the door opened. Ethan's smile was immediate and broad.

"Trick or treat!" Noah yelled and jumped up and down.

Ethan gasped, a hand to his chest. "It's Spider-Man! At my door!"

"It's me, Mr. Ethan!"

"Really?" Ethan leaned in, mock-surprised. "Are you sure?"

I couldn't help the laugh that bubbled up, warmth spreading through me as Ethan played along.

Noah lifted his mask and nodded solemnly. "Uh-huh. This is just a costume."

But Ethan continued the charade, which was one of the many things I liked about him. "You fooled me!" He grabbed a basket from a table in the entryway. "I think you deserve some candy for such a good costume."

Noah held out his pumpkin, and Ethan dropped a few mini chocolate bars into it. Noah would bounce off the walls when we got home and sampled his haul, but that was part of the fun of Halloween.

Ethan grabbed a jacket, armed his alarm system, and locked the door. My chest tightened at the simple but crucial acts of caution.

Together, we strolled the neighborhood, and our quiet footsteps mingled with Noah's chatter. Ethan lingered in the shadows at each house, letting Noah and me take the lead, but his presence felt significant.

Every so often, I caught his gaze on me, his expression unreadable but warm. I met his eyes once and the soft glow of a porch light caught the edge of a smile. My heart stumbled, and I looked away as heat crept up my neck.

This wasn't just another evening. This was something growing between us.

We strolled from one house to the next, Noah's small,

warm hand nestled securely in mine. The neighbors I'd known for years—the Vees, Wigfields, Carpenters, Hendershots, Moores, and others—were a mix of longtime retirees who'd lived there since the houses were built and young families settling into their first homes. At each door, I kept my tone casual, simply asking them to keep an eye out for anything—or anyone—unusual on the street. I didn't offer specifics. Just enough to plant a seed of watchfulness.

Ethan's phone chimed, the familiar sound instantly drawing my attention. I recognized the notification—it was from his security system. Someone was at his front door. My first thought was that it was probably just a kid trick-or-treating, but Ethan's sharp intake of breath told me otherwise.

I stopped in my tracks, instinctively pulling Noah to a halt beside me. "What's wrong?" My voice came out clipped, my senses on high alert.

Ethan turned the phone so I could see. A figure cloaked in a long, hooded robe approached Ethan's porch, their movements deliberate and unnerving. The person bent down, picked up Ethan's carefully carved pumpkin, and hurled it against the door. The sharp crack of impact reverberated in my imagination and sent a chill racing down my spine. Then the figure lifted their masked face toward the camera. They raised a middle finger with an air of casual defiance before disappearing into the night.

My chest tightened with an icy knot of dread. "Fudge," I muttered under my breath. My gaze flicked to Ethan, whose face had paled. "He's getting bolder. He's escalating. Why? What does he want from you?"

Ethan's shoulders sagged as he shook his head. "I don't know," he said, his voice barely more than a breath. "I swear, Garrett—I have no idea who he is or what he's after. He hasn't asked for anything. No demands. Just…messages.

Warnings. Threats. Like he's playing some twisted game, and I don't even know the rules."

I handed the phone back to him, my fingers brushing his, stiff with strain. "Send me that video."

Ethan's jaw worked as he nodded, his movements jerky.

Noah, attuned to the mood, tugged at my hand. "What's wrong?" His innocent voice cut through the tension, pulling both of us back to the moment.

"It's no big deal, buddy," Ethan replied, his tone carefully even. "Someone smashed my pumpkin." He forced a smile, but his rigid posture betrayed his attempt to stay calm.

Noah's face fell and his brows knitted in confusion. "Why would anyone do that? It was so cute." He hesitated, then mumbled, "Even though the smile was crooked."

Ethan's tense expression cracked, and he choked out a laugh. The sound, though brief, was enough to ease some of the weight pressing on my chest. "I'll do better next year," he promised, his voice thick with affection.

Would he even be here next year? The unspoken question lodged in my throat, but I swallowed it down for now.

Noah nodded solemnly. "Do that."

I snorted, glad for the comic relief. "Let's not turn this into a critique of Ethan's pumpkin carving skills. I think we need to—"

"No," Ethan interrupted firmly, his tone brooking no argument. "We're not cutting the night short. The guy is long gone, has probably already ditched the costume. We wouldn't recognize him in the crowd. He's not ruining Noah's night." With that, he turned on his heel and started toward the next house, his stride long and purposeful.

I opened my mouth to argue but stopped when Noah's hopeful face tilted up at me. "Please, Daddy?"

My resolve softened, and I glanced at Ethan. I appreciated his determination to protect the night for Noah's sake. I relented with a nod and followed. The photos I needed to take of Ethan's porch and the search for the costume could wait.

When we reached the next house and stopped beside Ethan, I called my sister. "Can you be at my house in thirty minutes? Something's come up."

"Is Auntie Harper coming over?" Noah danced on his toes. "Can we eat candy?"

"Yeah." Harper would have to deal with the consequences, and I held back a chuckle at her expense.

Ethan mouthed, "Thank you."

We finished the houses on our street and then circled back to Ethan's. The faint metallic tang of adrenaline still lingered in the back of my throat as I took in the mess on his door—the smashed pumpkin strewn like a garish warning. I snapped pictures while Ethan silently grabbed a broom, his movements unsteady but resolute.

When he was done, Ethan brushed pumpkin seeds from his hands and crouched in front of Noah. "Thanks for taking me trick-or-treating. I had fun."

"Look how much candy I gots!" Noah beamed and held up his bucket with pride.

"Wow!" Ethan exaggerated his amazement and earned a giggle from Noah. "That's a lot. Think you can share some with your dad?"

Noah scuffed the toe of his shoe against the concrete and thought it over. "Okay."

I laughed and ruffled Noah's hair. As Ethan straightened, our gazes locked. The warmth in his eyes and the unspoken longing between us made my heart skip a beat. For a moment, the world fell away, and it was just the two of us, possibilities stretching before us.

But not in front of Noah.

"Good night," I said softly, the words carrying more weight than they should. "Thanks for coming with us."

"My pleasure." His lips curved into a small smile, and my chest tightened with the unspoken connection between us.

By the time we reached home, Harper was already waiting. After a quick, generic explanation about a vandal, I grabbed my tactical flashlight and headed out to search for the discarded costume. The night air bit at my skin, and every shadow seemed alive, but the search turned up nothing. My frustration grew with every step.

When I finally texted Ethan to let him know, his reply was immediate.

Didn't find the costume.

Not surprised. Thanks for trying.

As I set my phone down, the heavy weight of uncertainty settled deeper. What would the stalker do next?

CHAPTER SEVENTEEN

ETHAN

The soft light of morning filtered through the slats of my blinds. I sat at my desk, pen poised over a page of the notebook beside my laptop. I tapped the pen on the paper, a metronome ticking away the seconds of my distracted thoughts. I was supposed to be brainstorming the next chapter of my book, but my mind refused to cooperate.

Instead, I kept replaying the events of the previous night.

The stalker's latest act felt like he'd crossed a line. Smashing the pumpkin wasn't just a petty, anonymous act of vandalism—it was a deliberate taunt. The way he had stared directly into the camera, raising his middle finger in mockery, sent a chill through me, even now. My stomach churned with a toxic mix of anger and unease. He was getting bolder. How long before he snapped?

I leaned back in my chair and scrubbed my hands over my face. The silence of the house felt oppressive, pressing down on me like a weight. Last night, I managed to maintain a veneer of calm for Noah's sake. But now, alone with my thoughts, the gravity of the situation bore down on me. What would the stalker do next?

My gaze drifted to the notebook on my desk, where I'd jotted down loose ideas for my next chapter. Jake Slate faced his own shadowy threat, an antagonist that lurked just out of sight. The book was just a story—a carefully crafted narrative to thrill readers—but now it felt like my life was bleeding onto the page. The parallels were too close, the lines between reality and fiction blurring in ways that left me unnerved.

I tried to focus, to force my mind back to the plot I'd been constructing, but my thoughts kept straying to Garrett. His staunch presence had been a balm against the chaos. The way he'd calmly handled the situation, prioritizing Noah's happiness while still quietly taking control, left me in awe. Garrett was a force of nature—unflinching, dependable, and protective.

And then there was the moment at the end of the night. Our gazes had locked, and for a heartbeat, everything else faded away. There had been a warmth in his eyes, a silent understanding that went deeper than words. My chest lightened at the memory, a flutter of something that was growing between us. Garrett made me feel…special.

It wasn't just the physical safety of knowing he'd protect me from the stalker. It was the way he made me laugh in the face of anxiety, the way he eased the constant tension in my shoulders. For a man whose life had become a tangled mess of fear and uncertainty, Garrett was a sanctuary.

I smiled to myself despite the heavy thoughts weighing me down. Garrett shouldered some of my burden.

My thoughts freed, I brainstormed the next chapter. The words flowed easily after that.

Before I knew it, the light outside had faded, and evening had crept in. I realized I'd worked through lunch without even noticing. My stomach growled in protest, a hollow ache that forced me to push back from my desk.

I stood and stretched until my spine cracked. A groan escaped my lips as I worked out the stiffness in my back and shoulders.

The backyard motion sensor floodlight flicked on.

The sudden brightness engulfed the room, sharp and intrusive. My pulse kicked up instantly. Probably just a cat or a breeze. Still, I parted the blinds and peered through the slats.

Nothing.

The bushes swayed in the breeze. No shadows, no movement shifted ominously along the tall wooden fence. Just me, overreacting. Again.

I let the blinds fall shut and blew out a breath. Still unsettled, I made my way to the kitchen. Food wouldn't fix the tension crawling up my spine, but it was a start.

Leftover chicken and vegetables called my name, and I set about reheating dinner. The clink of silverware and the hum of the microwave filled the quiet. Routine tasks, relaxing and familiar. I needed that sense of normalcy right now.

But normal wasn't what my life was anymore.

After eating, I loaded the dishwasher and wiped down the counters in wide swipes, lost in thought about my current chapter. Then my phone chimed.

The security camera notification.

I froze, and a shiver ran down my spine. Slowly, I meticulously dried my hands on a dish towel as I tried to steady myself. But my heart thumped hard against my ribs, an erratic beat of dread.

With trembling fingers, I pulled up the feed.

The screen was black.

Frowning, I rewound the footage, breath held tight in my

chest. There he was—the same hooded, masked figure as before, walking up to my porch like he owned the place. *Gutsy.* His movements were calm, almost casual, as he raised a can of spray paint. A cold rush of fear flooded me as I watched black paint splatter across the camera lens, blotting out the view.

Then, nothing.

The feed went dark.

I stood there and stared at my phone, the edges digging into my palm. My mind raced. Was he still out there? Watching? Waiting?

I texted Garrett, my fingers clumsy on the keys.

> Someone spray-painted the camera. Same guy. What do I do?

His response was immediate.

> Stay inside. Do NOT go out to clean the camera. I'm coming over.

> What about Noah?

> He's with my parents for the weekend.

Minutes stretched into eternity as I paced the entryway and glanced at the door every few seconds. Each creak of the house, each rustle of wind outside, set my nerves on edge. My heart hadn't stopped pounding since the notification.

The knock startled me, sending a rush of adrenaline through my veins.

"It's Garrett," he called, his voice steady, calming.

Relief hit me like a wave and crashed through the anxiety that had built inside me. I unlatched the door and pulled it open, the sight of him immediately easing the tightness in my chest.

Garrett stood there with a stepladder tucked under one arm, a bottle of rubbing alcohol in his hand, and a rag slung over his shoulder. His blue eyes scanned me briefly from head to toe. His presence was solid and reassuring, like an anchor holding me steady against the storm inside my head.

"You came prepared," I murmured, my voice hoarse.

His lips curved into a small smile. "I figured you wouldn't have this stuff lying around in a rental."

I held out my hands, suddenly wanting to take the task from him, to feel in control of something. "I can do it."

"No," he said firmly, his gaze locking on mine with authority. "I'm going to take pictures for the report, and then I'll clean it. You're staying inside."

"But—"

"No arguments." His tone softened, but the resolve remained. "I don't want you out here, Ethan."

His protective stance—always so calm, so sure—made my throat tighten. What would I do without Garrett? The thought of facing my stalker alone sent a shiver through me. He wasn't just offering the support of the sheriff's office. He was offering himself as a…friend. His strength, his time, his care.

Reluctantly, I nodded and closed the door. I locked it and flipped the deadbolt with a click that seemed to echo louder than it should have. As I walked in circles in the small entryway, the tension in my body built with each step. Every second Garrett spent outside felt like a century.

Finally, his voice came through the door. "Check your feed."

I pulled up the video. Garrett stood on the porch and gave the camera a small wave.

The image was crystal clear.

I smiled, warmth blooming in my chest despite the

anxiety still lingering there. "Looks good," I called through the door.

The porch light cast a glow over Garrett's face, highlighting his dark hair and the unruly lock that had fallen over his forehead. He brushed it back with one hand, but it slipped free again. For a moment, all I could think about was how good he looked standing there, framed by the soft light.

I opened the door. "Do you want to come in and wash your hands?"

He left his supplies on the porch and stepped in. His shoulders relaxed as he crossed the threshold.

I gestured toward the hallway. "Bathroom's straight ahead."

He disappeared for a moment, and when he returned, the faint scent of my woodsy hand soap clung to him. Something about that pleased me, a quiet, unspoken claim. My soap, my home. Garrett here.

"Thank you," I said, barely above a whisper.

His gaze softened. "I've got your back."

The air between us thickened with a buzzing current of electricity. My pulse quickened, my heartbeat loud in my ears as he took a hesitant step closer. The soft glow of the overhead light cast shadows across Garrett's face, highlighting the sharp angle of his jaw, the dark sweep of his lashes, and that unruly lock of hair.

His gaze locked on mine, and the intensity stole my breath. There was no indecision in his expression—only certainty, only want.

I swallowed hard, my throat suddenly dry. Everything I'd been holding back crashed into the need building inside me. My fingers twitched at my sides and ached to reach for him.

And then, as if something had snapped between us, we moved at the same time.

Garrett gripped my face with a desperate reverence. His

touch was firm yet trembled. I clutched his shoulders and pulled him closer. Any space between us was unbearable.

When his lips met mine, the kiss was anything but gentle. It was fierce and frantic, a collision of lips and breath that stole the air from my lungs. It wasn't careful or soft—it was raw, all-consuming, like the release of everything we'd been holding back.

My back hit the door, but I barely registered the impact. All I could focus on was Garrett—the way his fingers tangled in my hair, the way his lips moved against mine with a hunger that matched my own. His kiss tasted of heat and desperation.

I gasped against his mouth, and he deepened the kiss. His tongue slid against mine, and the velvety glide sent a shiver down my spine. My hands slipped from his shoulders to his chest, and I felt the rapid thud of his heart beneath my palms. His heartbeat matched mine, wild and erratic, as if we were both caught in a storm we had no desire to escape.

Garrett pressed closer, his body flush against mine. The bulge of his hard cock thrust against mine, and I groaned. I clung to him, needing the contact, needing him. Every touch, every brush of his lips, was a fresh experience. A step forward into whatever this was between us.

When we finally broke apart, we were both breathing hard and our chests heaved in unison. Garrett's hands remained on my face, his thumbs brushing my cheekbones in a tender contrast to the urgency of the kiss we'd just shared.

Garrett's gaze held mine, a promise lingering in the depths of his blue eyes. He leaned in again and brushed a softer kiss to my lips.

Everything had shifted between us.

Where would we go from here? We hadn't done anything more than kiss, yet they'd been the best kisses of my entire life. Hot, needy, earth-shattering.

What would it be like to take things further?

CHAPTER EIGHTEEN

GARRETT

Early morning light seeped beneath my eyelids. I slowly blinked them open, but my mind was already wide awake, replaying every detail of the night before. The stalker. The spray paint.

The kiss.

I sat up and scrubbed a hand over my jaw, the rasp of stubble loud in the quiet room. The previous night wasn't a dream. The timing hadn't been perfect—a stalker's threat wasn't romantic.

But the moment had felt charged, like a spark waiting to catch fire, and I'd leaned in and let instinct guide me.

And Ethan? He hadn't pulled away. Heck, he'd met me halfway with a quiet intensity that knocked the breath out of me. The kiss had been passionate and raw. Fervent. Hot. Eye-opening. And the way our hard cocks had ground together was a leap. Not just for me, but for us.

I swung my legs over the edge of the bed, and my feet hit the soft carpet. My mind wandered back to the moment when we had stepped into unfamiliar territory.

Ethan seemed interested in taking things further, but he was a patient, empathetic person. He was treading carefully. He knew I was still figuring out what this meant for me—what we meant. But I wouldn't pretend there wasn't something between us anymore.

For the first time in a long while—maybe ever—I felt like I was exactly who I was supposed to be.

The bathroom mirror reflected a version of me that seemed different this morning—a man who had crossed an invisible line the night before. I splashed water on my face, letting the coolness shock me back to reality before heading down the hall. As I passed Noah's room, I paused, and my eyes lingered on his neatly made bed, the Spider-Man quilt tucked perfectly at the edges. The emptiness of the room felt too loud.

A pang hit me square in the chest—I missed my little buddy. I could almost hear his laughter echoing through the house, his feet thumping down the hall as he raced to tell me some new fact he'd learned. But he wasn't here. He was with my parents. He was crabbing with my dad and probably loving every second. The thought brought a small smile to my face, but it didn't erase the ache.

He was safer there.

The thought sobered me instantly. Worry crept in and twisted my insides like a vise. I shuddered, the horrifying possibility of Noah ever being in the stalker's crosshairs too much to bear. The mere idea sent a chill down my spine, and I forced myself to push it away before it consumed me.

The mundane tasks of the day waited for me. I went through the motions, catching up on laundry and scrubbing the bathrooms while a true crime podcast played in my ears. The narrator's voice droned on about motives, timelines, and evidence, but I barely registered the details. Instead, my mind wandered, weaving between thoughts of Ethan, Noah, and the lingering fear that our peaceful life was teetering on the edge of something darker.

I folded a towel and realized how much I craved normalcy. The simple act of tidying up brought back a sense of control. But even as I wiped down the kitchen countertops, the weight of everything I couldn't control loomed large and pressed down like a storm cloud on the horizon.

But I would find that stalker and put the motherfudger behind bars. Ethan would live freely again.

And leave Seacliff Cove. Go back to his family. And I understood that—family was important.

Noah and I would remain behind. The thought settled heavily in my chest, like a weight pressing down on my ribs. Ethan's quiet laughter, his calm presence, his steadfast resilience—all of it would be gone from my life. A sigh escaped me, so deep it felt like it originated from the soles of my feet, carrying with it the ache of an inevitable goodbye.

As I slid the final fork into the dishwasher after lunch, my phone chimed with a text message. The familiar note, once tame, now sent a jolt of tension through me.

Ethan: *Received a threatening letter.*

Everything in me went still. A low, familiar chill crept up my spine as I grabbed the phone.

Garrett: *I'm coming over. Don't touch anything.*

I scooped up my keys from the counter and grabbed the small kit I kept by the door—gloves, evidence bags, a notepad. I hadn't needed them this often until Ethan arrived in Seacliff Cove.

I hustled across the street with a pair of nitrile gloves and an evidence bag in my pocket. My heart beat faster with every step. A mixture of professional urgency and personal need drove me forward. When I knocked on Ethan's door, it opened almost immediately.

The moment our eyes met, the formalities slipped away. I couldn't help myself. I pulled him into my arms, needing to feel him, to reassure both of us we were still here, still standing together against the dark shadows closing in.

Ethan trembled against me, his breath warm against my neck. His vulnerability, so rarely shown, hit me square in the chest. Watching Ethan go through this? That was the hardest part. Seeing the fear etched into his features, the way his voice shook slightly—this wasn't something I could easily fix.

"We're going to get through this," I said quietly. "Together."

He nodded against me. "I'm just so tired of wondering what's next."

I pulled back gently, my hands still resting on his arms. "Let me see it."

He turned and led me to the kitchen table, where a large manila envelope sat next to a stack of stapled papers.

"I—I wasn't thinking when I opened it, just figured it was junk mail." He raked a hand through his hair, frustration clear in every tense line of his body. "I didn't notice at first that the envelope didn't have a return address." He let out a shaky breath, his voice thick with self-recrimination. "So stupid. I know better than that."

I wasn't about to reprimand him. He was already punishing himself. But the thought of what could have been inside—something deadly—made a shudder run through me.

Pulling on my gloves, I approached the table. The envelope had Ethan's name—Ethan Cole—and local address spelled out in bold, black, all-caps lettering. The handwriting was jagged and angry, the pen pressed so hard it had scratched through the paper in places, leaving tiny tears. No return address. Generic postage stamps. A Seacliff Cove postmark dated two days ago.

Virtually untraceable.

A stack of stapled papers sat next to the envelope. I tugged on a pair of gloves and picked up the printout. I carefully opened the top sheet. The formatting caught my attention first—narrative structure, like a scene from a book. Then I read the words.

My stomach dropped.

"What is this?" I asked, flipping through the pages, already knowing I wasn't going to like the answer.

Ethan stepped beside me, his face tight. "It's a scene from book seven. Chapter forty-four, rewritten. The murder victim's name...it's been changed to mine."

I stared at the page, the detail. Goosebumps raised on my arms.

"I've never seen him escalate like this," Ethan murmured, voice low. "This isn't a warning. It's a script."

I didn't answer right away. I carefully slid the papers and envelope into an evidence bag, sealed and labeled it, my mind racing. "This is the clearest threat yet," I said. "More personal. Deliberate."

Ethan rubbed a hand over his mouth. "Garrett...I'm scared. And not just for me. What if you or Noah gets caught in this?"

I stepped forward, reaching for his hand and gripping it tight. "I'll keep Noah safe. Always. But we're done hiding that you're in town. It hasn't worked."

Ethan nodded, his jaw tight. "I hate that I brought this here."

"You didn't bring this here. *He* did. And I'm not letting him chase you into a corner." I hesitated, then added, "It's imperative you stay inside."

"I'm not fragile, Garrett," Ethan said, but there was no heat behind it.

I smiled, just slightly. "I know. But that doesn't mean you don't deserve someone at your side."

Ethan crossed his arms over his chest, his expression troubled. "I think we should—"

"No." I cut him off, my tone firm. "We're not letting him rule our lives."

"But—"

"I think we should do the opposite," I said and stepped closer to him, my gaze steady on his. "Your cover is blown. He knows you're here, and you're not running again."

Ethan's brows knit together, skepticism written all over his face. "What are you saying?"

"I'm saying I don't think you should go out alone. Not even to the mailbox at the curb," I clarified. "But I also don't think you should hide anymore. It hasn't helped."

There was a beat of silence, tension hanging in the air. Then, taking a deep breath, I made a decision—a leap of faith that could change everything.

"Go out to dinner with me tonight."

He blinked. "You're asking me out? Now? During all this?"

"I've been wanting to ask you for days," I said. "I just kept waiting for the danger to pass. But it won't. Not right now. So we live around it. We don't stop living because of it."

Ethan stared at me for a long beat. "We'll have to be careful. If Sarge finds out—"

"I know. I'm screwed. We'll be circumspect." My lips twitched. "I won't show up with roses, in uniform."

He let out a soft laugh, one that tugged something in my chest. "Okay. One date."

I gave his hand a squeeze. "One date, and a promise—we face this thing together."

His eyes met mine, and something shifted. A line drawn. A choice made.

"Are you sure you're ready to go public with our... relationship? Even if we're careful?" He cocked his head, his gaze steady but questioning. "You're a great kisser, don't get me wrong. But I get the sense that...that you've never been with a man before."

The weight of his words lingered between us. The implication was clear—this wasn't just about dinner. It was about stepping into the light, letting the world in on what we'd been carefully guarding. My heart beat a little faster at the thought, but instead of fear, I felt a curious calm settle over me.

I nodded. "But I want to be with you."

The statement was like an anchor dropping into place. For the first time in years, I felt settled in my own skin. The decision felt right, like it had been coming for a long time, maybe even since Leo, in high school.

Maybe that's why my relationship with Ava had always felt...tepid. Safe. A box checked off a list rather than a fire that burned deep. I hadn't been ready to admit it before, but now, standing here with Ethan, it was undeniable. I was attracted to men.

To *Ethan*.

"And what if the gossip gets back to your superiors? What about the repercussions to your career?" His brow furrowed.

That gave me pause, but only for a second. For the first time in a long time, I wanted something for myself. Not just as a deputy or a dad, but as a man. If Sarge found out, I'd deal with it. But giving up Ethan was not an option. Still, I wouldn't be stupid about it. "I'll pick you up at six," I said firmly. "And we'll go out of town." I grabbed the evidence bag, the smooth plastic slick under my fingers.

Ethan's lips quirked into a small smile. He stepped closer, and his familiar cedarwood scent washed over me. His kiss landed softly on my cheek, but the impact sent a flurry of butterflies crashing into each other in my gut. For a moment, I was transported back to high school. It felt like I was finally circling back to where I was supposed to be.

"I'll be ready," Ethan murmured, his voice brushing against my ear like a promise.

As I left, the bolt clicked shut behind me. I stood on the porch for a beat. A quiet resolve settled over me. This was a turning point—not just for me and Ethan, but for the rest of my life.

"Hey, buddy!" I crouched to a knee in Mom and Dad's living room. My heart lifted at the sight of Noah sprinting toward me with that grin that always knocked the wind out of me. He threw himself into my open arms with the reckless abandon only kids seemed capable of. His small body hit me with surprising force. The scents of sea salt and sand clung to him, tangled in his messy, windblown hair.

He gave me a quick, perfunctory hug before pulling back, his eyes bright with excitement. "We catched eight crabs this morning!" His tongue peeked out as he concentrated on his fingers and raised seven in triumph.

My dad chuckled from his spot on the worn leather recliner, where he sat nursing a cup of coffee. "Eight Dungeness. We threw the rock crabs back."

I rose to my feet, brushing sand off my jeans. "Sounds like an excellent dinner."

My mom, perched on the arm of the sofa, tucked a strand of graying hair behind her ear and smiled warmly. "Want to stay? We've got plenty."

I shook my head, the knot of nerves tightening in my

stomach. "Can't. I've got plans. Can you babysit this evening?"

"Of course." Mom's eyes lit with curiosity. "What are you doing?"

"I've got a date," I said, trying to keep my tone casual.

"That's wonderful! Anyone we know?" My mother raised her eyebrows.

I hesitated for half a second, then shook my head. "No. Not someone you've met."

She gave a small, expectant smile. "Well, what's her name?"

I took a breath, then let it out slow. "It's not a her."

She didn't say anything right away—just blinked once and studied me. My heart thumped once, hard.

"With a man," I said, quieter now. Steadier.

Her smile returned—smaller this time, softer. "I'm happy for you."

I rested my hand gently on Noah's small shoulder. His skin was warm beneath my palm, the soft, steady weight of him grounding me like nothing else could. He tilted his head up, wide blue eyes searching mine with a seriousness far beyond his five years.

"What's a date? Does that mean you're going to hold hands?" His brow furrowed in concentration.

I choked back a chuckle. "It means I'm going out to dinner with Mr. Ethan," I said softly.

My breath caught in my throat. I didn't know what I expected—a million questions, confusion, maybe even the echoes of things he'd heard other kids say.

"Can I go with you?" he asked, his eyes going wide with a hopeful sparkle.

I crouched to his level and brushed a hand over his tousled hair. "Sorry, bud," I said gently. "It's just going to be Mr. Ethan and me this time."

The brightness in his expression dimmed, his shoulders sinking just a little. But in true Noah fashion, the disappointment didn't linger. A beat later, he gave a tiny shrug and perked back up.

"Okay. Can I go play now?"

I grinned and stood. "Yeah, buddy."

But he was already bounding down the hall, his stockinged feet skidding against the carpet as he disappeared into his room like the question had never even existed.

I turned back just in time to see my dad watching me, his expression unreadable. "Who's Mr. Ethan?" he asked.

"A new neighbor," I said, keeping my tone light. "We've been…getting to know each other."

Dad nodded, slow and stiff. His jaw worked for a second before he spoke. "That's fine, Garrett. But I'm a retired sergeant. You think this'll come back on you at work?"

The words hit like a pebble dropped in a calm pond—small, but rippling.

I pressed my molars together, pushing back the sting of irritation. "There are openly gay men and women in the department now," I said evenly. "It's not like it was when you started. People are more open. More decent."

Dad lifted his chin. "You know we love your gay friends like our own sons."

"I know," I said, quieter now. And it was true. My parents had welcomed every friend I'd brought home with genuine warmth, even when they didn't fully understand.

Dad stood slowly, walked over, and rested a callused hand on my shoulder. His voice was low, gravel-thick with age and pride.

"I don't always understand everything in this world, Garrett. But I know this—you're a good man, a good father, and a damn good son. That's all that matters to me."

I swallowed hard, the words catching in my throat as I nodded.

And as he stepped away, I realized something had shifted.

My family didn't need to understand everything. They just needed to show up.

And maybe, just maybe, so did I.

I looked down the hall where my son had vanished, then toward the door where Ethan waited for a chance. I was done standing on the threshold. It was time to walk through it.

CHAPTER NINETEEN

ETHAN

Garrett expertly parallel-parked in a town to the south of Seacliff Cove with the precision of a trained cop, avoiding the curb by a breath. He shut down the SUV and silence reigned. The quiet felt charged—like something big was about to shift.

He cleared his throat and ran his fingers through his hair. Garrett Whitlock, unflappable deputy sheriff, was nervous.

My pulse kicked up a notch, and I braced myself. "Everything okay?"

"I, uh…" He clutched his hands over the steering wheel and his knuckles whitened. "I told my parents I was going on a date with a man."

My chest squeezed, and my eyes flew wide. "Garrett." I whispered his name like a prayer, reverent and full of meaning. "That's huge." I hadn't realized Garrett's parents didn't know he was interested in men. "How do you feel?"

He tilted his head toward me, a small, self-conscious smile playing on his lips. The streetlights cast soft shadows over his face and highlighted the crinkles at the corners of his eyes. "Good. Relieved." He exhaled slowly, like he was letting out years of tension. "I've spent so long suppressing this part of myself. Since high school. And now…it's like I can breathe easier."

A wave of emotion hit me and caught me off guard. Joy. Pride. "How did they take it?" I held my breath, hoping for the best.

"At first, they were surprised. They had questions. But once they got over the initial shock, they were supportive." A small smile crept over his mouth.

I released my breath. "I'm so happy for you."

His gaze dipped to his hands, fingers drumming on his thigh, before sliding back to me. "And…I told Noah I was taking you on a date tonight."

My breath caught. *Noah.* This wasn't just about Garrett. It was about his family—his son. And that he'd shared this with Noah felt monumental. I swallowed hard. "How did he react?"

Garrett chuckled. "He said, 'Yay!' Then he asked if he could go play."

"He was obviously traumatized," I deadpanned.

A snort escaped Garrett, and I smiled.

I blinked, emotions rising too fast to sort through. My heart ached with hope I hadn't expected. *I want to be around more, Noah.* But all I said was, "That's…great."

I reached across the console and rested my hand on his. "You've come a long way today," I whispered.

He squeezed my hand, his grip grounding me. "It feels right. You feel right."

He turned his hand over and entwined his fingers with mine. "I hope you understand, though, that I'm not ready for a lot of open affection in public. Guiding you through a crowd at the farmers' market is one thing, but…" He raised clasped hands between us as an example.

A small pang of disappointment ran through my chest, but this wasn't about me. While I was comfortable being out and open, Garrett was still adjusting to living authentically. "You need to proceed at your own pace. If you never feel you can hold hands with a man in public, that's okay."

I tried to withdraw my hand, but he pulled it to his lips and kissed my knuckles before letting go. A tingle ran down my spine at the gentle contact, warming me from the inside out.

"Thank you," he murmured, his voice thick with emotion. "For understanding." The clock on the dash caught his attention, and he cleared his throat again. "We should get going. We have a reservation in a few minutes."

I nodded, feeling lighter, almost giddy. He wasn't ashamed of me. He wasn't hiding me. He was walking his path at his own pace, but I was right there with him.

We strolled a block to an Italian restaurant, Garrett's hand brushing close to mine but never quite making contact. The restaurant glowed warmly in the dark, its large, mullioned, arched windows inviting.

Garrett opened the door for me, and I stepped inside. The scents of garlic and herbs hit me instantly and made my stomach growl. I took in the old-world charm—candlelit tables with crisp white linens. The atmosphere was cozy—intimate—exactly what I'd wanted for our date.

But this wasn't just any date. It was a statement.

Garrett stepped to the podium and nodded to the man standing behind it. "Evening, Luca. How are you doing?" Garrett greeted him.

The man's face broke into a grin. "Garrett. Good to see you." His gaze flicked to me, curiosity sparking.

Garrett straightened and stood a little taller. "Ethan, this is Luca, the manager and an old buddy. Luca, this is my... date. Ethan."

The word *date* hung in the air, loaded with implications. Luca's dark eyebrows shot up, and his gaze sharpened. "Your date?"

"Yes." Garrett's voice was steady, full of quiet strength.

Luca's expression shifted, and his curiosity melted into understanding. "I see." He reached out and shook my hand with a firm grip. "Welcome."

The word was like a benediction.

Garrett's shoulders relaxed visibly, the tension slipping away. I wondered how much that simple moment of acceptance had meant to him.

Luca grabbed two menus and led us to a small table in the back corner, tucked away from the main dining area. The privacy was a kindness, and I appreciated it—for Garrett's sake.

But I was touched that Garrett had chosen to bring me to a restaurant where he knew the manager. I wasn't his dirty little secret, and I reveled in that. The evening wasn't just about this dinner, it was about what it meant to Garrett—and to us. Whatever the future may hold.

Once seated, we fell into an easy rhythm. Conversation flowed effortlessly, and laughter rang out. Garrett told stories about his time on the force—like the time he tried to rescue a neighborhood cat from a tree and ended up splitting the seat of his pants—and I shared some of my more memorable fan encounters, including the woman who'd shown up at a signing with my books tattooed on her arm.

Several times, Garrett's hand hovered near mine, his fingers twitching like he wanted to reach out. But each time, he pulled back at the last second. *Maybe someday he'll get there. Maybe someday he'll be ready for more.*

And that thought was enough to fill me with quiet hope.

Before I knew it, the meal was over, and disappointment

tugged at my chest. I didn't want the evening to end. I wasn't ready to say goodbye yet.

"Want to come to my place?" The words slipped out before I could second-guess them. I held my breath, and my heart pounded in my ears.

Garrett's eyes darkened in a smoldering look that sent heat coursing through my veins. "I'd like that."

He signed the bill and stood quickly, the legs of his chair screeching against the hardwood floor.

As we stepped out into the cool night air, his hand brushed mine again—so close. Almost there.

One step at a time. I wouldn't push.

CHAPTER TWENTY

GARRETT

I drove us home and parked in my driveway. The walk to Ethan's house was quiet, the distant sound of the ocean waves a soothing balm for my nerves. But I could feel the tension in the air—the kind that made my skin hum and my thoughts spiral to what the evening could bring. His presence at my side anchored and electrified me all at once.

When we reached his front porch, he fumbled with his keys, probably as off-center as I was.

Inside, we kicked off our shoes.

He tilted his head toward the kitchen. "Glass of wine? Beer?" he asked, his polite question that of a gracious host.

I shook my head. "I'm good." I didn't want the alcohol talking tonight—I wanted a clear head. Anticipation curled in my gut, and I took a step closer.

"Ethan." My heart skipped a beat at the weight in my tone.

"Yeah?" he asked, barely more than a whisper.

I reached out and brushed an auburn curl off his forehead, and my fingers lingered against his skin. The touch sent a shiver down my spine, and I craved more. "I've been wanting to do this all evening," I murmured, and traced the line of his softly bristled jaw with my thumb.

"Then do it," he whispered and closed the distance between us, clutching my shoulders.

I didn't need more encouragement. I slid my hand to the back of his neck and pulled him into a kiss that was slow and deliberate. His lips were warm and soft, moving against mine with a confidence that left me breathless. I sank into him, my hands finding his waist and my fingers curled into the yarn of his sweater. My cock swelled. I wanted more—if he did. I broke the kiss, panting, and leaned my forehead against his. "Let's move to the couch."

He nodded and took my hand. With a gentle pull, he led me to the sofa.

When my butt hit the cushions, I pulled him close, thigh to thigh. My hands framed his face as I deepened the kiss, and his tongue teased mine in a rhythm that made my groin ache.

"I can't get enough of your kisses," I murmured against his lips, my voice husky and raw.

"Same." He ran his hands up my back, leaving goosebumps in their wake. "You're taking the lead tonight. Whatever you want to do—as much or as little—you let me know."

I nipped at his bottom lip. "I…I'm not sure. I've never done this before." I didn't know what to do with a man. I knew the basics, of course. I *was* a man, and I knew what I liked. But what would Ethan enjoy? How could I please him?

How could we pleasure each other?

Here I was, thirty-six years old, and yet I hadn't felt so inexperienced and vulnerable since I was a teenager first exploring sex.

"Hey." His gaze was soft, understanding. "You're thinking too hard. Just go with your gut and explore."

It was as if he'd yanked the thought from my mind. *That* I could do. I wrapped my arms around him and pulled him closer until there was no space left between us. I kissed him again, more frantically this time, tracing fervent patterns down his neck and around his shoulders.

"We don't have to rush," he whispered against my ear. "We can do whatever you want at your pace."

"I want... I don't know what I want." I adjusted my hard cock, trapped in my jeans. "I just want to..." I couldn't finish the sentence, but he got the picture.

He chuckled darkly. "I think we can manage that." He rubbed his hand against the bulge of my jeans, then fingered my belt buckle. "May I?"

"Please," I whispered. But I didn't know exactly what I was begging for.

He opened my belt and slid my zipper down while I held my breath. I levered off the couch and shoved my briefs and jeans to my knees. My dick sprang free of its confinement, stretching toward my belly. I sighed in relief.

Ethan made a little noise in the back of his throat that sounded like approval. He reached out and lightly ran a warm, soft finger up my length. I gasped at the electrifying sensation.

"Wait!" exploded from me.

He immediately jerked his hand back. "We can sto—"

"I want to touch you, too." I licked my lips. "At the same time."

He grinned playfully. "I won't say no to that." He made quick work of shedding his jeans and boxer briefs to his knees, his dick bobbing free.

I reached out and grasped his long, thick cock, warm in my encircling fingers. My heart thundered at the heady feeling of another man's erection in my hand. I didn't think I could get any harder. Until Ethan licked his palm and enclosed my dick with his slick hand. I nearly flew off the couch, and my balls ached. But this wasn't only about me.

I began pumping Ethan slowly, running my hand up and down his hard yet silky length, paying attention to the head, and getting a feel for his minute responses. A slight hitch of breath. A tensing of his stomach muscles. A soft moan. His reactions spurred me on, and I pumped him faster and with a bit more pressure.

But my ministrations stuttered, and I lost my grip when he expertly played me like a fine instrument. With my heightened senses and the knowledge that this was a *man's* hand—*Ethan's* hand—on my dick, it wasn't long before the telltale tingling began at the base of my spine. Ethan fused his mouth with mine, his tongue pulsing in and out to the rhythm of his strokes, and tipped me over the edge. I thrust into his hand erratically, threw my head back with a cry, and came with sparklers lighting the backs of my eyelids. I collapsed onto the cushions, gasping. His hand left my softening cock, leaving me bereft.

The soft *swooshing* of skin rubbing frantically on skin filled the room, and I opened my eyes just as Ethan came, dick in hand, with a low, drawn-out moan.

"Hey! I was supposed to do that." My voice betrayed my post-orgasm fatigue.

Ethan blew out a breath and sat back. "Couldn't wait. You were *hot*."

I chuckled, ridiculously proud that I could reduce him to impatience.

He stood and pulled his pants up to mid-thigh. "Wait here." He awkwardly waddled down the hallway and returned in a few moments with his pants zipped. He sat and gently cleaned my stomach with a warm, wet washcloth.

I raised my hips and dressed. "Thank you. That was…" I shook my head, hardly able to express the contentedness inside me. "You made my first time easy—and phenomenal."

Ethan responded with a quick kiss to my lips. "I'm glad you don't regret it."

"Absolutely not." The experience further cemented my attraction to Ethan, and I wanted more. What that entailed, I didn't know. I was ready to explore with him. But exhaustion hit me like a rogue wave, and I suppressed a yawn.

Ethan chuckled and stood. "Time for you to go to bed." He pulled on my elbow, and I climbed to my feet.

I wiggled my eyebrows. "Is that an invitation?" I teased.

His cheeks flushed. "Well, if you—" he said, hesitantly.

"Just kidding. I don't have my toothbrush with me." I'd never slept the entire night with a girlfriend—not even Ava —but the thought of sleeping with Ethan appealed to me on a deep level. *Goals.*

Covering another yawn, I followed Ethan to the door and slipped into my shoes. With one last, lingering kiss, we said goodnight.

I stepped out the door and listened as the lock engaged. I walked across the dark street, my senses on high alert. Footsteps scuffed along the pavement down the street and faded around the corner. Was it a dog walker? Someone out for a stroll late in the evening?

Or someone more sinister?

CHAPTER TWENTY-ONE

ETHAN

Monday at noon, I paused my writing. Hunger drew me to the kitchen, but my thoughts were focused on anything but lunch. As I mindlessly slapped sliced turkey onto whole wheat bread, memories of Saturday night stole my attention.

I could still feel Garrett's warm breath against my skin, his strong hands gripping me. How did he feel about what had happened between us? Did he regret it? Or was he like me—reliving every electrifying moment? The mere thought sent a charge through my body, tightened my chest, and quickened my pulse.

He could've chosen anyone. Someone with less baggage. Someone safer. But he chose me.

The realization settled in my chest like warmth melting an ice cube. He'd handed me that moment, that trust, not just with his body but with a part of himself he'd never offered anyone before.

And that…meant something.

It wasn't just sex. It wasn't curiosity or impulse. It was Garrett stepping into something new—with me.

And I'd be damned if I wouldn't treat that like the rare, complicated, beautiful thing it was.

The sudden ringing of my phone on the counter jolted me. I glanced at the screen. *Garrett.* A mix of relief and nervous anticipation bloomed in my gut, fluttering like a flock of hummingbirds taking flight. I wiped my hands on a paper towel, grabbed the phone, and swiped to answer before it could click over to voicemail.

"Hello?" My voice carried a smile I couldn't suppress.

Garrett's tone, however, was all business. "I've been thinking. This creep has to be close by to follow your movements, so it stands to reason he's staying in town, at least part of the time. Sarge gave me the go-ahead to canvass motels this afternoon. Just wanted to keep you in the loop."

My stomach plummeted. The idea of my stalker staying in Seacliff Cove sent a shiver racing down my spine. "Take me with you."

Garrett hesitated. "Ethan…I can't. That's not protocol. I could be—"

"I could help," I argued, and gripped the phone tighter. "What if…what if I recognized someone? Or a name?"

A long sigh came through the line. "Pick you up in ten," he murmured, his voice low and quiet, almost resigned, before he ended the call.

My appetite evaporated. I wrapped my unfinished sandwich and stuffed it into the fridge with trembling hands. The thought of confronting the man who had been haunting me was terrifying, but this could be the break we needed.

I barely had time to throw on a jacket and grab my phone before the sheriff's department SUV pulled up outside my house. The rumble of the engine sent a ripple of tension through me. I stepped onto the porch as Garrett climbed out of his Ford Police Interceptor, his uniform crisp and his presence reassuring.

He confidently walked toward me as his eyes scanned the area. "Ready?" A protective edge laced his deep voice.

"As I'll ever be." I tried to match his calm demeanor, but my heart thundered in my chest.

Inside the vehicle, the faint traces of gun oil and the fresh smell of Garrett's body wash enveloped me, oddly comforting despite the nerves dancing in my stomach. As we pulled onto the main road out of the neighborhood, I glanced at him. His jaw was set, his hands firm on the wheel at ten and two. There was something about the way he carried himself—a mix of determination and control—that made me feel safer, even as my mind raced with worst-case scenarios.

"Any idea where to start?" I broke the tense silence.

He nodded. "Cheap, cash-friendly places. If this guy's staying local and under the radar, they're the most logical spots."

Logical. But beneath that calm exterior, I knew Garrett was just as concerned as I was.

The weight of what we were about to do settled over me. I stared out the window as the streets of Seacliff Cove passed by. This town was supposed to be my sanctuary, my fresh start. Now it felt tainted, with every corner holding the possibility of danger.

But as Garrett reached over the console and gave my knee a brief, reassuring squeeze, I knew I wasn't facing this alone. And somehow, that made all the difference.

The first motel looked like the definition of seedy. The single-story structure sat awkwardly along the highway outside the cozy town of Seacliff Cove. The neon vacancy sign flickered faintly, one of the tubes completely burned out. The whole place screamed *bad decisions*. My stomach tightened as I followed Garrett through the cracked glass front doors into the reception area.

The linoleum floor peeled in places and revealed a sticky

underlayer that clung to my sneakers as I stepped inside. The smell of old cigarette smoke mingled with something sour, and I fought the urge to gag. Behind the counter, a pot-bellied man in a stained T-shirt barely glanced up until he caught sight of Garrett's uniform. His small, watery eyes widened, and he stiffened and flicked the butt of his cigarette into an overflowing ashtray.

"Don't want no trouble," the man muttered, his voice a gravelly smoker's rasp. He shifted nervously. A cockroach skittered across the counter. He slammed his hand down on it and wiped the dead bug on his pants. My stomach churned.

Garrett didn't miss a beat, his tone calm but firm. "Then you'll cooperate. We're looking for someone who might've been here for a few weeks. Single man, average build, about five feet ten, maybe coming and going a lot. Ring any bells?"

The man's lips pressed into a thin line. He leaned back, scratching at his greasy hair. "Need a warrant for that kinda thing." He smirked, though his darting eyes betrayed his nerves.

I clenched my fists at my sides, disappointment bubbling to the surface. This was a waste of time.

Garrett, however, didn't flinch. His voice dropped, low and commanding. "You'd rather I call the health department? Pretty sure they'd be interested in this place."

The man grimaced but didn't respond.

Garrett's eyes narrowed at him, but he said to me, "Let's go."

Outside, the bright sunlight assaulted my eyes after the dim, grimy interior.

"Is this pointless?" I already felt defeated.

"Maybe not." Garrett strode toward his SUV. "These vehicles might tell us something." Inside, he ran the plates through the onboard computer while I held my breath.

Southern California…Nevada…Seacliff Cove…rental car. My pulse quickened at that one. But when Garrett ran the plate and contacted the rental company, I didn't recognize the driver, Edward Johnson, age seventy-four. The only red flag was an unpaid parking ticket. Not exactly a lead.

The second motel was even worse, wedged between a smoke shop and a dingy pizza place in another sketchy area outside of town. The faint stench of burned coffee lingered in the air as we walked in. The man behind the counter was younger, with a scruffy beard and a cynical smile that made my skin crawl.

Garrett repeated his questions and asked about suspicious guests.

The guy chuckled. "Everyone here's suspicious. That's why they come here. What they do ain't my business."

"What about Halloween night?" Garrett pressed.

The man shrugged. "Privacy's what they pay for. I don't snoop."

I tensed, and Garrett gave me a brief glance, his expression unreadable.

Once again, we ended up in the parking lot, Garrett running plates while I scrubbed my face. "How do you have the patience for such uncooperative people?" I asked, anxious for answers.

He shrugged. "It's part of the process."

I admired Garrett's calm focus. His investigative style was deliberate, steady, like he could untangle any knot if given the time. If anyone could make sense of this, it was him.

He'd run the plates of every car in the parking lot, cross-checking the registered owners against the licenses. None of the faces meant anything to me.

"We don't even know where he's from," I murmured, anxiety creeping into my voice. "He could be from New York. Maybe he followed me here." I scrubbed a hand down my face. "Hell, he could be from anywhere in the country—found me in New York, tracked me here. Who knows how long he's been watching?"

Garrett glanced over, his voice even but laced with concern. "He could be," he said. "But if he knows your routines—where you live, when you're home—chances are, he was close to you in New York. That kind of access doesn't come from casual observation. It's personal. Do you know of anyone with a grudge against you?"

The weight of that truth settled in my chest like a stone. "I've been trying to figure that out since the feather, but I can't think of anyone."

Garrett started the engine and backed out of the parking slot. "One more cash-friendly motel to check out. I doubt he is staying at any place nicer and paying with a credit card." He added under his breath, "Unless he's stupider than I think he is."

The final motel, perched near the coastal freeway, had a weathered exterior that inspired little confidence. Inside, the air reeked of mildew, and the woman behind the counter barely looked up from her magazine as Garrett asked his questions. She waved him off with a dismissive grunt.

The vehicles in the lot here were a mix of locals and out-of-staters, and none of the names associated with the plates seemed familiar. By this point, the frustration was a dull ache in my chest. Every time we approached someone, I hoped for something—a lead, a clue, a reaction. Instead, we encountered indifference or hostility.

I leaned my head against the passenger-side window, the cool glass soothing my overheated skin.

"What now?" I asked, my voice flat. "We've got nothing."

Garrett started the engine with a low rumble and shifted into gear.

"We're not done," he said, eyes fixed on the road ahead.

I turned to him, brows lifting. "You have another lead?"

"Not a lead," he said. "A gut feeling."

He didn't elaborate, and I didn't push. I trusted his instincts more than I trusted my own heartbeat right now.

We headed back into town, navigating through the historic district until we pulled up in front of the Sea Glass Suites. The boutique hotel sat prim and elegant on Main Street, all soft blue paint and white trim, like it belonged on the cover of a travel magazine. A small sign in the window welcomed guests with hand-lettered charm.

Inside, the lobby was warm and coastal in a tasteful way —bleached oak floors, soft lighting, and subtle sea glass accents in shades of green and blue. Behind the desk stood a man I didn't recognize, but who exuded charm like it came with the job. Dark hair styled to perfection, silver bracelets on one wrist, and a smile that could probably convince even the grumpiest traveler to extend their stay.

Garrett approached the desk with quiet authority. "How are you, Landon?"

"Wonderful, Garrett." The man raised an eyebrow and eyed me like I was a snack. "And this is Ethan," he purred. "Nice to finally meet the man who likes pumpkin spice lattes."

My eyes widened. "You…how…?"

"Oh, darling, I know everything that goes on in Seacliff Cove." He turned to Garrett. "Which is why you're here."

Garrett glanced back at me and nodded slightly. "Has anyone tried to check in recently using cash?"

Landon's brows lifted, thoughtful. "Not many people do that anymore. But…yes. About a month ago. A man tried to pay in cash. Said he didn't like using credit cards. I told him I don't accept cash for rooms—policy. He wasn't happy, but he left without causing a scene."

"Can you describe him?" Garrett asked.

Landon paused, his fingers tapping lightly on the counter. "Unusual guy. Under six feet. Scruffy. But what I remember most—his eyes. One was blue, the other brown. Hard to forget."

A chill slithered down my spine, cold and sharp. I hadn't thought about him in years.

Two different colored eyes. One blue. One brown.

The image snapped into focus. "I knew someone like that," I said quietly. "Years ago, before I was published. We met at a writers' group in Brooklyn. He was writing a thriller and gave me the creeps even then."

Garrett turned to me, alert. "Do you remember his name?"

I searched my memory, the tension in my chest tightening like a vice. "Ted. No, wait…Theo? Yes, Theo. Flynn?" I shook my head, frustrated. "No. It was the name of a bird." I snapped my fingers. "Finch! Theo Finch. That's it."

Garrett moved fast. Back in the SUV, he pulled up the department's database on the onboard computer and ran the name. A few moments later, his screen lit up with a match. "Theodore Finch. New York address. No known criminal record, but he fits the description."

He turned the screen so I could see the DMV photo. My breath hitched.

"That's him," I said. "Oh my God. That's him." A shudder ran through me.

Landon had followed us outside, arms crossed over his chest. He glanced at the screen and nodded. "Yeah. That's the guy who tried to pay in cash. I watched him leave. Pretty sure he was driving an older, banged-up white car. Maybe a Civic?"

Garrett reached for his radio. "Thanks, Landon. That's exactly what we needed." Garrett notified patrol to be on the alert for Finch.

As he spoke in clipped, efficient tones, I stared out the window at the historic street in downtown Seacliff Cove, heart pounding with the realization: we had a name now.

Finch was real. And he was here.

Garrett started the engine, his jaw tight. "Keep an eye out for Finch's white Civic. If you see it near your house, call me immediately."

"And if we don't find him?" The words escaped before I could stop them, the weight of my fear spilling over.

Garrett glanced at me, his expression softening. "We will. Trust me."

I turned my head away, staring out at the quaint shops as we drove down Main Street. Garrett's confidence was unshakable, but mine felt like it was crumbling by the second.

CHAPTER TWENTY-TWO

GARRETT

I barely had time to grab my morning coffee at the end of roll call before Sergeant Rodriguez called my name. His voice was clipped, sharp—dangerous.

"Whitlock, my office. Now."

My stomach dropped. This wasn't going to be good. Sarge wasn't the kind of guy who yelled when he was mad—he got quiet, cold, and precise. That was worse. I caught Holt Larson's glance from across the room. His brows lifted in silent question. I shook my head and headed for the office.

Sarge was standing when I stepped in, arms crossed over his broad chest. He nodded toward the chair across from his desk. "Sit," he ordered.

I closed the door behind me, lowered myself into the chair, and forced myself to keep my posture relaxed—even though my gut was twisted into knots.

Sarge didn't sit. He paced behind his desk like a caged animal before turning and leveling a hard look at me. "Tell me why I got an anonymous call this morning about you playing detective with a civilian."

I fought the instinct to stiffen. *Shoot.* Was the caller Finch? Had he been watching us?

"Sir, if this is about canvassing the hotels—"

"Of course it's about canvassing the hotels!" he snapped. "What the hell were you thinking, Whitlock? You took a victim—a witness—and dragged him through the shitty motels in town? What part of that sounded like a good idea to you?"

I kept my voice steady as I took full responsibility. "I thought maybe he'd recognize someone, a name. And he did. We discovered the name of the suspect."

"You don't bring a civilian into an investigation like this." Sarge's tone was razor-sharp. "I don't care what your reasons were. *Your* job is to investigate, not to play detective duo with him."

"I understand, sir."

"Do you?" He narrowed his eyes. "Because from where I'm standing, this investigation has become too personal for you. Maybe *Cole* has become too personal to you."

A tense silence stretched between us. I wasn't going to give him the satisfaction of a defensive reaction, but my pulse hammered.

Sarge exhaled sharply and sat down, leveling me with a look that felt like a verdict before he even spoke.

"I can't trust you to be objective on this case. Effective immediately, you're off it."

The words hit me like a sucker punch to the ribs. "Sir—"

He held up a hand. "Detective Ballard is taking over. You'll hand over any reports, notes, or evidence you've collected. You're done."

I gripped the arms of the chair, anger flaring hot and fast. "Sir, with all due respect, Ballard is buried in other cases. You and I both know this investigation will get pushed to the back burner."

Rodriguez's jaw tightened. "That's not your concern anymore."

"The heck it isn't!" I snapped, my control slipping. "The stalker has escalated. If we back off now, we're giving him more time to plan his next move."

Sarge's face darkened. "And if you keep pushing, you're going to find yourself with a suspension. Maybe worse. You're too close to this, Whitlock."

I sat there, jaw tight, hands clenched into fists. I couldn't argue without proving his point.

"I know you want to protect him," Sarge said, quieter now, but no less firm. "But your job is to protect this town— all of it. You can't play bodyguard for one man."

"I can't just pretend this isn't happening," I said through gritted teeth.

"Then trust your team to do its job."

I let out a sharp breath and looked away.

Sarge sighed and rubbed a hand over his face. "Look, Whitlock. You're a damn good deputy. But if you don't step back now, you're going to step right over a line you can't uncross. I don't want to see you lose your badge over this."

The words carried weight. It wasn't just an order. It was a warning.

I nodded stiffly and stood. "Am I dismissed, sir?"

He exhaled heavily. "Yeah. But compose yourself before you walk out there. You look ready to punch something."

He wasn't wrong.

I left the office, shoulders tight, barely registering my coworkers' glances as I stormed out of the station. Crisp air hit me like a slap.

I pulled out my phone and scrolled to Ethan's number, hesitating only for a second before I hit *Call.*

He picked up on the first ring. "Hey," he said, but I

could hear the strain in his voice. "Do you have news for me?"

I blew out a breath. "Sarge found out about yesterday. About us canvassing the hotels together. He pulled me off the case. Detective Ballard's taking over."

Silence.

Then Ethan swore softly. "Garrett, I'm sorry. I didn't mean to get you into trouble."

"You didn't." I shook my head even though he couldn't see me. "I knew better. I knew the risk. But I genuinely thought it might help to have you along."

He sighed, and I could hear the frustration mixed with guilt. "But now what? If Ballard's too busy—"

"I'll still protect you, Ethan," I said firmly. "Badge or no badge. I'm not backing off."

I ended the call and shoved my phone into my pocket, exhaling slowly. Sarge could take me off the case, but that didn't change a damn thing. Ethan was still in danger, and I wasn't about to let him face it alone.

CHAPTER TWENTY-THREE

GARRETT

The house felt too quiet, a hollow, echoing kind of silence that pressed into my chest. Saturdays were usually a noisy affair—Noah running around, building caves out of couch cushions, or begging me to watch another episode of *Bluey* with him. But today, he was in San Francisco with Harper, marveling at the lionfish and laughing at penguins waddling along the rocks.

I should have been grateful for the break, glad he was safe and having a great time—Harper's texted pictures proved as much. Noah's smile beamed back at me from a photo. A stuffed penguin perched in the crook of his arm. My chest tightened with an ache that bordered on ridiculous.

But I missed my boy.

Weeknights with him were too short—dinner, homework, bedtime. And now, with this darn stalker targeting Ethan and hovering like a dark cloud over my life, too, I couldn't risk having Noah home on the weekends. Not until I had that bastard behind bars.

My jaw clenched as my thoughts spiraled, and anger

bubbled up from a deep well of frustration that I was off the case. I scrubbed harder at the countertop with the sponge in my hand, my fingers gripping it like a lifeline. The soapy water spilled over and pooled into a messy puddle that dripped onto the floor.

"Fudge," I muttered under my breath and tossed the sponge into the sink with a little too much force.

I grabbed a dish towel and mopped at the countertop, more aggressively than necessary. The frustration wasn't about the mess, though—it was about *him*. The faceless creep who had turned our lives upside down. The man I hadn't been able to find fast enough and now would probably fall through the cracks. My family deserved peace. *Ethan* deserved peace.

My phone buzzed in my pocket. I paused and wiped my damp hands on the towel before pulling it out. The message lit up my screen.

ETHAN

> Could we go for a walk on the beach?
> Maybe out of town? Trying to figure out a
> plot twist.

A small smile tugged at my lips and broke through the storm cloud in my head. Leave it to Ethan to make everything feel a little brighter, even when his book stumped him.

I quickly typed back:

> Be over in 5.

I grabbed my keys and headed to Ethan's.

At a beach a few miles north of Seacliff Cove, the wind whipped off the ocean and carried the sharp tang of salt and the distant cries of gulls. I shoved my hands deeper into the pockets of my jacket and glanced sideways at Ethan. He'd hunched his shoulders against the chilly breeze, his curls ruffled and messy around the edges of his ball cap. He spoke animatedly about plot holes and red herrings. Most of it went over my head, but I sensed that what he needed was a listening ear, someone to bounce ideas off of.

I could do that. Occasionally, I interjected with what I hoped was an intelligent question, but otherwise, I let him talk about his sticky plot problem.

The pounding of footsteps behind us broke through the sound of the waves. A runner, moving fast, barreled into Ethan.

"Hey!" Ethan yelped as he went down hard onto the sand.

The guy—a man with a dark hoodie pulled low over his face—stumbled, barely catching himself. "Sorry!" he barked over his shoulder, but he didn't stop.

Adrenaline shot through me like a bullet. "Stay here," I growled, already breaking into a sprint.

"Garrett! Stop! That's not him!" Ethan's shout carried on the breeze.

The guy was fast, but I was faster. My sneakers dug into the sand as I closed the gap between us. I launched myself and tackled him to the ground. He grunted as we hit the sand, and I whipped out my badge, shoving it in his face.

"Who are you?" I demanded, my voice low and dangerous. "Why were you following us? Why did you attack Ethan?"

The man raised his hands defensively, his face twisted in confusion. "I wasn't following anyone! It was an accident!"

I tightened my grip on his arm. "Accident?" I spat the word. "You're not getting away with assault."

I glanced back to see Ethan hurrying toward us as he

brushed sand off his jacket. My heart squeezed at the sight of him—rumpled, vulnerable, too damn close to danger.

"Let him go," Ethan said, his tone soothing but firm. "He's not the stalker. He's too big." He shook my shoulder.

I turned back to the runner. He was tall, broad-shouldered, and definitely not the wiry figure from the security footage.

I exhaled through clenched teeth and released my grip. "Fine. But if I find out you're lying, I'll track you down myself."

The man scrambled to his feet. "You're insane," he muttered and glared at me before jogging away.

"Are you okay?" I stepped closer to Ethan. My hands found his shoulders, then his arms, checking him over for injuries. "Did he hurt you? Are you dizzy? Did you hit your head?"

"I'm fine." His mouth flattened into a tight line. "I promise. But…" He shook his head.

But I couldn't stop. My fingers brushed over his jacket, then his sides, then his arms again, searching for any sign of damage. My heart thundered in my chest, louder than the waves crashing nearby.

When I found nothing wrong, I exhaled heavily, pulled him into a hug, and wrapped my arms tightly around him. I didn't care that we were in public. I didn't care who was watching.

"He scared the hell out of me," I murmured into his ear. "He could have—"

Ethan stiffened in my arms and pushed back with his hands against my chest. His face was flushed, but not from embarrassment or the chilly wind—it was anger.

"You can't do that, Garrett," he snapped, low but sharp enough to cut through the sound of the waves, mindful of our wide-eyed audience.

I froze, caught off guard. "Do what?"

"That." He gestured toward the sand where I'd tackled the runner. "Overreact. That guy wasn't the stalker—you should have seen that."

"I was trying to protect you," I shot back and felt the heat rise in my face.

"Protect me? Garrett, you went full-out deputy on some random jogger." His eyes blazed, hurt laced through the anger. "You didn't even think. You just *reacted*. That's not protecting me. That's putting yourself at risk."

The words hit me like a slap. My jaw tightened as I tried to push down the frustration bubbling up. "I wasn't going to let him get away if he *was* the stalker," I said more quietly, but no less defensively.

Ethan shook his head, his shoulders tense. "You didn't listen to me. You didn't trust me when I said he wasn't the guy."

I opened my mouth to argue, but the look in his eyes stopped me cold. He wasn't just angry—he was hurt.

"I know you want to solve this case, officially or not," he said, his tone softening. "But you can't bulldoze through it. It won't help either of us."

For a long moment, I just stood there, the wind biting at my face. I clenched and unclenched my fists at my sides. He was right. As much as I hated to admit it, he was right.

"I'm sorry," I said finally, the words heavy on my tongue. "I just...I can't stand the thought of anything happening to you."

Ethan's expression gentled, but the tension didn't entirely leave his shoulders. "I know. But you have to trust me. Can you do that?"

I nodded and swallowed past the lump in my throat. "Yeah. I can do that."

Ethan studied me for a moment, then sighed. "Come on. Let's go. I'm cold."

As we started walking again, the weight of his words settled over me. He was right—I couldn't overreact. I was allowing my feelings for Ethan to color my reflexes. I needed to step back and act like a professional.

But I couldn't find it in my heart to step back. He was beginning to matter more than I ever expected.

I held out my hand. "Let's warm up with a pumpkin spice latte." I knew a place nearby. It wasn't The Coffee Cove, but it would do.

He slotted his hand in mine, and my heart steadied. As we left the beach, I felt a surge of pride at having him by my side, Sarge's warning be darned.

———

The familiar creak of my front door announced our arrival as I nudged it open with my shoulder. I juggled my keys and my coffee. Ethan followed close behind, his quiet footsteps loud in the house's stillness. The faint scent of roasted beans wafted between us, mingling with the crisp salt air that clung to our jackets.

"Shoes off, coat on the rack." I flashed him a sheepish grin, my cheeks heating. "Please," I added. "I'm used to reminding Noah."

Ethan smirked. He set down his pumpkin spice latte, toed off his shoes, and shrugged out of his jacket. He took a moment to glance at the coat rack, where my uniform jacket hung neatly beside Noah's small hoodie. The juxtaposition was enough to make anyone smile—or at least that's what I told myself when I noticed the corners of his mouth twitch.

"Make yourself comfortable," I invited, as I led the way into the living room and sank into the cushions of the couch.

He sat beside me, close enough to feel the warmth radiating from his shoulder. "You were saying something earlier about the plot," Ethan started. "Before the jogger…" He trailed off, his voice faltering.

I didn't let him finish.

"Ethan," I said quietly, and waited until he turned his head to meet my gaze. "I don't want to talk about that right now. As much as I admire your talent, I'm not interested in dissecting your book."

His brow furrowed, and he shifted toward me, coffee cup lowering just enough for me to catch the way his lips parted, maybe to ask a question, maybe to protest.

I didn't give him the chance. I plucked the cup out of his hand and placed it beside mine on the coffee table.

"What I need," I said, steady but softer, "is to know you're safe." My chest tightened, the vulnerability sneaking into my tone despite my best efforts. "And…I need your kiss. Right now, that's what I need most." I needed the reassurance, the comfort of his body. The incident with the runner had shaken me more than I cared to let on.

The air between us stilled, thick with unspoken tension and something else—something electric. Ethan's lips curved into the smallest smile, his coffee forgotten as he leaned just a fraction closer.

The air between us crackled with something undeniably charged. Ethan's smile flickered, and his lips parted as though he had something to say, but I didn't want words. I wanted him. Needed him.

Before he could utter a sound, I closed the gap between us, and my hand cupped the side of his jaw. His breath hitched, and his eyes fluttered shut just as my lips crashed into his.

The kiss wasn't tentative. It was everything I'd been holding back. Desperation. Desire. The need to reassure myself—and him—that he was safe. His lips were soft but responsive and yielded to the pressure of mine, just as hungry, just as determined.

Ethan's hand came up to clutch the front of my sweatshirt. He pulled me closer and anchored me like he was afraid I'd disappear.

I shifted, and my free hand slid to his waist. My fingers gripped the fabric of his sweater to bring us closer. I deepened the kiss and felt his sigh against my lips, warm and fulfilling.

When we finally broke apart, it wasn't because I wanted to. It was because breathing had become nonnegotiable. Our foreheads rested together, and my thumb brushed absently over the trim beard along his jawline as I tried to steady my pulse.

"I needed that," I murmured, low and rough, my lips still close enough to graze his as I spoke. "But I need…" My cock thickened, demanding the comfort of physical intimacy.

"What do you need?" he whispered. "I'll give it to you."

"I need to touch you." I ran my hand down his neck to his broad shoulder. "All over. Skin to skin." I needed to ground myself in him and reassure myself of his safety, though I wouldn't admit to that aloud.

He seemed to understand my unspoken words. He whipped his sweater over his head, followed by his T-shirt, and revealed a defined chest lightly dusted with auburn hair.

I'd seen plenty of bare chests before—in locker rooms, at the beach—but none had affected me like this. My body reacted as if struck by lightning, and I couldn't shuck my sweatshirt fast enough.

Ethan chuckled at my eagerness. We unbuckled, unzipped, and tossed our jeans and socks aside in a flurry of movement until we were naked, thigh to thigh—his light, fine hair against my dark, coarser hair. My heart thundered in my chest at the simple touch, yet we were only getting started.

"Trust me?" he asked, his voice husky. "I think you'll enjoy what I have in mind."

My dick hardened even further at just the words. At the simple promise of pleasure. "Of course. Anything you want to do."

He twisted, swung a leg over my thighs, and straddled my lap. Our cocks and balls aligned, and the feel of his warm length against mine sizzled. A shiver shot through me.

He leaned forward and kissed me, long and deep, ratcheting up my anticipation. When he finally broke away, I was panting and ready to beg for release.

He didn't make me wait. He took both of our erections in hand, swiped our pre-cum for lubrication, and pumped, twisted, and paid extra attention to the heads. The pressure of my orgasm built, and I couldn't help thrusting into his hand. Crying his name, I came in long spurts. With a grunt, he followed soon after.

I collapsed into the sofa cushions, completely spent. "That was...that was definitely reassurance that you're alive."

He chuckled. "Thought that would do the trick." He carefully climbed off my lap. "Wait here." He sauntered out of the room with a light step and returned a short time later with a warm, wet washcloth.

I took it from him, cleaned my stomach, and tossed the cloth onto the floor. I'd throw it into the laundry later. At the moment, Ethan needed a kiss. I stood, took him into my arms, and crashed my mouth to his. Naked body to naked body. Stubble to beard. Hairy chest to hairy chest. The foreign sensations were arousing and comforting at the same time.

He shivered, and goosebumps rose on his arms, the flush

of the heat we'd created cooling. The house was chilly—I hadn't thought to fire up the heat while I cleaned.

"Let's get you dressed and warmed up," I said softly, reluctant to let the moment end. My fingers lingered on his skin for a beat longer than necessary before I forced myself to pull away and hand him his clothes.

He took them without a word, his expression unreadable in the dim light. We dressed in tandem, the previous intimacy replaced with companionship. I pulled my sweatshirt over my head, the fabric almost like armor after the vulnerability we'd just shared.

"Want to stay for dinner?" The words slipped out before I could second-guess them, my voice tinged with hope that he'd say yes, and we could extend this fragile thread of connection a little longer.

He sighed, and the corners of his mouth tugged downward. "Rain check? I'd better get back to work."

Disappointment hit me like a sudden wave, sharp and cold. I nodded and tried to mask the sting. "I get it." I forced a small smile. His job wasn't a neat nine-to-five, no matter how much I might wish our schedules meshed. "I'll walk you home."

He opened his mouth, the beginnings of an argument forming in his eyes, but I shook my head and cut him off before he could start. "No argument." Sarge couldn't prevent me from protecting a neighbor.

A twitch of his lips broke through his frown, and he nodded in surrender. "Okay."

He slipped into his jacket and tied his sneakers with quick movements. I grabbed my keys, gestured toward the door, and held it open as we stepped into the brisk late afternoon air.

Our footsteps fell into rhythm as we walked the short

distance to his house. Neither of us spoke, but the silence felt amicable, the kind that didn't need filling.

That comfort shattered the moment we reached his porch.

I saw it first—a paper flapping in the breeze, just a corner of it caught beneath the edge of the doormat.

I froze. "Hold up."

Ethan followed my gaze, the last trace of relaxation draining from his face. We both crouched.

It was a single sheet of printer paper, the kind you'd barely glance at if it weren't for the bold black letters across the top:

Author Ethan Quinn Dead At 38

My pulse thudded in my ears. The rest of the page was filled with the details of a fake obituary—his *untimely passing*, the *loss to the literary world*, and a funeral date for the following week. It was sick. Calculated. Meant to terrify him.

And judging by the way Ethan's breath hitched, it worked.

"Inside," I ordered. "Now."

"Garrett—"

"I'll handle this," I said firmly. "Lock the door. Don't open it for anyone but me."

He nodded, eyes wide but trusting, and stepped inside without another word.

I'd take it to Ballard, do everything by the book. But the bitter truth lodged itself deep in my chest as I straightened up.

Ballard wasn't going to do a damn thing.

So, I would continue to protect Ethan.

CHAPTER TWENTY-FOUR

ETHAN

Just after lunchtime the next day, my phone chimed with a text.

GARRETT

Beautiful day. Want to take a break, get out of town, and visit a lighthouse?

I glanced at the word count on my manuscript. Progress had been solid this morning, a flow I'd been missing lately due to the worry hanging over my head. The thought of spending the afternoon with Garrett, away from my keyboard, away from the stalker, made me smile. I flexed my shoulders, trying to work out the knot from sitting too long, and typed back.

Love to.

Pick you up in fifteen.

The sound of his Escape pulling into my driveway sent a little jolt through me. I grabbed my jacket and headed out. Garrett greeted me with an easy smile, and I climbed into the passenger seat.

The drive south along the coast was breathtaking. Sunlight danced on the waves, the ocean stretched endlessly to the horizon, and the salty air, tinged with the faintest hint of kelp, infiltrated the SUV's interior.

In the background, the radio softly played "More Than a Feeling," and I caught Garrett tapping the beat on the steering wheel with his thumb.

"You know, for a guy who is all business on the job, you've got a serious soft spot for seventies rock." I watched him from the corner of my eye.

He didn't deny it. Just gave me a shrug and the faintest grin. "Good music is good music."

"I'm starting to think you've got layers, Deputy Whitlock."

He glanced at me, amused. "You just now figuring that out?"

"Maybe," I said. "So far, I've learned you like classic rock, you and Noah live on boxed mac and cheese and chicken nuggets, and you own exactly zero spices besides salt."

"I have pepper," he said, deadpan.

"Oh, forgive me. A kitchen wizard." I laughed. "Do you cook anything that doesn't come from a box?"

"I make grilled cheese," he said with mock pride.

"What a gourmand," I teased. "But points for effort."

He chuckled, then added, "You want to know something else?"

"Always."

"I watch a lot of home renovation shows," he admitted. "Like…a lot. I redid my bathroom after bingeing six episodes of *Modern Fixer*."

I blinked. "Seriously?"

"I find it satisfying," he said. "Taking something broken, putting it back together better than it was. Demo day is therapy."

"I had no idea you were a secret shiplap enthusiast."

He gave me a look. "It's about texture and warmth. You wouldn't understand."

I snorted. "You're right. I wouldn't. The last time I tried to build a bookshelf, it leaned so hard it basically collapsed under the weight of a single paperback. And I followed the instructions. With pictures."

"Tragic," he said, but his grin softened. "Noah's better with an Allen wrench than you, huh?"

"Embarrassingly so. I think the cat I had growing up had more construction instinct."

He glanced at me with quiet amusement. "So, you cook to relax, and I build things. Not a bad balance."

"Until we need shelves," I said. "Then it's all you."

He smiled, and the lines at the corners of his eyes deepened just enough to make something tighten in my chest.

Maybe it was the music. Maybe it was the way the sunlight caught in his hair. Or maybe it was just the way we kept peeling back layers without even trying. But whatever it was—

We fit.

When the lighthouse came into view, perched on a rugged promontory, I drew in a breath.

"Wow," I whispered.

The Pelican Point Lighthouse was stunning—a 115-foot conical tower of whitewashed brick rising stark against the vivid blue of the sky. At its base, waves crashed against jagged rocks, and beyond them, at low tide, a colony of harbor seals basked in the sun on a rocky reef. Their barks punctuated the rhythmic sounds of the surf. Above the seals, pelicans glided in long, graceful lines, their wings skimming the water.

Garrett pulled into the gravel lot and shut off the engine. "You're going to love this," he said with a grin. "It's one of Noah's favorite places."

As we walked toward the lighthouse, gulls wheeled above us, their sharp cries carried by the breeze. The chilly, briny air stung my cheeks, but Garrett's presence beside me kept me warm.

The lighthouse itself was closed for restoration, but we wandered the grounds, taking in the view. Nearby lay an enormous chunk of a schooner's hull—a haunting relic of a shipwreck.

"This place has history," Garrett said with a quiet reverence.

In the old fog signal building, we explored exhibits detailing the lighthouse's 145-year-old story. The centerpiece was the original first-order Fresnel lens, a massive, brass-encased beehive that had once sent its beacon miles out to sea. The prisms and bull's-eye lenses captured the light pouring through the narrow windows, casting rainbows that shimmered across the room.

"It's beautiful," I murmured and stepped closer to study the intricate glasswork.

"It is." Garrett stood close beside me, his eyes on me instead of the lens. "Let's get a picture of us with it in the background."

I hesitated for a split second. Garrett had been wary of public displays of affection. But something in his tone told me this moment was a step forward.

He raised his phone and angled it to capture us in front of the lens. At the last second, he turned and pressed a soft kiss to my cheek.

The click of the photo startled me almost as much as the

warmth of his lips. I turned to look at him, our lips a breath away, and my heart caught at the softness in his expression.

"What?" His crooked grin teased me.

"Nothing," I said, though my throat was tight. "Just... thank you."

"For what?"

"For this." I gestured to the lens, the room, the day. But what I really meant was *him*. For showing me that this—*us*— wasn't something to hide. At least, outside of Seacliff Cove. The implications for his career if we were found out in town were something I understood.

His hand found mine as we left the building, fingers intertwining. The simple touch sent heat radiating through me.

The drive back was quieter, a silence that felt like companionship rather than awkwardness. My thoughts lingered on the moment he'd kissed me, the casual ease of it, and the weight of what it meant.

When we pulled into the driveway, Harper's car was there. Garrett frowned, and he reached for the door handle. "She wasn't supposed to be here yet."

Concern tightened his voice, and I reached out and brushed his arm with my hand. "Maybe it's nothing."

But the worry didn't leave his face as he stepped out of the vehicle. My heart, still full from the day's quiet revelations, now held a flutter of unease. Whatever awaited us inside, it couldn't erase the implications of his actions at the lighthouse—but I knew our time was over for the day. I rushed after Garrett, my chest tight.

The front door flew open as we approached, and Noah launched himself onto the porch like a small whirlwind. "Daddy! I missed you!"

Garrett dropped to one knee just in time to catch Noah and wrapped him up in a hug that looked like it was the answer to every unspoken prayer. "I missed you, too, buddy," Garrett murmured, his voice thick. He kissed Noah's cheek and held him close.

My heart squeezed. The sight of them together was enough to make my guilt blare to life like a warning siren. I'd kept them apart. Because of me, Noah had been homesick. Because of me, Garrett had missed his son.

A woman—a few years younger than Garrett—appeared in the doorway and leaned against the frame with her arms crossed and an affectionate smile tugging at her lips. Her dark hair fell in waves around her face, and her piercing blue eyes—so much like his—darted to mine with an assessing glance.

"He wanted to come home early," she said. "Kept asking for his daddy, so here we are."

Garrett stood, his arm still draped protectively over Noah's shoulders. "I'm glad you brought him back," he said, his gaze full of gratitude. "Thanks, Harper."

She waved him off with a grin. "You know I'd never keep him from you." Her eyes flicked to me again, her expression curious but kind. "I'm Harper. You must be Ethan. My parents mentioned you."

"Uh, yeah," I said, my voice uneven. I extended a hand, feeling more exposed than ever. Did Garrett's family know I'd brought danger to his doorstep? Judging by Harper's grin, I doubted it. So I simply said, "Nice to meet you."

Harper's handshake was firm. "Same here. Don't let him scare you off," she added with a nod toward Garrett.

"Too late for that." I tried for humor but was unable to shake the weight of my guilt. I glanced at Garrett. "I should go. I don't want to intrude."

"No!" Noah piped up, his bright eyes fixed on me. "We're having burgers for dinner, and Auntie Harper's making fries! You should stay!"

My gaze darted to Garrett, who shrugged and grinned. "He's already invited you. Can't let him down." He mussed Noah's hair.

I hesitated, torn between the warmth of being included and the persistent fear of bringing the stalker to the house. But the hopeful look on Noah's face and the casual acceptance in Garrett's smile tipped the scales. "Okay," I said, my voice soft. "Thank you."

Dinner was noisy and joyful. Noah dominated the conversation with tales of his weekend adventures with Harper—a visit to the library, hot chocolate at The Coffee Cove, and a blanket fort to read in. Harper provided occasional commentary. I found myself pulled into Noah's orbit, asking questions and laughing at Noah's animated storytelling. For a moment, the weight I'd been carrying lifted, replaced by the fullness of belonging.

Harper watched my interactions with Noah and Garrett with a smirk that only grew as the evening went on. When dinner was done and we were clearing the dishes, I lingered at the table, unsure whether to help clean up or play with Noah in the living room. Then I heard Harper's teasing voice from the kitchen.

"I like him," she said, light but pointed. "He's good for you."

Garrett quietly mumbled his agreement.

My cheeks heated. I wasn't used to being the subject of approval. But her words settled something inside me, a quiet reassurance that I hadn't entirely misstepped by staying for dinner.

Harper lingered long enough for Garrett to walk me home. The cool night air was a welcome relief after the warmth of the house, but the silence between us was charged with the significance of the day.

I approached my porch with trepidation, but I breathed a

quiet sigh of relief when there was no "gift" waiting for me. Had we escaped the stalker by leaving town?

Garrett turned to me and cupped my jaw with strong fingers. "I had a great day with you. And thanks for staying for dinner," he said, low and husky. "It meant a lot to Noah."

I met his gaze, the sincerity in his eyes making it hard to breathe. "It meant a lot to me, too."

He took a step closer, and his lips met mine. The kiss was soft and unhurried, the fitting end to a day of belonging. When we finally pulled apart, Garrett's smile was small but teasing. "Now get your ass inside and lock the door."

I chuckled. "Yes, sir."

As I threw the deadbolt and armed my alarm, I knew I was in trouble in a way no security system could save me from.

My feelings for Garrett Whitlock, with his tender heart and fierce protectiveness, were growing stronger by the moment.

CHAPTER TWENTY-FIVE

GARRETT

My car's tires crunched over gravel as I pulled into the parking lot at the ark. The towering trees framed the lot like silent sentinels. Noah and I had walked this easy loop trail many times over the years, his small hand in mine as we marveled at banana slugs and chased the echoes of birdcalls.

Noah. The thought of him tightened my chest, guilt worming its way in. Another weekend apart. Another missed adventure with my boy. I could picture his eager face as he'd climbed into Ava's parents' car last night, bundled in his puffer jacket and gripping his mittens. He'd been so excited about the trip to their cabin in Tahoe, giddy at the chance to see snowflakes dust the world in white. I'd hugged him fiercely before he left, breathing in the scent of his shampoo and telling myself it was okay—he deserved that fun, even if it meant the house felt emptier.

But my guilt wasn't just about Noah. A part of it, if I was being honest, stemmed from the anticipation humming in my chest. Spending the weekend with Ethan was something I'd looked forward to all week. He'd made significant progress on his book and taken the day off, something I knew didn't come easily.

I glanced at him across the console, his profile lit by a shaft of sunlight breaking through the clouds. His jawline was strong, his short beard neatly trimmed, and his expression relaxed. I reached over and squeezed his thigh, firm under my hand. "Thanks for coming with me."

He turned toward me. "Looking forward to it. It's nice to get out of the house." His lips curved into a teasing smile. "Oh, and to spend time with you, I guess," he added with a wink.

I laughed, a low snort that broke the quiet, but inside, his words warmed me.

We climbed out of the car, the cool, damp air wrapping around us as we made our way toward the grove. His hand found mine, fingers lacing together in a way that felt both new and natural. A couple walking their dog gave us a sidelong glance, but I kept my chin high and refused to let their judgment touch the quiet joy buzzing between us. Fudge them.

Under the towering canopy, the temperature dipped. The air smelled of pine and rich, damp earth, with a hint of bay leaf that made me inhale deeply. A woodpecker's rhythmic tapping echoed, answered by the mournful cry of a dove somewhere deep in the grove.

We started down the well-worn trail, our pace unhurried. This wasn't a hike to conquer, but a chance to soak in the towering redwoods and, more importantly, each other. I pointed out a banana slug inching through a patch of redwood sorrel, its vibrant yellow standing out against the green. Ethan glanced at it but seemed distracted, his gaze distant as if he were somewhere else entirely.

"What's on your mind?" I asked, my voice low and laced with concern.

He rubbed his hand along his short beard. I recognized it as a sign he was weighing his words. "I hate taking you away from Noah," he said finally, quiet but heavy. "I want to find the stalker so you and your son can spend your weekends together, without this hanging over you."

His words hit like a stone in my chest, and I squeezed his hand tightly. "Don't worry about Noah. He's having a great time this weekend." The truth of my words didn't stop the ache in my chest, that hollow spot left by my boy's absence. But having Ethan there helped fill it.

"Has there been any progress with forensics? The email I got?"

I shook my head, and frustration knotted my stomach. "There hadn't been before Sarge took me off the case. Tech hadn't cracked the source of the email. If Finch is as smart as he seems to be, he probably covered his tracks too well for us to trace. Since then, Ballard hasn't kept me updated."

Ethan's jaw tightened, his mouth flattening into a thin, hard line. "I just want this to be over."

I did, too, for Ethan's safety. But I swallowed against the lump forming in my throat, my stomach twisting at the implication of his words. *But then you'll leave and return to your real family.*

The thought settled heavily in my mind, unspoken but loud enough to drown out the whisper of the wind through the redwoods. I clung to the moment instead and focused on the warmth of Ethan's hand in mine and the comfort of the towering trees around us. Whatever the future held, I would hold on to this—for as long as I could.

Ethan stopped so abruptly that I nearly stumbled. His entire body went rigid, and his hand clamped down on mine with a grip that bordered on painful.

"It's him," he whispered, his voice tight with fear.

My heart skipped a beat. "What?" I followed his wide-eyed gaze and scanned the forest until I saw him: a slim, average-height man partially concealed behind a massive redwood. His phone was raised, the lens pointed directly at us. Hollow cheeks, a strong jaw—features burned into my memory from the driver's license photo I'd studied. *Theodore Finch.*

Adrenaline surged through me. I dropped Ethan's hand and reached for my phone. My fingers trembled as I prepared to call for backup.

Before I could dial, Ethan let out a raw, guttural cry—a sound that spoke of months of fear, frustration, and helplessness all boiling over at once. Finch's head jerked up, his eyes wide with alarm, and then he bolted and disappeared into the dense woods.

"Ethan, no!" I shouted as he tore after Finch.

Fuck. My pulse hammered as I sprinted after them. The underbrush grabbed at my legs with clutching fingers. Ferns whipped against my thighs, and vines clawed at my ankles as I pushed through the forest. I was distantly aware of the damage we were causing to the fragile ecosystem, but the pounding urgency in my chest drowned out everything else. Finch was a stalker, a predator, and I couldn't let him get away.

And I had a…boyfriend…to stop before he did something even more stupid.

And Ethan was charging headlong into danger. It hit me like a punch to the gut: this was exactly how he'd felt when I'd chased down the jogger who'd plowed into him. Fear, frustration, and helplessness rolled into one sickening knot in my stomach.

I dodged around tree trunks. Branches slapped at my arms. My breath sawed in and out. I strained to keep them in sight.

Ethan slowed. His steps faltered as the uneven ground took its toll.

I surged ahead and pushed past him. Finch was wiry and fast. But I was in peak shape.

The forest suddenly gave way to the gravel parking lot. The trees parted like a curtain to reveal rows of parked cars.

Finch darted between the cars. He glanced over his shoulder, his expression wild with desperation.

"Stop! Sheriff's department!" I bellowed. My voice cut through the still air. Finch didn't even hesitate.

He dove into a beat-up white Civic just as I closed the gap. Gravel sprayed from under his tires as he slammed the car into reverse. He narrowly missed me and a young couple walking toward the trailhead. They screamed and plunged to the ground.

The Civic peeled out of the lot in a cloud of dust.

Panting, I skidded to a stop, whipped out my phone, and dialed 9-1-1. My badge number rolled off my tongue as I issued a BOLO on Finch and his vehicle and requested immediate assistance from the local sheriff's office.

As I ended the call, I turned to see Ethan kneeling next to the couple, his voice low and soothing. Even shaken, he had a kind, reassuring nature.

I approached, my footsteps crunching on the gravel. "Are you both okay?" I asked the couple, keeping my tone as calm as I could manage. They nodded, wide-eyed and trembling, but they agreed to file a report with a deputy when I asked.

Once they were settled, I pulled Ethan aside, my emotions teetering between relief and fury. "What the heck were you thinking?" I snapped, my voice sharp and tight. "You put yourself in danger. You could've been hurt—or worse."

He ran a hand through his hair, the usually neat curls now wild and disheveled. He'd lost his ball cap. "I know," he said, his voice soft and filled with regret. "I didn't think—I just acted. Like you did on the beach." His gaze locked on mine, shame and a plea for understanding mixing in his expression. "I want to stop looking over my shoulder, wondering when he's going to show up again."

The fight drained out of me in an instant. My chest ached for him. But the thought of what could've happened—what Finch might've done—made my breath catch. Without a word, I grabbed him and pulled him into a fierce hug, my arms wrapping tightly around his shuddering frame.

He sagged against me, his chin lowering to my shoulder as his hands fisted in the back of my jacket. "I'm sorry," he murmured.

"Just don't do it again," I said roughly. The deputy in me pushed through the raw emotions swirling inside.

I felt his lips curve into a faint smile against my neck. "Yes, sir," he teased.

I held him a moment longer and silently vowed that no matter what it took, I would end this. For him.

So he could return to New York—leaving Noah heartbroken and confused—and taking a piece of me with him.

CHAPTER TWENTY-SIX

GARRETT

When we reached Ethan's door hours later, exhaustion dragged at every part of me—body, mind, and soul. The weight of the chase, the near-miss, and the mounting tension settled like a lead ball in my chest. Ethan's shoulders sagged as he unlocked his door, his silence heavy with unspoken thoughts.

The shrill ring of my phone shattered the quiet. I snatched it from my pocket and answered with a clipped, "Whitlock."

"Deputy Sheriff Banks, South County sheriff's office," came the professional voice on the other end. "Finch abandoned his car in a residential neighborhood. No sign of him, no witnesses."

My stomach sank. "Fudge," I muttered under my breath and pinched the bridge of my nose. "He probably stole another car that hasn't been reported yet."

"That'd be my guess," Banks agreed. "I'd advise you to keep an eye out. I'll update you if we get anything."

I thanked him for the courtesy call and stabbed *End*, the

tension in my body coiling tighter. A long, heavy sigh escaped me as I tucked the phone away.

"What?" Ethan's voice cut through the silence, edged with concern.

I relayed the information and watched as his expression shifted from worry to something darker—fear, maybe, or frustration. Or both. "No telling what Finch will do now that he's cornered. He could disappear entirely, try to hide. Or he might become bolder, even more dangerous." I clenched my fist around the phone, the need to protect Ethan burning in my chest. "Pack an overnight bag."

Ethan's brows pulled together, confusion flickering in his eyes. "Why?"

"Because you're staying with me. Or I'm staying with you."

His jaw tightened. "But I've got a security system—"

"It's not good enough." I cut him off, my voice firm. "I'm not leaving you alone tonight."

For a moment, it looked like he might argue, his mouth opening as if to protest. But then his shoulders slumped, the fight draining out of him. "Come on in while I pack."

We stepped into his house, the quiet stillness almost eerie. The soft chime of the security system reassured me, but it wasn't enough to ease the knot of anxiety in my chest. While Ethan moved through the house, packing a duffel bag and grabbing his laptop, I kept my eyes on the windows, the door, the shadows shifting in the corners.

At my place, the comforting normalcy of hanging our jackets and toeing off our shoes anchored me briefly, though the tension lingered beneath the surface. My stomach growled and broke the silence with almost comical timing.

"Chili okay for dinner?" I tried to keep things light. Normal.

"What can I do to help?" Ethan followed me into the small kitchen.

"I've got it." I pulled ingredients from the fridge. The simple rhythm of preparing dinner was a balm to my frayed nerves. We chatted as I worked, Ethan sharing his favorite New York haunts—Central Park, a hole-in-the-wall pizza place in Brooklyn, the Cloisters. I countered with stories of fishing trips and whale-watching tours, but we danced around the elephant in the room. We wouldn't be going to those places together after he left.

After dinner, Ethan settled at the kitchen table with his laptop, diving back into his writing while I relaxed with the third Jake Slate novel. The quiet domesticity of it all—the soft tapping of his keyboard, the turning of pages, the hum of the heater—wrapped around me like a warm blanket. I wanted more evenings like this.

I was immersed in a heart-pounding action scene when Ethan swore, long and colorful enough to make me glance up sharply.

"What's wrong?" My voice came out tense, my senses instantly on alert.

He rubbed his temple, his laptop still open in front of him. "Another email. From EyeSeeYou." His throat worked as he swallowed hard. "It reads, *This isn't over. You stole my voice, so I'll take yours.*"

"What the heck does that mean?" I muttered, even though I was already trying to piece it together. "You stole his voice…?"

Ethan didn't look at me. His fingers hovered uselessly over the mouse. "He used to write," he said finally. "Not professionally, but in that writers' group I told you about. He shared a few stories. A lot of rambling ideas. Nothing polished."

"So maybe he thinks you took something?" I asked. "A plotline, a character?"

"I didn't." He shook his head. "Maybe we were inspired by similar events and people, but I never plagiarized him."

I studied him for a moment. "He thinks you did. And now he's talking about taking your voice. That could mean a few things, Ethan—and none of them are good."

Ethan swallowed. "Like silencing me?"

"Yeah. Either professionally or…" I trailed off, jaw tightening.

Physically.

I didn't say it, but we both felt the weight of it. The threat wasn't veiled anymore. It was staring us dead in the face, written in black text on a glowing screen.

"Well," I said, my voice low and grim, "one thing's clear. He's not gone into hiding. He's getting desperate." My stomach churned with the realization. "You're in more danger now than ever. Forward that email to Ballard." I rattled off his email address.

After a few strokes, Ethan snapped his laptop shut and abruptly pushed back from the table. He began pacing the living room, his steps quick and agitated. "There's got to be something we can do. We've got to be proactive."

The urgency in his voice set off alarm bells in my head. "Whatever you're thinking, forget about it."

He stopped pacing and turned to face me, his hands on his hips. "I can't just sit around and wait for him to make a move. I can't do nothing."

"What you're going to do is keep yourself safe while the sheriff's department does its job," I ordered, leaving no room for argument.

"But—"

"No."

His mouth pressed into a tight line, frustration clear in the way his jaw worked and his hands flexed at his sides.

I sighed, the tension easing slightly as I softened my tone. "I don't want to fight you on this, Ethan. I just want you safe."

He dropped onto the couch beside me, his arms crossed defensively over his chest. His rigid weight pressed against my side.

I placed my hand on his thigh and squeezed gently. "I'll keep you safe," I promised. "No matter what it takes."

Ethan didn't reply, but his hand covered mine in a silent acknowledgment of the trust he placed in me.

I stifled a yawn. "It's been a long, hard day. Let's go to bed." I pushed myself to my feet, my joints protesting.

Ethan remained seated; his shoulders slumped as if the strain of the evening had finally drained every ounce of fight from him. His face looked pale and drawn in the soft light, the spark in his eyes dulled by exhaustion and lingering anxiety.

"Do you have an extra blanket and pillow?" he asked tentatively.

"Why?" I tilted my head, my brows drawing together.

"So I can make up the couch," he said, a faint crease forming on his forehead, confusion in his expression.

I studied him for a moment, his question striking me as almost absurd. "You're sleeping with me," I said, the words firm but calm. "I'm not letting you out of my sight."

His mouth fell open, his surprise flickering into something softer, more vulnerable. "Are you...? Are you sure you're ready for that?" His tone was cautious, like he was treading on fragile ground, unsure of where we stood.

I stepped closer, my gaze steady on his, trying to reassure him. "I'm sure I'm ready to sleep," I said with a faint smile, letting a bit of humor creep into my voice to ease the tension. "Anything else, well…" I allowed the sentence to hang for a beat before finishing with a wink. "We'll see."

Ethan blinked, and his lips twitched into a hint of a smile.

"C'mon." I led Ethan to my bedroom. He followed, his duffel bag slung over his shoulder.

"You can use the bathroom first," I offered and nodded toward the cramped ensuite.

Ethan rummaged in his bag and pulled out a neatly folded pair of flannel pants and a T-shirt, then disappeared into the bathroom. The door clicked shut, and a moment later, the sound of running water filled the quiet bedroom.

I exhaled, ran a hand through my hair, and pulled open my dresser drawer. I traded the boxer briefs I usually slept in for a pair of soft sleep pants. A tiny smile tugged at the corner of my mouth as I thought about Ethan's reaction if I chose otherwise.

The bathroom door creaked open, and Ethan stepped out, mint toothpaste scenting the air. He wore flannel pants similar to mine and a faded T-shirt that clung to his frame, worn from years of washes. The sight of him, casual and unguarded, made my chest tighten in a way that had nothing to do with exhaustion.

I cleared my throat, slipped into the bathroom, and closed the door behind me. Leaning on the counter, I caught my reflection in the mirror, and my gaze locked on the shadow of stubble along my jawline. Determination set my features. Tonight, I'd ask for what I wanted—for more. And if Ethan said no, I'd take it in stride. No pressure, no harm, no foul.

I finished my routine and returned to the bedroom.

Ethan stood at the foot of the bed, hands on his hips,

studying the neatly turned-down covers. "Which side is yours?" He glanced at me with an almost shy smile.

I gestured to the left. "Closest to the door. Easier for Noah to find me when he has a bad dream."

Ethan nodded, his face softening. "Makes sense," he murmured. He circled the bed and slipped beneath the covers with a sigh that seemed to come from the very depths of his soul.

I turned off the light and slid into bed beside him, the cool sheets quickly warming as I settled on my side. I hesitated for a beat, my heart thundering, then shifted closer and spooned him. "This okay?" I asked hesitantly.

For a moment, he didn't reply, and I wondered if I'd overstepped. But then he relaxed against me, his body melting into mine, and he murmured, "Mm-hmm."

The soft sound of his approval sent a rush of relief through me. He snuggled closer, pressed his ass against my hard groin, and let out a soft moan.

I had my answer. He wanted more, too.

I kissed the nape of his neck, and he stretched to give me better access. I slid my hand from his waist to the hem of his T-shirt and slipped it underneath. Warm, firm abs tightened beneath my touch. My hand roamed to a pebbled nipple, which I tweaked between my thumb and forefinger. He hissed in pleasure.

"Are we wearing too many clothes?" I whispered in his ear.

In answer, he sat up, whipped off his T-shirt, and tossed it…somewhere. His pants and boxer briefs followed, freeing his hard cock.

The sight in the dim light made my dick ache, and all I could think about was my mouth on his erection. I'd never done that before, but heat pooled in my belly. I wanted to try. For him.

And selfishly, for me.

I shucked my clothes in record time to the music of Ethan's chuckle.

I pushed him flat on his back, my gaze on his dick. I licked my lips. "I've never sucked a guy before, but can I try it? I'll do my best to make it good for you."

He groaned and stroked himself. "Just watch your teeth, and you can't do it wrong."

I batted his hand away. "Mine." I spread his legs, settled between his thighs, and lightly gripped his penis. I tenderly licked around the head and blew on the damp skin. He pulled in a sharp breath. Empowered, I sucked, licked, stroked, and gently pulled on his balls until he was making nonsensical noises and fucking my mouth. I gagged, and he backed off, but I could tell the effort to keep still cost him. He clenched his fists at his sides and panted.

"Oh God, Garrett," he moaned. "You're doing so good," he praised. "Pull off. I'm gonna…" He tapped my shoulder.

I doubled down, wanting him to come in my mouth. Wanting the intimacy. The connection. A moment later, he spurted onto my tongue, the taste salty and slightly bitter.

I couldn't stand the pressure in my balls anymore. I quickly pulled off his dick, rose to my knees, and jacked myself. I came in long ropes onto his stomach. "*Fudge.*" I collapsed onto my elbows, gasping. "That was…"

He ran his hands along my shoulders. "I know."

I felt like I'd run a marathon, but I climbed off the bed. I cleaned myself up in the bathroom and wet a washcloth with warm water. I returned to the bedroom and took care of Ethan, finding satisfaction in the act. I threw the cloth toward the hamper and climbed back into bed, spooning him once again.

The soft sound of his approval sent a rush through me.

He cuddled closer, his shoulders pressing against my chest. I tightened my arm around him and held him there.

Despite the fear and uncertainty that still loomed over us, in this moment, we were together. And that was enough for the night.

CHAPTER TWENTY-SEVEN

ETHAN

A few days had passed since Garrett told me about the written warning he'd received from Sergeant Rodriguez, but the anger still simmered beneath my skin. A fucking written warning for going to the redwoods together.

I paced the length of my living room, frustration buzzing like static in my chest. He was in trouble because of me. Because we had chased Finch through the redwoods, because Garrett had filed an honest report instead of covering it up. And now, his department was punishing him for it.

But that hadn't stopped Garrett. We still exchanged text messages, then late-night phone calls, filling the distance between us with quiet conversations. I told myself it was just to check in, just to make sure he was okay, but we both knew that was a lie. I needed to hear his voice.

Still, it gnawed at me. What if this was just the beginning? What if his sergeant escalated things? If we kept ignoring the department's warnings, would they suspend him? Take him off the force entirely? The thought made my stomach twist.

Should I break things off with him?

I barely glanced at my phone when it rang, expecting another spam call, but the moment I saw *Garrett Whitlock* lighting up my screen, a slow smile spread across my lips.

Over the past few days, our conversations had shifted— what had started as brief case updates via text had morphed into calls, ones neither of us seemed eager to end. I started piecing Garrett together like one of my character profiles. He hated noisy, crowded cities—said they made his skin crawl— but the quiet, unhurried rhythm of Seacliff Cove suited him. He told me that driving with the windows down and breathing in the salty air made him feel alive, like something inside him unlocked. He loved teaching Noah basic life skills —how to check the oil, sort laundry, hammer a nail straight. Things I'd never learned growing up in a city where grocery delivery and maintenance men were the norm.

Garrett was built to protect, like it was coded into his DNA. He didn't talk about it as a job—it was just who he was. Me? I found comfort in control. I labeled my file folders, color-coded my outlines, and found peace in tidy structure. I could lose myself for hours in a bookstore, running my fingers over spines, building worlds in my head. He confessed he was a potato chip junkie—barbecue flavor, specifically. I admitted that junk food made me feel like I'd swallowed a paperweight. Different worlds. But every message, every call, felt like a bridge between us.

I swiped to answer the call and sank back into my couch with a grin. "If this is another attempt to convert me into a home reno addict, I should warn you, it's working. I watched three episodes of *Dream House Disaster* today, and now I have strong opinions about exposed beams."

Garrett's low chuckle came through the line, warm and easy. "Knew I'd get you hooked. Next step is convincing you that undermount sinks are superior."

"I'm team integrated quartz."

"Ugh. You're killing me."

I laughed, stretched my legs out, and rested my socked feet on the coffee table. "What's up, Deputy?"

A pause, and then, "What are you doing for Thanksgiving?"

The question hit me sideways, and my grin faltered. I hadn't expected the conversation to shift there. "Uh, not much?"

"You're...not?" He sounded thrown.

I rubbed the back of my neck. "It's just me this year."

Silence stretched for a beat. Then Garrett's voice turned firm. "Nope. Not happening."

I frowned. "What do you mean, 'nope?'"

"You're not spending Thanksgiving alone." His tone brooked no argument. "Come to my parents' place."

A warmth curled through me at the offer, but I tamped it down, my practical side kicking in. "Garrett..." I sighed. "That's really generous, but I don't want to intrude. Thanksgiving is for family."

Garrett scoffed. "So? My mom will be thrilled to have another person to feed. And they won't tattle to the department about us."

I huffed a quiet laugh, and my fingers traced the seam of my jeans. "Still. I don't want to impose. Or...put anyone at risk from Finch." My voice dipped at the last part. The thought of his family being dragged into the mess with Finch knotted my stomach.

Garrett exhaled heavily. "There's been no sign of Finch for days. And you're not imposing. Trust me, if my mom knew I let you sit at home alone on Thanksgiving, she'd disown me."

I hesitated. The idea of being in a warm, bustling house for the holiday, surrounded by food and conversation, instead of alone in my silent rental, eating a baked chicken breast, was more appealing than I wanted to admit. "Are you sure?" I asked, still uncertain.

Garrett's voice softened. "Yeah. I'm sure."

Something in my chest eased. I let out a slow breath, finally allowing a small smile to return. "Well…if I can bring a pie, I might be convinced."

Garrett chuckled. "You can bring as many pies as you want. And my mom will probably send you home with enough leftovers to feed a small army."

"That's a hard sell," I admitted and feigned deep contemplation. "Fine. I'll come. But if your dad tries to interrogate me about my intentions, I'm blaming you."

Garrett laughed, and the sound lit me up. "Deal. I'll pick you up at noon on Thursday."

As I hung up, I stared at my phone for a moment, that lingering warmth still curling inside me.

———

A knock sounded at my door, and when I swung it open, I barely had time to register Garrett's warm smile before Noah launched himself at me.

"Mr. Ethan!" He wrapped his arms around my legs in a tight hug. "I missed you!"

My chest squeezed, and the simple affection hit me with a pang, easing the ache of not spending Thanksgiving with my own family. I rested a hand on the back of his head for a moment and let the warmth settle in my gut. "Hey, buddy. I missed you too." Honesty rang in my voice.

Garrett stood behind him and shot me a knowing look, his eyes crinkling with a grin that made my stomach flip. "Hope you're hungry. Mom's been cooking since dawn."

I gestured toward the pie sitting on the side table, neatly wrapped in cling wrap. "I brought reinforcements."

Noah gasped dramatically. "Is that *apple* pie?"

"Sure is."

His eyes widened. "You made it yourself?"

"Sure did."

Noah turned to Garrett and stage-whispered, "He can bake apple pies. That's even better than dinosaur nuggets."

Garrett rolled his eyes. "All right, pie expert, let's go before Grandma sends a search party."

We piled into Garrett's Escape, and Noah chattered away in the backseat about how many rolls he planned to eat.

"You have to eat turkey too," Garrett admonished.

I turned my head to see Noah pouting and suppressed a grin.

When we pulled up to the house, a sixties ranch home with a festive fall wreath on the door, my nerves kicked in. I was new to meeting parents, and this felt significant.

Garrett's mom opened the door before we even knocked. Her face lit up as she pulled Garrett into a hug. "You're late," she scolded, but she said it with affection. Then her gaze landed on me. "I'm Carol. You must be Ethan."

"That's me." I offered the pie. "Happy Thanksgiving. I come bearing gifts."

Her eyes twinkled as she accepted it. "A man who bakes? I already like you." Then, with a pointed glance at Garrett, she added, "You must be someone special—because my son has never brought a man home before."

Heat crept up my neck, but I forced a casual smile. "Good to know I'm breaking new ground."

Garrett groaned. "Mom, *please*."

"Don't 'Mom, please' me," she shot back. "It's true. Come on in. Food's ready."

Inside, the scents of roasted turkey, stuffing, and something sweet and spiced filled the air. Garrett's dad gave me a nod and a firm handshake. "John Whitlock."

Harper greeted me with a hug. "I'm glad you're here," she whispered in my ear, settling the nerves in my stomach.

Dinner was a spread straight out of a holiday commercial —a golden turkey, mashed potatoes heaped in a steaming pile, cranberry sauce shimmering in a delicate glass bowl. Plates were passed, wine poured, and before long, conversation flowed as easily as the food.

"So, what's it like being a bestselling author?" John asked with polite interest.

I took a sip of wine and considered my answer. "Equal parts amazing and exhausting. There's nothing like seeing your book in readers' hands, but the pressure to follow it up with another hit is real."

Carol leaned in, intrigued. "Where do you get your ideas?"

Garrett cut in before I could answer. "Mostly by people-watching at Thanksgiving dinners."

I shot him a mock glare. "Hey, I also make things up sometimes."

Harper smirked. "But do you get writer's block?"

"All the time," I admitted. "It helps to step away for a bit. Or, you know, kill off characters from Thanksgiving dinner."

The table erupted into laughter, though Noah scrunched his forehead in confusion. The warmth of the family surrounded me, and I felt something I hadn't in a long time —belonging. This wasn't just a meal. It was a home.

Then, as if to cement that thought, Noah piped up. "Grandma, tell Mr. Ethan about the time Daddy got stuck in the fence."

Garrett groaned. "Oh, come on."

His mom grinned. "It's a classic."

"I like this story already." I smirked as Garrett glared at me.

Carol launched into a tale about five-year-old Garrett, a game of hide-and-seek gone wrong, and a broken redwood fence. By the time she finished, my stomach ached from laughing, and Garrett had dropped his head into his hands.

"I should never have brought you here," he muttered.

Noah patted his arm. "It's okay, Daddy. I got stuck on top of the jungle gym this week."

Garrett sputtered. "How did you get down?"

Noah shrugged his shoulders. "I fell." He stuffed a roll in his mouth.

A look of horror swept across Garrett's face, and he paled.

I chuckled and shook my head. "This is the best Thanksgiving I could have asked for."

And it was.

As I looked around the table—the way Harper teased Garrett, the way his mom beamed at her grandson, the way Garrett's hand lingered just a little too long against mine when we reached for the same dish—I felt something shift inside me.

I wanted this. Not just today. Not just a dinner invitation. But *this*. A life that included Garrett and Noah and embarrassing childhood stories told over pumpkin pie.

Could I really walk away from this?

Would danger always keep me at a distance?

Garrett caught my eye then, his expression questioning. As if maybe he was wondering the same thing.

And for the first time since I'd come to Seacliff Cove, I wasn't sure I wanted to leave when Ballard caught Finch.

As we finished dinner, Carol turned to Noah and smiled. "Would you like to stay the night? You can help me decorate the Christmas tree tomorrow."

Noah's eyes flew wide. "Really?"

"Of course," she said warmly. "You have extra clothes and a toothbrush here, so you don't even have to go home and pack a bag."

Noah turned to Garrett, bouncing in his seat. "Can I stay, Daddy? Huh? Huh? Please?"

Garrett chuckled. "All right, buddy. But be good for Grandma and Grandpa."

"Yay!" He threw his hands into the air.

"It's settled." Carol stood and started gathering dishes.

"Please, sit down and relax. We'll do the dishes." I raised my eyebrow at Garrett and dared him to disagree.

He shot from his seat. "Uh, yeah. Sit down, Mom. You cooked. We'll clean up."

Harper smirked and mouthed to Garrett, "Kiss ass."

I suppressed a grin as I stood and stacked the dirty plates. Harper and Garrett joined me in the kitchen with loads of dishes.

Harper stored leftovers while I scraped plates, and Garrett filled the sink with soapy water. "Looks like you two have the night to yourselves." She wiggled her eyebrows.

Garrett rolled his eyes. "Thanks, Harper."

But I couldn't help the thrill that ran through me at the thought of spending another evening with Garrett.

After cleaning the kitchen and saying goodbye to his family and Noah, we left with enough leftovers for an apocalypse. But when we arrived at my house, a chill settled over me. Sitting on my doorstep was a photo of Garrett and me at the redwood grove. During our lively conversation at dinner, I hadn't noticed the chime of my security feed. When I pulled up the video, I discovered that Finch had looked directly into the camera.

Garrett tensed beside me. "He's getting bolder."

My stomach churned. "What now?"

"Call it in. But I'm staying here tonight," he said firmly. "No argument."

I just nodded and unlocked the door, knowing sleep would be impossible tonight.

CHAPTER TWENTY-EIGHT

ETHAN

Hours later, a trio of knocks sounded a quick tattoo on my door. "It's me," came Garrett's muffled voice.

My pulse thrummed as I quickly unlocked the door. The moment I swung it open, a gust of cold, briny air rushed in with him, curling around us. I locked the door behind him. The click of the deadbolt was the exclamation mark at the end of the sentence.

Garrett's mouth was set in a grim line, his posture rigid, as if the weight of his job pressed down on him. My stomach sank.

"Larson said canvassing the neighborhood was a bust. No one saw Finch or a suspicious character in a hoodie come or go. Unfamiliar cars were parked on the street, but Thanksgiving visitors could have been responsible. He ran the plates on any remaining unknown cars, but none were stolen."

I exhaled slowly and frustration settled deep in my chest. It was as if Finch had vanished into thin air, leaving behind nothing but the photo—a taunt, a reminder that he was always watching. The thought sent a prickle of unease down my spine, but even that couldn't quite drown out the low hum of anticipation beneath my skin. Garrett was staying the night.

Sure, he was here to protect me. But the last time we'd spent the night together, we'd crossed an unspoken line, acknowledging something more between us. Something fragile, new. I had spent years knowing who I was, what I wanted. But Garrett was still navigating those waters, feeling out his own sexuality. And so, I followed his lead, waiting, hoping. I wondered if tonight we'd cross another line together.

Garrett set his duffel bag down with a heavy clunk, pulling me from my thoughts.

I raised an eyebrow. "What do you have in there? A copper pipe for the plumbing?"

My joke fell flat. Garrett's lips didn't even twitch. "My service revolver."

I frowned, and my stomach tightened. "Is that necessary?"

His eyes, dark and serious, met mine. "I'm not taking any chances with you," he said low, dangerous.

A shiver ran down my spine. It wasn't just the words—it was the way he said them, the raw protectiveness in his tone. Like he wasn't just guarding me out of duty, but because losing me wasn't an option he was willing to consider.

I swallowed hard, my throat dry. "Okay," I whispered.

Garrett nodded once, his expression unreadable, but I caught the flicker of something deeper behind his eyes. Tension coiled between us, a charged energy neither of us seemed ready to name.

He moved first. One second, we were standing in the thick silence, the next, he'd pressed me against the wall, his hands firm on my hips, his body crowding into mine. The breath rushed out of my lungs, and my pulse hammered against my ribs. Garrett's grip tightened, and his fingertips dug into my sides like he needed to anchor himself—or maybe me.

"Tell me to stop," he murmured, voice rough, but I heard the restraint, the barely leashed control behind the words.

I didn't want him to stop. I wanted more.

Instead of answering, I reached for him, curled my fingers into the fabric of his sweater, and tugged him closer. His breath ghosted over my lips, and then he kissed me.

It wasn't tentative. It wasn't careful. It was heat and pressure and raw intensity. Garrett kissed like a man making up for lost time, like a man who had been holding back and refused to any longer. His mouth moved against mine with purpose, with demand, and I met him every step of the way, drinking in the taste of him, the scent of him, the sheer force of *him*.

My world narrowed to the feel of Garrett—his broad frame pressing into me, the rough scrape of stubble against my skin, the intoxicating mix of power and tenderness in the way he took control. Every other kiss I'd ever had felt distant, forgettable in comparison. This was fire licking at my skin, setting every nerve alight.

Garrett groaned against my mouth. His fingers slid up my sides, over my ribs, and traced the outline of my body like he wanted to memorize it. When he pulled back just enough to breathe, his forehead resting against mine, his chest rising and falling in time with my own, I barely had the strength to keep standing.

He exhaled a shaky breath. "Ethan…"

I swallowed hard, and my heart pounded so loud I was sure he could hear it. "Yes?"

He hesitated for a moment, and then he ground his hard

cock into mine. "I want… I want to fuck you." He sucked in air. "Is that something you'd want?"

My cock throbbed, onboard with the possibility. "Yes, I'm vers. And I'd love that." *With you.*

"I don't—you'll have to lead the way." His voice was unsteady, uncharacteristically unsure.

I reached up and cupped the back of his neck, tethering us both. "We'll work it out. Together."

Garrett let out a breath that sounded almost like a laugh, but his grip on me never loosened. I saw it in his eyes—not just the protectiveness, but the desire, the want. The willingness to take this leap with me.

A shiver shot through me in anticipation, and then our lips met again in a scorching kiss. We staggered down the hall toward my bedroom, reluctant to release each other. We fell onto the bed in a tangle of arms and legs.

He pulled back far enough to strip us of our clothing, tossing them to the floor. His hands roamed my chest, my abs—the sensitive area of my groin—as I arched off the bed and goosebumps rose on my skin. I whispered his name in reverence.

I turned away long enough to grab a bottle of lube from my nightstand drawer. "Do you have a condom?" I hoped he came prepared. I hadn't brought any with me.

He vaulted off the bed, rummaged in his pockets until he found his wallet, and triumphantly held up a foil packet.

Thank God.

Garrett climbed onto the bed and eyed the lube. "How do I—"

My pulse fluttered as Garrett looked down at me, his expression curious and open. I reached up, fingers brushing his jaw.

"Kiss me," I whispered.

He did—slowly, tenderly—like I was something fragile

and worth holding on to. His lips met mine with a warmth that stole the air from my lungs. He broke away and peppered kisses down my neck, leaving goosebumps in their wake, until he reached a nipple. His tongue laved the sensitive skin, and I hissed in a breath.

"What else do you want?" he asked, low and husky, his pupils dilated.

I spread my legs and pulled them to my chest. "Grab the lube." I taught him how to open me with his fingers—one finger, two, then three—and he was a fast learner. I was a trembling mess of need by the time he finished.

He rolled on a condom, coated his dick with more lube, and lined himself up. He licked his lips nervously and began to press inside. I breathed through the initial entry.

He watched me carefully as he slid farther into me. "You okay?"

I nodded. With his gaze locked on mine, the moment was even more intimate than the physical touch, but I couldn't look away. I wanted this closeness of mind and body. With him.

As he inched into me, wonder mixed with pleasure crossed his face.

I thrummed with the pleasure-pain, and the discomfort receded.

He bottomed out, and we both groaned. He leaned forward to crush my lips with his. "Had to kiss you," he said when he broke away. "You feel amazing. So tight. So hot."

"And you fill me up." More than just physically.

He thrust into me tenderly and gently. I hooked my legs around his waist and urged him on. I angled my hips, and he hit me in just...the right...spot. I gasped. "Yes! Like that."

Garrett repeated the stroke. He propped himself on his hands and set up a rhythm guaranteed to push us both over the edge. "Too good. Can't hold on much longer." The cords on his neck strained.

"Right there with you." I slipped a hand between us and gripped my steel-hard cock. It only took a few tugs before I said, "I'm—" Cum spurted onto my stomach in long ropes, and colorful fireworks burst behind my closed eyelids.

Garrett tumbled over the edge soon after, my name on his lips, as his dick pulsed inside me. He collapsed to his elbows and panted. "That was…that felt…right."

I wrapped my arms around him and squeezed. That felt right to me, too.

After a few moments of clinging to him like I never wanted to let go, I caved to the inevitable and dropped my wobbly legs from his waist.

He gently pulled out of my tender hole, backed off the bed, and disappeared into my bathroom. Water ran, and then he returned with a warm, wet washcloth and cleaned me up, smiling softly.

Naked, we climbed under the covers. I snuggled against him, my head on his shoulder and my hand over his heart. I could get used to this. To making lo—having sex and then taking care of each other.

Could we have this closeness if I stayed in Seacliff Cove? Would Garrett want me to stay after the danger passed, or was our relationship built entirely on the crisis? Would it fizzle out once Ballard caught Finch? The questions circled in my mind, relentless, impossible to answer. The warmth of his body against mine grounded me, but my thoughts still churned with doubt.

One thing was certain—I was tired of being a sitting duck. I wanted to be proactive, not reactive. Could I end this stalking if I took charge? I exhaled slowly and steeled myself for the coming argument. "I want to turn the tables on Finch."

Garrett's body tensed beneath me, and his muscles tightened like bowstrings drawn too taut. His arm around my waist went rigid, and his voice dropped into a deep, dangerous growl. "Whatever you're thinking, forget about it."

But I wasn't backing down. "I want to be in control for once," I pressed. "I want to draw him out in public. He'll be in the open, and you can arrest him."

"No." The finality in his tone was sharp as a knife. "I'm not using you as bait."

I pushed up onto an elbow and met his scowl with my own. The shadows in the room carved hard lines into his face, and his eyes burned with emotions—fear, anger, something deeper that gave me hope for us as a couple.

"I'm going to have a book-signing at the bookstore," I continued, unwavering. "There will be lots of people around, and I'll be perfectly safe. Finch won't be able to resist attending."

"You don't know that."

"Call it a gut feeling," I said, my voice softer, but no less determined. "Somehow, I feel like I know him. He's…acting like a character would in one of my books." My throat tightened. And if that was the case, the ending of this story wasn't looking good for me.

I could hear his molars grind and see his jaw work as he tried to find a way to dissuade me. He scrubbed a hand through his hair. "You'd need a heavy presence from the sheriff's department. I'd have to see if Larson can get Sarge to agree to that. Ballard is useless."

Relief poured through me and left my chest light. He was considering it.

"I'll set up the book-signing with Mason." Resolve hardened my voice.

Garrett's eyes searched mine. "You're sure about this?"

I nodded. "I'm ending this. On my terms."

CHAPTER TWENTY-NINE

GARRETT

Over a week had passed since Ethan had floated the idea of a book-signing, and the Saturday evening of the event had finally arrived. I managed the front door of Tides & Tales, ostensibly placing stickers on the books readers brought with them. In reality, my eyes never stopped scanning the sea of faces, searching for the one I dreaded and needed to find—Finch. Mason, stationed across the doorway, mirrored my vigilance, his usual easygoing nature overshadowed by tense focus. We'd had to confide in him about the stalker, and he'd been livid—fear and protectiveness warring in his expression. He was more than eager to help catch Finch, but I could tell the weight of it sat heavy on him, just as it did on me.

"What a disaster," I muttered under my breath.

"What?" The man in front of me furrowed his brow, his fingers curled around a hardcover copy of Ethan's latest novel.

I straightened and offered a tight smile. "I said, welcome to Tides & Tales. The line for the book-signing ends over there." I gestured to the queue snaking around the store, winding between bookshelves and display tables.

Hundreds of fans had turned out, more than I'd expected for our small town. Ethan was more popular than I'd realized —so many people were eager to meet him. But the sheer volume of bodies, the constant shifting of movement, the open doors—it was a logistical nightmare.

My sergeant hadn't approved any extra deputies for the shift, leaving just one on-duty officer at the event, and he was stuck with traffic control. Larson had volunteered to watch the back-alley entrance on his night off. And me? Well, I was here under the radar. We were spread thin. Too thin. And Finch—if he was here—was going to slip through the cracks.

Occasionally, the crowd parted, giving me a clear line of sight to Ethan at his table. Caleb Sullivan, Mason's boyfriend, stood guard at Ethan's side and controlled the crowd.

Ethan was in his element, pen gliding effortlessly across pages, posing for photos, exchanging smiles and laughter with fans. He looked radiant, feeding off the energy of the crowd, glowing with the quiet humility and grace that made him so darn easy to admire.

My heart swelled with lo—*affection*. I swallowed hard and forced my gaze away.

Ethan deserved this. He belonged to the world, not to some sleepy coastal town with more fishing boats than traffic signals. He needed a city that could match his ambition, where he could network, attend events, and flourish in the literary industry. Seacliff Cove didn't even have a department store, let alone a thriving writing community. He had a future mapped out, one that didn't include quiet nights with me and trick-or-treating with Noah. He had a family waiting for him back in Brooklyn. A niece who missed him.

I'd have to let him go.

My chest tightened, a weight pressing against my ribs,

making it hard to breathe. But I forced the emotion down, focused on the next visitor, and ushered them inside.

Hours later, as the last of the fans trickled out, Mason closed the door with a weary sigh. Inside, only a handful of books remained on Ethan's table, their glossy covers reflecting the soft glow of overhead lights.

Ethan stretched his fingers and shook out his hand before scribbling a last message inside the front cover of the last book. "Thanks for coming." He handed it back to its owner with a tired but sincere smile.

The woman clutched the book to her chest like it was a treasured artifact, beaming as she made her way out the door. The moment it clicked shut behind her, Ethan exhaled, his shoulders slumping.

"Did you see him?" he asked. He stood, every line of his body trembling with exhaustion.

Larson entered the main room of the store from the back entrance and shook his head, his expression grim.

"He didn't show up," I answered.

"Fuck." Ethan's face fell. He braced his hands against the edge of the table. "I was sure he would." His head dipped forward as if frustration and fatigue pulled at him. "Now what?" he murmured, more to himself than to me.

The defeat in his voice cut through me. Without thinking, I stepped behind him, placed my hands on his tense shoulders, and worked my thumbs into the knots. He stiffened for only a second before melting under my touch, a low, appreciative moan escaping him.

"We wait for his next move," I murmured, my fingers kneading slow, steady circles. "My guess? He's going to retaliate tonight."

Ethan tilted his head and glanced up at me. "You think so?"

I nodded. "Yeah. And I'm going to be watching your porch until dawn."

Ethan's lips parted like he wanted to protest, but something in my expression stopped him. He let out a slow breath and nodded. "Okay," he murmured.

Whatever Finch had planned next, I'd be ready. Because there was no way in heck I was letting him get near Ethan again.

———

When we returned from the event, I backed my SUV into my driveway, lining it up just right. From this vantage point, I had a line of sight to Ethan's porch for the night. I wasn't taking any chances.

I walked Ethan home, my senses on high alert, and scanned for any sign that Finch had been there. The porch was undisturbed, the locks intact. But that didn't mean Finch wasn't lurking somewhere nearby.

As soon as we stepped inside, I took Ethan into my arms and pulled him against me. The weight of the night, the tension, the unknown, all poured into the desperate kiss I gave him—deep, consuming, as if I could hold on to him tightly enough to make the danger disappear.

"I'll be watching," I murmured against his lips.

"Stay safe." There was worry in his voice, but I feared more for him than for myself.

I pulled back reluctantly. We swapped phones and passcodes, a sign of his complete trust in me that I didn't take lightly. I would receive any security notifications on his phone, and he could call me from my phone. I returned to my house, full of determination. I put together a couple of sandwiches, poured fresh coffee into an insulated mug, holstered my weapon, and headed back out into the night.

The wind whipped down the street with an approaching storm, but the street was eerily empty. Was Finch watching me? Was he already here, waiting for the right moment?

I settled behind the wheel of my Escape and checked my view. If Finch made a move, I'd be ready—on foot or by car, whatever it took.

Time dragged. The cold seeped into my bones, and I regretted not bringing a blanket, but I couldn't risk turning on the heat. Any movement, any sound, could tip off Finch.

At one a.m., I finished my sandwiches. At two a.m., I drained the last dregs of my coffee and yawned. At three a.m., my eyelids grew heavy. I shifted and forced myself upright—stretching, blinking against the exhaustion threatening to pull me under.

At four a.m., I startled awake with a sharp inhale. My heart pounded. I had fallen asleep.

I jerked forward and immediately checked the porch. My stomach plummeted.

"Shoot."

Something lay on Ethan's doormat.

A cold dread settled over me as I wrenched open my door, my Glock already in hand. My breath puffed in the chilly, damp air as I scanned the street, and my pulse hammered.

Nothing. Not a single shadow out of place. Finch was gone.

I approached the porch warily, setting off the motion-activated security fixture. The bright light illuminated the item left behind—a book. One of Ethan's hardcovers. My fingers flexed around my weapon before I exhaled and slid it into its holster. I forced myself to stay methodical. I pulled out Ethan's phone, snapped photos from multiple angles, then slid on a pair of nitrile gloves and carefully picked it up.

Had Finch been at the event? Had we missed him in the crowd?

I flipped open the cover. My breath caught as my gaze landed on the inscription:

To Theo—Good luck with your book! Ethan

The date beneath it was from last spring.

A fresh unease slithered through me. What did that mean?

I needed answers. *Now.* I rang Ethan's doorbell.

After a few moments, he appeared, bleary-eyed and disheveled, his curls tousled from sleep. He blinked, and then his eyes sharpened, hope lighting them. "Did you catch him?"

Failure sat like a boulder on my chest, and I shook my head. "I'm sorry. I fell asleep," I confessed.

His expression flickered—disappointment, then understanding. "Oh…" His voice softened. "I get it. You're exhausted."

I didn't deserve this kind, forgiving man.

I lifted the book. "He left another 'gift,' but I don't know what it means."

Ethan's brow furrowed. "One of my books?"

I nodded. "And it's signed. Dated last spring. It says, 'Good luck with your book.'"

Ethan stepped back, gesturing me inside. "Come in. I'll take a look."

The warmth of his home enveloped me and chased away the chill that had settled under my skin. I could feel the coming storm in my bones.

"Want some coffee?" Ethan asked, already heading toward the kitchen.

I followed him. "Love some."

He popped a pod into the machine as I re-read the inscription and tried to make sense of it.

Ethan leaned over my shoulder, his nearness a steadying force. "So, Finch came to one of my book signings. But I can't make sense of what I wrote on the title page. Did he mention a book he'd written? Had I read it in the writers' group and just...forgotten?"

The coffee machine burbled. Ethan grabbed the full mug and placed it on the counter beside me, the rich scent filling the kitchen.

I bagged and tagged the book and called for a deputy. I took a grateful sip of the hot brew while we waited. I'd hear from Sarge in the morning about my involvement, and my gut clenched. I was walking a razor-thin wire and could fall off at any moment.

Ethan brewed a second cup, added a splash of creamer—pumpkin spice—then stirred it absently, lost in thought.

I studied him. "Why does he think you stole his voice?"

Ethan spread his hands. "I don't know." His tone was heavy with frustration. "I wish I knew what motivated him. Maybe it would help."

I shook my head and set my mug down. "We're not dealing with someone rational."

Ethan sighed. "No, we're not."

Silence stretched between us, but it was filled with the weight of what we didn't know—and what we feared was still coming.

CHAPTER THIRTY

ETHAN

The crack of thunder tore through my restless sleep and jolted me upright. My pulse pounded in my ears as I blinked into the dark, my breath coming fast and uneven. Wind howled outside, rattling the window like an intruder, and rain lashed against the glass in furious bursts. The storm raged with an unrelenting ferocity. I reached for my phone and my fingers fumbled against the nightstand until I found it.

4:03

Too damn early for a Monday. I exhaled, sank back against the pillows, pulled the covers tighter around me, and willed myself to sleep again. The wind could shake the house all it wanted—I had no intention of leaving the warmth of my bed.

Then came another gust that slammed against the window hard enough to shake the pane. A second later, a nearby, earsplitting car alarm shattered the night.

My car alarm.

The relentless wail cut through the storm and demanded

attention. I cursed under my breath, threw off the blankets, and swung my feet to the floor. A shiver raced up my spine at the shock of cold hardwood under my bare skin, but I ignored it as I padded across the room. The house felt different—the storm's wild energy made it come alive.

I reached the front window and spread the slats of the blinds just enough to peek outside. The street shimmered under the downpour, slick with rain and barely visible between the flashes of lightning. My car's headlights strobed along with the blaring alarm, turning the street into a chaotic display of light and sound.

Another crack of thunder rumbled deep in my chest, and my gaze flicked to Garrett's house across the street. If he woke up, he'd be at my front door in an instant. He'd insist on escorting me to the car, weapon in hand, ready to play bodyguard whether I wanted him to or not. But I couldn't let him leave Noah alone—not for this.

A deputy would take too long to arrive, and in the meantime, the entire neighborhood would curse me for the ungodly wake-up call.

I inhaled slowly and tried to shake the unease curling in my stomach. The storm must have set it off. A strong gust of wind, some loose debris, a random sensor malfunction. It was *not* Finch.

Even Finch wouldn't be out in this weather.

Lightning split the sky and momentarily banished the shadows along my driveway, illuminating empty spaces where someone could lurk.

No one was there.

My pulse settled—a little—as I forced a breath into my lungs. I could turn off the alarm from the porch. A quick step outside, just long enough to press the fob and make this storm a little quieter. *Easy.*

Still, my heartbeat matched the hammering of thunder as

I shoved my feet into my sneakers, grabbed my key fob, and unlocked the door. The moment I stepped onto the porch, the wind stole my breath. Cold rain pelted my face and soaked my T-shirt in seconds. I squinted against the sheets of water, raised the key fob—

A shadow moved.

I barely had time to register the dark figure lunging from the oleander bushes at the end of the porch. Too fast, too close.

A long object in his hands.

The dark figure swung.

The last thing I saw was Finch's wild eyes and the arc of his swing before pain detonated in my skull and obliterated the world in an explosion of white-hot agony.

———

I woke to a pounding headache, a sickening pulse of pain that radiated from the side of my skull. My thoughts were sluggish, my body heavy, but the cold seeping into my skin jolted me to awareness. The ground beneath me was wet sand. And the air—thick, briny, damp—told me I was somewhere close to the water.

A wave crashed in the distance, and the low rumble sent a spike of adrenaline through my system.

I tried to move, but my arms wouldn't cooperate. My wrists were tightly bound behind my back. Plastic zip ties cut into my skin. My ankles were the same, locked together, and reduced my movement to helpless squirming. The sharp bite of duct tape pulled at my mouth and sealed it shut. Panic surged. I twisted and arched my neck to look around, but my vision blurred, and darkness pressed at the edges. I could just make out the rocky walls of a cave in the dim light of a flashlight lying on the ground.

Then a shape emerged.

Lightning flashed and silhouetted the figure.

Finch.

The man stopped a few feet away and parked a beach utility cart—the same one he must have used to haul me here. Water dripped off his hair from the storm, but his expression was eerily composed, like he was just tying up loose ends.

I thrashed, muffled sounds escaping behind the gag.

Finch chuckled. "Yeah, I figured you'd be a little freaked out."

I jerked against the restraints, muscles straining, but the zip ties didn't budge. The more I struggled, the deeper they cut. I tried shifting my legs, but something rattled and yanked hard at my ankle.

My stomach clenched. *A chain.*

I twisted, my heart hammering, and searched for the source.

Finch smirked. "You're chained to a fluke anchor buried deep in the sand."

The chain was thick and secure. Even if I could get free from the zip ties, it ensured I wouldn't be going anywhere. I regulated my breathing to keep panic at bay.

Finch squatted in front of me and rested his elbows on his knees. He regarded me like a scientist studying a bug. "You don't recognize this place, do you? Well, you should." He gestured toward the mouth of the sea cave, where sheets of rain slanted sideways in the wind. "Noah pointed it out to you, didn't he? It was flooded by high tide at the time."

A new kind of fear slithered through my chest. *The tide.*

"Yeah, you get it now," Finch said smugly. He leaned in and his eyes gleamed with satisfaction. "Five hours, Ethan. Until ten o'clock. That's all you've got before this whole place is underwater. Your deputy's not gonna find you in time."

His eyes gleamed with a dark, triumphant satisfaction, the kind that made a shiver crawl up my spine. "But *I* found you, didn't I?" His lips curved into a smirk; his gaze locked on mine like a predator to its prey. "You thought you could run from me. Clever of you to try." He leaned closer. "That Priority Mail Express envelope you got?" His voice swelled with pride. "That was from me. I tracked it the moment it was forwarded to Seacliff Cove. After that, it was easy—just a matter of watching the bookstore. I knew you wouldn't be able to stay away. I counted on it."

I growled behind the duct tape and bucked against the restraints, but it was useless. I was trapped.

Finch sat back on his heels. "You're probably wondering why, huh? Why I've been following you? Why I went through all this trouble?"

I shook my head, a desperate, jerky denial. Not just of the question—but of all of it. The cave. The cold. The panic that scraped at the edge of reason.

Finch tilted his head like he was examining a bug. "You really don't get it. You read my story in that little writers' group back in the city—years ago. You told me you liked it. Said it had potential." He let out a soft laugh that echoed like something broken. "And then your first book came out. And I saw it. The twist, the setting, the character arc—it was mine."

I shook my head harder. My books were mine. Every plot twist, every character—I had written them through sleepless nights and bloodshot mornings. I hadn't even remembered Finch until Landon described him. But none of my writing was his.

Finch stood abruptly, pacing a slow circle. "But you got all the book deals. All the praise. The tours. The fans. I kept waiting for you to come clean. To give credit where it was due. But you didn't." He stopped and turned, eyes dark. "So,

I'll fix it. Once you're gone, there'll be space for my voice. My books. I won't be in the shadow of a thief."

A scream built behind the gag, helpless and raw. I thrashed, the chain biting into my ankle, wrists twisting against the zip ties. Pain flared, sharp and useless. There was no escape. No leverage. No one coming.

He thought I stole his voice.

And now he wanted to silence mine.

Finch stepped back and lifted the hood of his jacket. Then, without another word, he turned and walked into the storm.

I growled, raw and desperate, but the churning, roaring tide swallowed it. The waves were closer. The rain battered the entrance of the cave, and the ocean crept higher, inch by inch.

I twisted against the zip ties, against the unyielding chain.

I had five hours, and Garrett probably didn't even know I was missing.

Was this the end of my—*our*—story?

CHAPTER THIRTY-ONE

GARRETT

Monday morning, I loaded Noah into the car, my mind already running through a hundred different tasks for the day ahead. Rain drummed steadily against the roof of the SUV, the storm still raging, and wind gusted through the trees lining the street. As I buckled Noah in, my gaze flicked to Ethan's house across the road. Something about it sent a sharp prickle of unease down my spine.

Then I saw it.

Someone had damaged Ethan's car. The rear bumper bore a deep dent, the passenger-side taillight was smashed, and glass littered the driveway. My pulse kicked up. That hadn't been there yesterday.

Finch. It had to be him. He'd escalated his game.

I shut the car door, rounded the rear of my Escape, and climbed into the driver's seat, out of the rain. I quickly typed out a message to Ethan.

You okay?

I hit send and waited. Nothing.

I dialed his number. The phone rang and then went to voicemail.

Dread twisted in my gut.

I forced my hands to stay steady on the wheel as I pulled out of the driveway. I had to drop Noah at school first. I had to go to roll call. But the entire drive, my mind kept circling back to the smashed taillight, the silence from Ethan. Something was wrong. I felt it in my gut.

Noah chattered in the back seat, oblivious to the storm raging both outside and inside my head. I forced a smile when I kissed his forehead at drop-off and watched him run inside. The drive to the station was a blur. I barely registered roll call, barely heard my sergeant rattling off incidents that happened during the night shift, and assignments. The second I got the chance, I requested permission to perform a wellness check on a neighbor. Maybe it was nothing. Maybe Finch had only damaged the car to mess with us.

But my instinct told me otherwise.

Rain lashed against my slicker as I climbed out of my Interceptor at Ethan's house, and my boots splashed through puddles. The damage to his car seemed worse up close—a deep indentation with the taillight shattered completely. I doubted there would be any trace evidence left in this rain, but I pulled on a pair of gloves. I crouched and ran my fingers over the dent. Made by a blunt object. And still no answer from Ethan to my many calls. My stomach clenched.

I ran to the door and pounded on it. "Ethan!"

The door creaked open from the force of my knock. My breath caught. Unlatched and unlocked.

I stepped to the side of the door and pulled my gun. "Sheriff's department! Come out with your hands where I can see them!"

No answer. I wasn't waiting for backup, though I'd

probably receive disciplinary action for it. But Ethan could be injured.

Or worse.

I peered around the doorframe and cautiously stepped inside. The home was eerily silent. I swept the house, room by room.

Nothing seemed out of place—until I saw his bed.

The sheets were rumpled, twisted, as if he'd just gotten out of bed. As if he'd planned on returning. My chest tightened.

"Ethan?" My voice was sharp, urgent. Still no answer.

Then I saw his phone on the nightstand.

He wouldn't have left his phone behind. Not willingly.

I snatched it up. He'd given me his passcode when we'd switched phones during the stakeout. My fingers flew across the screen as I pulled up the security feed. I fast-forwarded through the night.

And my blood ran ice cold.

At four in the morning, the night vision footage showed Ethan stepping onto his porch. A shadow moved in from the side—then a blur of motion.

A long, blunt object connected with Ethan's skull.

My breath left me in a ragged exhale. Ethan crumpled instantly, limbs limp, and his body hit the wet concrete of the porch. My grip on his phone tightened as I watched a figure step forward—Finch. He bent, grabbed Ethan under the arms, and dragged him off the porch, his unconscious body trailing down the rain-soaked walkway. They disappeared out of sight around the corner of the garage.

I scrubbed a hand down my face, and my stomach twisted. Finch had taken him.

I rewound and watched the footage again, scanning for clues. I focused on the long object in Finch's hands.

Was that…an oar?

I fast-forwarded through the footage after the attack. Finch never passed in front of the house heading east, which meant he'd headed west. Toward the coast. We'd concentrate the search in that direction.

I toggled my radio and called in the abduction, my voice taut. Dispatch confirmed that assistance was en route, ETA five minutes. I paced while I waited.

Think.

Where could Finch have taken Ethan? He couldn't have gotten far on foot—not while dragging an unconscious body. That meant he had to have had some kind of transport. A car? But there hadn't been any unusual vehicles caught on the security footage. Finch was too smart for that. Had a car been down the street, toward the beach, and out of sight of the camera?

What other options were there?

I tried to remember roll call, but my mind had been on Ethan, too distracted to focus on details. Had there been any new reports of stolen cars? I forced myself to search my memory. There'd been a traffic accident, a downed tree across the coastal highway, a breaking and entering at Seacliff Beach Rentals...

I froze.

Beach rentals.

My pulse kicked up as I toggled my radio and requested a report on the B&E. "What was stolen?"

The radio crackled before the response came through. "An oar and a beach utility cart."

A cold weight settled in my gut. *An oar.* The same kind of weapon Finch used to knock Ethan out. And a beach utility cart—perfect for transporting an unconscious body.

On the beach.

I raked a hand through my damp hair, frustration and adrenaline surging through me. *This was it.* Finch took exactly what he needed to carry out the abduction. And now I had a direction to follow.

I checked my watch, my jaw tightening as the numbers glared back at me: 8:42 a.m. Ethan had been missing for almost five hours. Five hours of uncertainty. Five hours of Finch having him—God knew where. The weight of that realization pressed against my chest, suffocating.

Where was my backup? The storm slowed response times, but every passing minute felt like a lifetime. The wind whistled around the corner of the house and rattled a loose gutter. Rain hammered against the windowpane in a relentless rhythm. I flexed my hands, trying to stop them from clenching into fists. Every second that ticked by was another second Ethan was vulnerable, injured, or…my mind couldn't go there.

I forced myself to take a breath, but it was shallow, useless. I was wasting time while I just stood there. And time was the one thing I couldn't afford to lose. I needed to search the beach.

I left the house, paced in front, fists clenched, and watched the street. Waited.

Finally, the wail of sirens cut through the downpour. Two cruisers skidded to a halt, lights flashing, and sent flickering red and blue streaks over the rain-slick pavement. I rushed forward as deputies Holt Larson and Nate Decker jumped out, their faces grim.

I toggled my radio. "Where's Detective Ballard?"

A crackle, then dispatch responded, "He was at the sheriff's headquarters. ETA forty-five minutes."

Too long. We didn't have forty-five minutes.

I took charge, not worried about a reprimand. Sarge could suspend me, for all I cared. "Nate, start canvassing. Someone had to have heard or seen something. We need a witness, anything that gives us an edge."

Nate nodded and took off toward the nearest cluster of my curious neighbors watching from under umbrellas.

"Holt, you're with me. We're checking the beach."

Together, we pushed through the wind toward the beach path, our boots squelching through the rain. The storm had already tried to erase any sign of Finch, but as we reached the path, I spotted faint, washed-out tire tracks in the wet sand. *Beach utility cart.* My gut clenched.

At the beach-end of the path, Holt said, "Tracks lead north."

I nodded. "Let's go."

Sheets of rain turned the world into a swirling gray blur, but I could still make out the churning, frothy, violent waves. The rising tide had obliterated the tire tracks along the beach.

I turned my gaze north and spotted the sea cave, half-submerged beneath the surging tide. My pulse hammered against my ribs. That had to be it.

"He's got Ethan in the cave." I raised my voice above the noise of the storm. I could feel Holt's stare on me, but I was already moving. Fear tightened my chest, but I shoved it down. Ethan needed me.

I sprinted forward and sand shifted under my boots as I charged toward the jagged rocks. Holt followed, but he was a step behind. My mind screamed that I was too late, that Finch had already won, but I didn't let myself believe it.

Then—a blur. A dark shape emerged from a fissure between the rocks.

Finch.

He swung at me, and I barely had time to twist out of the way before the oar whooshed past my head, missing me by mere inches.

"No!" Finch bellowed, his face distorted with something wild and unhinged. "I won't let you save him!"

Rage and adrenaline exploded in my veins.

I ducked and dodged the second swing. I sprang forward and tackled Finch, slamming him into the wet sand. He grunted and thrashed beneath me, but I was stronger, fueled by something raw and unstoppable.

We struggled, rolling once before I gained the upper hand. I wrenched the oar from his grip and tossed it aside. Finch snarled, trying to claw at my face, but I yanked his arms behind his back and snapped the cuffs around his wrists.

"I've got him!" Holt's voice cut through the wind as he arrived. He grabbed Finch and hauled him to his feet. Finch struggled briefly before sagging in defeat. "Go!" Holt shouted.

I turned my gaze to the sea cave and my stomach wrenched. The water was already waist high, waves crashing violently against the rocks, surging deeper into the cave's entrance. If Ethan was in there—

I ran.

The first step into the water stole my breath. Frigid. Ruthless. The undertow nearly yanked my feet out from under me, but I powered through. The closer I got to the cave, the deeper the water became, dragging at me like unseen hands.

But I didn't stop. Ethan was in there. Trapped.

A wave slammed into me, shoving me back. I caught myself against a jagged rock, ignoring the sting of torn flesh, ignoring the exhaustion burning in my limbs.

I pushed forward.

Darkness yawned before me. The cave.

I plunged into the mouth of it, chest heaving, muscles screaming.

"Ethan!" I roared, but my voice was lost in the storm.

Nothing.

I fought against the waves, forcing my way deeper. He had to be there. He had to be alive.

The water was higher out here on the promontory, swirling and churning inside the sea cave, the tide creeping ever upward. *Chest-high.* Every second mattered. The icy waves slapped against my torso, the current threatening to pull me off balance as I fought forward.

I yanked my flashlight from my tactical vest and flicked it on; the beam sliced through the cavernous dark. My breath caught. *Ethan.*

He was at the back of the cave, before it narrowed, struggling against bonds. Water lapped at his chest, and his movements were sluggish from the cold. Duct tape gagged his mouth, but his eyes met mine. Relief flashed in them, but worry drowned it out.

"I've got you." I pushed through the water with renewed urgency. It wasn't fast enough. The tide rushed in with every wave, higher, colder, stealing precious time. Ethan needed to be out of here hours ago.

I reached him with my heart slamming against my ribs. I cupped the side of his face for half a second—just to ground myself, just to confirm he was real and alive.

"This is gonna hurt." I gripped the duct tape covering his mouth. "I'm sorry." With a sharp yank, I tore it off.

Ethan sucked in a ragged gasp and winced. "Garrett," he rasped, shivering violently. "You have to go. He—he chained me to a buried anchor. You can't—"

My blood turned to ice. *Chained.*

He shook his head, desperation in his voice. "Please. Think of Noah. Get out while you can." The water licked at his shoulders.

"Baby," I said, voice low and firm, my hands gripping his trembling shoulders. "I'm not leaving you. We're getting out together."

I radioed Nate. "I need bolt cutters and a bus. Yesterday. Ethan's chained to an anchor. Tide's coming in fast."

Static. Were we too deep in the cave for a signal? I held my breath and tried to not panic.

Relief poured through me at Nate's voice. "On my way. Hold on, Garrett."

I turned back to Ethan, every instinct screaming at me to move faster. I pulled my multi-tool from my vest and slashed through the zip ties binding his wrists. He sagged against me, exhausted, his skin too pale, his lips tinged blue. Symptoms of hypothermia and concussion.

I held him close and rubbed his arms, trying to transfer warmth, trying to anchor him in the rising tide.

"Stay with me," I murmured. "I need you to hold on."

Ethan's fingers curled into my slicker. "Trying," he whispered, voice thready.

The wait for the bolt cutters stretched into eternity. The water was up to my chin, my grip on Ethan tightening as the tide dragged at us, its pull insidious, relentless. The cave was a tomb waiting to happen.

A flashlight cut through the dim light.

"Garrett!" Nate struggled toward us, holding the bolt cutters above his head. "Here!"

I seized the cutters and dove under. Salt water burned my eyes, stung my skin, and chilled me to the bone. I fumbled with the chain, my fingers numb, my lungs burning.

One cut. The metal groaned but didn't give.

I adjusted my grip. Another cut.

The chain snapped.

I quickly cut the zip ties around his ankles, rose, and gasped for breath. "I've got you, baby. Let's go."

The three of us fought our way through the roaring waves, the current trying to suck us back into the cave. I held

Ethan against my side, my legs burning as I forced us forward, step by step.

A wave crashed over us, knocking us under. Blackness. Cold. Salt filling my nose.

I surfaced and dragged a coughing, sputtering Ethan with me.

"Almost there!" Holt was waiting at the shore, arms outstretched. The paramedics were just behind him, blankets ready.

One last push. One last struggle.

Finally, we broke free of the ocean's grasp.

I collapsed to my knees, Ethan still in my arms. His body shuddered violently, lips quivering, but he was breathing. *Alive.*

I cradled his face and pressed a kiss to his cold lips, not caring about our audience. "You're safe. You're okay."

A paramedic crouched beside us. "Let's get him warmed up. You too, Deputy. You're half-frozen."

I let them bundle him in a first-aid blanket, but I kept his hand in mine. I refused to let go, even when they wrapped me in my own blanket.

I'd almost lost him. *Almost.*

But I hadn't. I squeezed his hand, and he weakly squeezed mine. "Let's get you to the ambulance."

We'd caught Finch and rescued Ethan, but Ethan wasn't out of the woods yet.

CHAPTER THIRTY-TWO

ETHAN

The late afternoon sky was a dull gray when Garrett pulled up to the medical clinic to pick me up. The storm had passed, leaving the world damp and cold, the kind of chill that settled deep into my bones and refused to leave. I shifted in the chair in the waiting area, the fluorescent lights overhead too bright, and my head pounded with every movement. The soft sweatshirt and sweatpants Garrett had brought from my house were a comfort against my skin, itchy from the salt water, but nothing could fully erase the exhaustion clinging to me.

The door swung open, and Garrett strode in.

His gaze swept over the bruise on my temple and the abrasions on my wrists. I sat slumped in my seat, too drained to pretend I was okay.

Guilt flickered across his face as he stepped forward, his voice rough with apology. "I'm sorry I wasn't here earlier," he murmured and crouched beside my chair. "I had reports to file."

I shook my head, regretting the motion instantly as

dizziness washed over me. "You caught him," I said simply. "That's what matters."

"No, you're alive. That's what matters." His jaw clenched, his hand hovering near mine as if he wanted to touch me but wasn't sure if I could handle it. I wanted him to. I grasped his hand.

"Come on," he murmured. "Let's get you home."

The drive to Garrett's house was quiet, but not uncomfortable. The sound of the air blowing out of the heater vents filled the silence. I pressed my hands to the warm louvers and tried to chase away the lingering cold that clung to me like a second skin. My head throbbed with each bump in the road, but I focused on Garrett's presence beside me, on the steady way he drove, on the way he kept glancing at me, like he needed to reassure himself I was still there.

I glanced at him, taking in the tense line of his jaw. He was holding something back.

"So," I started, my voice a little hoarse. "How'd it go with Sergeant Rodriguez?"

He let out a breath and rubbed the back of his neck. "Suspended," he admitted, glancing at me before turning his attention back to the road. "A week. But at least it's with pay."

I winced. "Garrett—"

"Before you say anything," he cut in, throwing me a quick look, "I'd do it all over again. No hesitation."

My chest tightened, and I swallowed hard. Damn him for saying things like that. Things that made me feel too much. I sighed. "Still. I don't like that you got in trouble because of me."

He smirked, but there was something sheepish about it. "Well, if it helps, I might not be in trouble for long."

I raised an eyebrow. "Oh? How's that?"

Garrett exhaled and shook his head. "Reporters picked

up the story. Turns out, the kidnapping and rescue of a famous author makes for a pretty darn good headline."

My stomach twisted. "Wait—what?" I straightened in my seat despite the dull ache in my skull. "Are you telling me the whole world knows about this?"

Garrett chuckled. "More like the whole country, at least. News outlets got wind of it, and now I'm being hailed as some kind of hero. They're even calling me a real-life Jake Slate, can you believe it?" He shot me a wry look. "And get this—bowing to public pressure, the sheriff's talking about a commendation."

I chuckled, despite it all. "You're getting a commendation? For breaking department protocol and getting suspended?"

His grin turned downright smug. "Apparently, saving a well-known author from certain death outweighs a little insubordination. My suspension won't stick as much if they slap a shiny medal on my chest."

I eyed him and suppressed a grin. "That's really why you did it, huh? For the commendation?"

Garrett smirked. "Oh, totally. That, and maybe…I didn't want to lose you."

Warmth spread through my gut, settling somewhere deep. Despite being an author, I didn't have the words for what I felt. But I knew one thing—Garrett Whitlock wasn't just some deputy who'd saved my life. He was my safe place.

When we pulled into his driveway, the porch light was already on, casting a warm glow against the damp pavement. Harper opened the door when we reached the porch, concern in her gaze.

Inside, Noah's face lit up when he saw me, but there was hesitation in his step as he took in the bruise. "Mr. Ethan?" His small voice wavered, his blue eyes wide with concern.

Garrett squatted beside him, his voice gentle. "Hey, buddy. Remember how we talked about bad guys?"

Noah nodded slowly.

"A bad man hurt Mr. Ethan," Garrett explained carefully, "but he's safe now. He's going to stay here for a few days while I take care of him. We're going to have a sleepover."

Noah's lower lip trembled, and my stomach twisted at the sight of his worry.

"Did you catch the bad guy?" He glanced between his dad and me.

Garrett nodded, firm and certain. "I did. He's in jail."

Noah let out a small breath, and relief settled onto his narrow shoulders. Then, without hesitation, he turned and ran down the hall. I blinked, caught off guard, until he returned seconds later, clutching a stuffed animal—a well-loved, slightly floppy sea lion. He held it out to me with serious eyes.

"This is Flippy. He helps when you're sick. You can borrow him."

A lump formed in my throat as my fingers closed around the plush fabric. "Thanks, kiddo."

Noah nodded, seemingly satisfied, and ran off to play with his cars.

Harper stepped forward then, worry etched in every line of her face. "How are you feeling?" She reached out as if she wanted to touch my arm, then seemed to think better of it.

I forced a small smile. "Like I got hit with an oar and almost drowned."

Her lips pressed together, and Garrett shot me a look. "Not funny," he muttered.

"A little funny," I countered, but my voice was raw.

Harper exhaled, then gestured toward the kitchen. "I made chicken noodle soup. Thought it might help warm you up."

Warm. Would I ever be warm again?

Still, I nodded gratefully, and Garrett led me to the table with his hand on the small of my back. The smell of fresh rolls and steaming broth filled the air and wrapped around me like an embrace. It felt like it had been so long since we'd first sat down for dinner weeks ago. The simple family supper comforted me.

Garrett pulled out a chair for me. Harper ladled soup into a bowl and set it at my place. Noah climbed onto his chair across the table. He watched me closely, as if to make sure I was okay.

I wrapped my hands around the warm ceramic and let the heat seep into my fingers. For the first time since the cave, I felt something like safety.

————

The night pressed against the windows, the storm long gone, but its echoes still lived inside me. My body remained tense, my mind unwilling to let go of the past night and day. Curled up against Garrett in his king-sized bed, wrapped in the safety of his arms, I couldn't shake the feeling that if I closed my eyes, I'd wake up drowning.

My head rested against his chest, and I listened to the steady, reassuring beat of his heart. The warmth of his body was a stark contrast to the icy grip of the sea from earlier. I knew I should sleep—I was beyond exhausted, physically wrecked, emotionally drained—but fear had me in its hold.

I swallowed hard and stared at the darkened room. "I think I'll have nightmares for years," I whispered.

Garrett's arms tightened around me.

I squeezed my eyes shut, emotion thick in my throat. Relief crashed over me again—the same overwhelming, suffocating relief that I was still here, still breathing, still alive. I had thought, more than once, that I wouldn't make it out of that cave. That the tide would take me under before Garrett could reach me.

"I shouldn't be here," I murmured, and guilt settled heavily in my chest. "You're a single dad. You had Noah to think about. You shouldn't have—"

Garrett cut me off by tilting my chin up and forcing me to meet his gaze in the low light. His touch was firm but gentle. "Don't. Don't you dare blame yourself. Finch did this. Not you. And I'd do it all again to protect you. Save you."

His conviction made my breath hitch. I wanted to believe him. But deep down, the fear lingered.

I turned my face into his chest and inhaled familiar scents—warm skin, fresh body wash, and fabric softener. His presence, his steadiness, was the only thing keeping me tethered to the present instead of spiraling.

"I'm glad I'm here with you," I admitted quietly. "I don't think I could be alone in my house. Not yet."

Garrett exhaled softly and his finger traced soothing patterns over my back. "You don't have to be. Stay as long as you need."

The words settled something deep inside me. I wasn't a burden to him. I wasn't an obligation. He wanted me here.

Garrett's hand slid up to tangle gently in my hair, as if he needed the reassurance just as much as I did. He held me closer, and his lips brushed over the top of my head in a quiet, unspoken promise.

But safety wasn't the only thing keeping me in his arms. The warmth between us, the way he held me like I was something he didn't want to lose—it wasn't just comfort. It was something more. Something real.

At least, it was for me.

I hesitated before whispering, "Garrett, do you still want this? Us? Now that the danger is over?"

He pulled back just enough to look at me, his expression unreadable. "Is that what you think? That I only wanted you because I needed to protect you?"

I swallowed hard. "I don't know. I just... I keep wondering if you only see me as someone who needs saving."

Garrett's jaw tightened, and he let out a slow breath. He tenderly cradled my cheek, his fingers rasping against my stubble.

"Ethan, I wanted you before any of this. Before I knew about Finch. Maybe from that first awful sip of your pumpkin spice latte. I wanted you when you gave Noah your undivided attention and made him laugh. I wanted you when we were just figuring this out, when I didn't know there was a darn thing to protect you from. And I want you now. Not because I saved you. Because you're *you*. I know it's fast, and maybe too soon for me to say this. But you're...the man I love."

My breath caught. Warmth spread through my chest and mitigated the steady ache in my head. My fingers curled into the fabric of Garrett's T-shirt, as if holding on to something tangible would make this moment more real. "I love you too," I admitted, my voice barely above a whisper. "And I think I have for some time. I just hadn't admitted it to you— or even myself."

The words tumbled free, and with them, so did the weight of hesitation I hadn't realized I'd been carrying. This was home. Sanctuary. Not just the town. Not just the safety of Garrett's arms. *Us.*

I took a steadying breath and forced my tired limbs to shift just enough so I could see his face. "I want to stay in Seacliff Cove. With you."

Garrett froze, and his grip on me tightened.

Had I misread the situation? "If...if you want me to."

His throat bobbed as he swallowed, his expression

unreadable for a long beat. "But what about your family? Your niece?"

I shook my head, wincing as pain pulsed behind my temple. "That's what airplanes are for—I can see my family whenever I want to. And it's time my parents stepped up for my niece. I've been putting everyone else first. Don't I deserve a little happiness, too?"

He searched my face, and his eyes flickered with vulnerability. "You'd really do that? You'd stay?"

My lips curved into a slow smile. "I think I was always meant to end up here."

Garrett exhaled, the breath shaky, his relief palpable. Then, without hesitation, he kissed me.

It wasn't desperate. It wasn't urgent. It was steady, deep, grounding—a promise, a beginning, a homecoming all at once.

When we finally pulled apart, his forehead rested against mine. "Then stay," he murmured. "Stay with me."

I nodded and my heart hammered, no doubt in my mind. "I'm staying."

Outside, the waves gently washed to shore in the distance, no longer violent, no longer a threat—just a part of the town I now knew I would never leave. The storm had passed, the tide had settled, and with Garrett's arms around me, I knew I'd found something unshakable.

The final chapter of my old life had ended, and in its place, a new story had begun—with Garrett as my favorite plot twist.

EPILOGUE

ETHAN

I stood at the end of the beach path, the scent of salt and sun-warmed sand filling my lungs. This place had once been tainted by fear, by memories that still gripped me in the dead of night. But today, it was something new. Today, I was taking it back.

I patted the folded papers in my vest pocket, reassuring myself that they were still there. My fingers trembled slightly —not with nerves, but with the weight of how much this moment meant.

Barefoot, I stepped forward. Into our future.

Two rows of white chairs came into view, set on either side of an aisle lined with driftwood lanterns and soft ivory flowers. Beyond them, nestled beneath a tule-draped cabana, stood Garrett—with eight-year-old Noah at his side.

My breath hitched.

The sun hung low on the horizon and cast a golden light over the waves. A soft breeze ruffled the hem of my linen pants and carried with it the sound of waves kissing the shore. It was a perfect June evening for a beach wedding, as if the universe had conspired to give us this moment of peace, of love, of reclaiming something once lost.

I'd never been happier.

It hadn't been an easy two and a half years since my kidnapping. Healing had been a journey, one that didn't end just because Finch was in prison serving a life sentence. There had been therapy, restless nights, shadows that lingered even in the brightest moments. But Garrett had been my harbor. He was always there, holding me close, whispering me back to safety whenever my nightmares tried to pull me under.

Just like he had that day.

I never lived in my rental house again. The thought of returning had been too much, and even though it had been early in our relationship, moving in with Garrett and Noah had been the easiest decision I'd ever made. Over the past two years, we had poured ourselves into renovating Garrett's house together, and we had transformed it into something that was ours.

And in doing so, we had built more than a home. We had built a little family.

One night, Noah had hesitantly asked if he could call me *Papa*. I had been so choked up I could only nod and pull him into a hug so tight he had to squirm away, giggling.

As I walked closer to my fiancé and Noah, my heart pounded—not from anxiety, but from the sheer intensity of my love for them.

The small congregation—family and friends from Seacliff Cove, my family from New York—turned to watch, and a few beachgoers paused, drawn in by the ceremony. But I barely noticed. My world had narrowed to one person.

Garrett.

His broad grin was the first thing I saw, his face alight with unguarded joy. My lips curved into a soft smile in return.

Noah stood beside him, beaming, his light-gray vest and pants a match to ours. The only difference between us was the colors of our ties—Garrett's a cobalt blue, mine a dusty pink, Noah's a bright pop of yellow. My men, my family, looking impossibly handsome.

I reached Garrett, and my heart thundered against my ribs, my emotions barely contained.

"Hi," he whispered, and his eyes danced. Before I could answer, he leaned in and pressed his lips to mine. "Let's get married."

I chuckled, warmth flooding me, and the officiant cleared her throat with a smirk.

"Sorry, had to do that," Garrett said, completely unapologetic as he winked at me.

Laughter rippled through our guests as I shook my head, my chest aching with so much love I thought I might burst.

The officiant smiled and lifted her hands. "Welcome, everyone. We are gathered here today to celebrate the love between Garrett and Ethan…"

She continued speaking, but I barely heard her. All I could see was the man before me, the man who had saved me in more ways than one.

Then she turned to us, eyes warm. "Garrett and Ethan have written their own vows. Please face each other and hold hands. Garrett?"

Garrett squeezed my hands, firm and sure. "Ethan, from that first sip of your pumpkin spice latte, I knew you were trouble."

I snickered inelegantly.

"The best kind of trouble. You took my quiet, predictable life and filled it with laughter, warmth, and love I never saw coming. I promise to be your safe place, your home—no matter what storms may come."

I could barely breathe after his heartfelt declaration, but

it was my turn. I swallowed past the emotion clogging my throat.

"I've spent my life writing stories, creating larger-than-life characters. But no thriller, no fictional story, will ever compare to this—to you, to us, to the family we've built together. We are my greatest story, and it has a happy ending. I promise to spend the rest of my life proving that to you."

Garrett's normally steady hands trembled in mine, his eyes shining.

The officiant asked for the rings, and Noah stepped forward, solemn in his duty. He pulled two bands, tied together with a ribbon, out of his pocket and handed them to the woman. She thanked him with a smile. During the ring ceremony, we stacked our gold wedding bands snuggly against our diamond-encrusted engagement rings, glinting in the late evening sun.

The warmth of Garrett's hands never left mine, steadying me. This was forever.

"And now, Ethan has something he'd like to say. Noah, would you stand in front of Ethan?"

Confusion crossed Noah's face. This part of the ceremony hadn't been in the rehearsal. But he came to me, and I crouched down in the sand, so we were eye to eye.

I removed the papers from my pocket and held them up. My heart pounded; my throat constricted.

"Noah, these are adoption papers. Do you know what those are?"

He shook his head, curiosity flashing across his young face.

"They mean that I'd like to adopt you as my son. I'd be your legal father—your real father—along with your dad. Would you like that?"

For a moment, Noah just stared at me, wide-eyed. Then, without warning, he threw himself into my arms, nearly bowling me over. His arms wrapped around my neck with a strength that shattered me in the best way.

He whispered in my ear, "Yes. I want you to be my papa for real."

I clutched him tight, fighting back tears, my throat thick with love and relief. Above us, Garrett sniffled, and I knew without looking that he was just as overwhelmed as I was.

A collective *aww* rose from our guests, the moment washing over them like a gentle tide.

Noah stepped back and wiped his eyes, his face breaking into a mischievous grin. Then he whispered conspiratorially, "Is this when I'm supposed to go sit with Grandma?"

I chuckled and ruffled his hair. "Yes. Just like we practiced. I love you."

"Love you too, Papa!" he yelled, quickly recovering from the emotional moment. He ran to Garrett's mother, who scooped him up in a hug.

I stood and took my husband's hand, his grip as solid as the promise in his eyes.

The officiant smiled and concluded in her warm voice, "By the power vested in me, I now pronounce you married. You may kiss—again."

Garrett grinned. "Thought you'd never say it."

His lips met mine, firm and familiar. The guests erupted into cheers, Noah's "Eww" carrying above them all. The wind, the waves, the warmth of Garrett's body against mine —everything was exactly as it was meant to be.

We broke apart, breathless and grinning, and I leaned in, voice just for him. "Looks like we finally got our happy ending."

Garrett chuckled, his fingers lacing through mine. "No, baby. This is just the beginning."

———

Want more of Garrett and Ethan's story? Read their bonus scene at bit.ly/TidesOfChange-Bonus.

———

It started with a kiss…and a lie.

Want to read Cooper and Jack's story? Download *Tides of Discovery*, Seacliff Cove Book Three.

———

Want more MM romance? Join my newsletter at www.lisalinden.com/newsletter for sneak peeks and new release alerts!

———

Thank you for reading! If you enjoyed *Tides of Change,* please consider leaving a review on Amazon or Goodreads to help other readers discover it. Your feedback is greatly appreciated!

ABOUT THE AUTHOR

Lisa Linden is an author who took a leap of faith, changing both her genre and pen name to write in the category she loves to read—MM romance. The sticky note on her monitor saying, *You can do it!* serves as her daily inspiration. Her Seacliff Cove series stands as a testament to her willingness to follow her heart into new territory.

See Lisa's links at linktr.ee/lisalinden.

ALSO BY LISA LINDEN

Seacliff Cove

Tides of Redemption

Tides of Change

Tides of Discovery